Haunted Decisions of the Heart

Haunted Decisions of the Heart

Charlotte's Voices of Mystery Series

C.L. Bauer

For information contact:

www.clbauer.com

ISBN: 978-1-957015-05-7

First Edition: August 2023

10 9 8 7 6 5 4 3 2

Charlotte's Voices of Mystery Series

The Haunted Lost Rose
Haunted Decisions of the Heart

Dedication

My book covers for this series offer a view of Kansas City places. This time it is a bench in the Laura Conyers Smith Municipal Rose Garden in Loose Park. Many weddings and engagements have taken place in this lovely setting. When the roses begin blooming in May it is one of the best sites in the city to just sit and think, or to think about nothing at all! Here's to all of the wonderful, hard-working volunteers who perpetually make this a magical garden.

Chapter One

"I'm not fond of the news," I commented as I shoveled my hand into my bowl of popcorn.

"Well, I am, and I want to see the coverage on Max's case."

I really didn't want to see anything about Max Shaw, but my dad did. He loved the man. Why? Dad had three perfectly good sons still living. He didn't need another one. Yet, he wanted to see Max. And soon there he was the devil, in all his glory, on the television screen.

"My office believes the indictments are indicative of our aggressive prosecution. The arraignment of Cynthia Martin is just the beginning for our office."

"Mr. Shaw, will the federal government indict any other suspects?" the reporter asked as she thrust the microphone into the prosecutor's face.

Maxwell Shaw smiled slightly. "We will follow the evidence. I began my investigation when I was in Atlanta, and it has led me to this day. We will not limit our investigation or be satisfied until all involved are behind bars." He took a step forward, but the reporter stood her ground. Slowly, the well-dressed man raised his hand in front of the microphone.

"That's all for today. You can contact my office for any further information, and of course, we'll keep you all updated."

As Max passed by, he heard the question. "Isn't this a personal vendetta because your old family home was involved?"

"It doesn't matter whose house. These people hurt so many, including a family who lost their father. The man's finances were stolen. He took his own life. If it's personal on my part, it is because I want justice for all of their victims." Max's dark eyes flashed in anger, but he checked his tone. "Thank you, everyone."

I threw a handful of popcorn at the television screen. Mickey, Dad's dog, scrambled to reach the treat before it hit the floor.

"Charlotte Rose," my dad scolded. "What are you, five years old?"

"Dad, you know how old I am. But just look at Max. He's such a pompous a–"

"He's a good prosecutor. That reporter was attempting to goad him." My father, the illustrious retired federal judge, perched his glasses on his nose. When he did that, I knew I was in for it. I had disrespected the great Maxwell Shaw.

"Charlotte, you two could've been killed in that arson attempt at the house that night. That woman wanted both of you dead."

I nodded and stuffed three kernels into my mouth at once, chased down with a slurp of root beer. Mickey waited patiently at my feet hoping for another outburst of anger toward the television. "She's being tried for that. All of these federal indictments are just a cherry on top of Max's banana split. It's all about him."

My father sighed. "Charlotte, you don't have to answer, but I just have to ask. Your mother would ask. What the heck happened on that date?"

"Nothing. It was fine."

"Fine doesn't usually mean good."

"No, it doesn't, does it? He was a perfect gentleman. We laughed a little and ate a wonderful dinner, and then he took me home and gave me this weak peck on my forehead like he was the big brother taking out his forlorn little sister. It was like something happened somewhere along the way, but I don't know what it was."

My father was examining my face, but I remained stoic. I wasn't about to share my devastation. I had been examining what had happened for days. I thought…I didn't know what I thought now. "Saturday night at the charity auction, he was with that lovely girl. She works for one of the news stations."

"I saw, and you were with me."

I rolled my eyes. "Yes, you and I went together. Max kissed her. Her hands were all over him."

Dad's smile was infuriating. His happiness taunted me. "I saw the performance. He made sure you saw him, and what I saw was a man desperate to make you jealous."

I continued to chew the popcorn in my mouth. "I saw someone moving on and very quickly. He had no intention of a serious relationship with me. Max kissed her ferociously like he was devouring her." I shielded my face with my hand. Just the thought of Max kissing me in that way made me warm. I would only have my dreams of what that would feel like, how my body would feel when his hands roamed over my lower back…

"Charlotte, look at me."

I had been caught. I was flushed not out of anger but from lust. Why did Max Shaw make me feel? Couldn't another man do the job? I just needed a good…cold shower.

"Call him. Just be an adult and ask him. You like him, and he likes you. Something is going on with the man. Rip the band aid off and call him."

"Dad, I'm not sure."

"Not sure about what? Sometimes you have to take a chance. You don't do that very well. You have never been the risk taker. I'm not sure why. Your oldest brother once dove off of a cliff, your sister rode motorcycles like a daredevil, Sean stayed five seconds on a mechanical bull, Tom risked his savings on the real estate agency, but you--"

"I play it safe. Always." I sighed as I looked at the screen. They still had Max's photo on the screen. The man was too handsome for his own good. "Even though he's the devil, Max looked good in that live interview, didn't he?"

"I suppose."

There was an awkward silence. It was a good time to share my career idea. I had been thinking about taking a chance. "Dad, I've done well with the real estate job, but I think I want to head in a different direction." I concentrated on one popcorn kernel before flinging it into the air for Mickey to enjoy.

Dad removed his glasses and sat on the edge of his chair. "Yes? What are you thinking?"

"I'm thinking." I hadn't said it out loud yet to anyone. I was scared to turn my life upside down. "I have savings."

"Charlotte, out with it. What do you want to do?"

"I want to practice family law. I've always wanted to, but I was so afraid. I want to help people with adoptions, wills, and everyday things that matter."

Surprisingly, my father clapped his hands. "That's wonderful. You'll be great. Now, what do you need to do?"

"I want to begin my own practice. It won't be easy, and I've figured I have enough savings for a year if things don't work out. I've been looking for a small office in the area."

"Excellent. Let's go tomorrow and look around. You know, Tom might know of a few available spaces. This is exciting, honey."

Dad's wide smile offered the positivity I needed to go forward. "Do you really think I can do this?"

"You can do this, Charlotte, and I'm so proud of you."

My father could say just a few words and turn me into jello.

His eyes seemed to have tears housed in them as he swiped his hand across to prevent them from trailing down his face. "It's because I'm going into law again, isn't it?"

"No," he answered rather adamantly. "It's because you are doing something you are passionate about. Life has gotten in your way before, and finally you're going to do what you want to do. I'm not the only one in this family who knows how much you sacrificed when your mother became ill. You took the safe job with Tom, and ultimately your relationship fell apart with the man who will never be named."

I managed a weak grin. Since the night I very publicly had an altercation with my ex-boyfriend and future father of my imaginary children, I requested one thing from my family. We should never utter that man's name again. Surprisingly, everyone followed the rule, even my diabolical brothers who could've used the entire display and subsequent photograph in the newspaper to prod and poke me for the remainder of the time I had on earth. Now, Max's name would have to be erased from my lips, never to be spoken again.

"Dad, I may need your help. I'm thinking about selling my house if I can move back in here. I'll be out within a year if all goes well."

"I will always help you, and I'd love the company. But I need you to do one thing for me."

Ah, now the judge wanted to negotiate. "Fine, what's the deal?"

My father stood up, looming over me. There was no intimidation, just a sense of respectable power. "I need you to talk to Max and work out whatever is going on. I want to have him over to my house now and then, and I don't want any uncomfortable situations between the two of you."

I quickly placed my popcorn on the coffee table and paid attention. "You want me to do what?"

"Fix this with Max, whatever **this** is."

My father began to walk out of the room, and I stood up to follow. "Just like that? You want me to talk to Max and find out what the heck is going on, or not going on between us? Dad, that's death."

"Maybe, maybe not." Dad continued toward the kitchen. "Do you want a cup of coffee? Or maybe some lemonade? I made fresh-squeezed yesterday. It was my first attempt, but it was good."

I almost walked into his back as he stopped in front of the refrigerator and turned to face me. "Dad, I can't talk to Max. He is the devil. You saw him in that interview. He was cool, calculated, and dressed to kill."

My father turned back to the refrigerator and pulled out the pitcher of his touted homemade beverage. "So, he's the devil again? I thought we'd gotten past that?"

"No, we did not." I placed my hands on my hips to emphatically show him I meant business, but he went to the cabinet and pulled out two glasses. "Dad!"

He spun around with one finger raised in the air. "Talk to him, Charlotte. Do it for me. I like Max. I won't have any animosity in this house. Now, what do you want? Lemonade or…"

What did I want? "For now, lemonade. After I talk with Max, I'll need an exorcism and at least two Irish beers, none of that light stuff."

"Fine, I'll pour you a glass, and later our family priest can take care of the other. We'll need about a gallon of holy water, candles, and a sturdy cross."

"Amen." So, the deal was done, and now I had my marching orders. I wasn't sure exactly what I was going to say, or what I was supposed to say, but I would do it for my father, and only for him. Dad was right about one thing. Something was up with Max, and I was the one to uncover it.

Chapter Two

Downtown Kansas City, Missouri

"Max, Charlotte O'Donohue called again this morning. There are five messages from her since yesterday. She seems insistent to speak with you."

Max grabbed up the pieces of paper that his assistant Carolyn Westen waved in the air. After three hours of depositions, he was in a foul mood. Charlotte made him feel, well, made him feel. "I know. She's left a couple of messages on my cell too."

His comment was met with a raised eyebrow. "She's the daughter of an old friend. She must want some legal advice." He didn't answer any questions but strode straight into his office and closed the door. He immediately removed his necktie and threw it in a chair with his jacket and briefcase.

"Charlotte, what the hell do you want?" Max asked out loud as he stared out the wall of windows. His avoidance wasn't working. He thought Saturday's little act might have worked to dissuade her. Prior to his doubts about his parentage, Max would've taken Charlotte to the event. Instead, he called upon an old friend who just moved from Atlanta to take a job at one of Kansas City's news stations. The lady was recently divorced and amiable to participate in Max's charade if necessary. When Charlotte first saw him that night she smiled nicely, but as soon as she saw his partner, Max felt like he was a voodoo doll, and Charlotte was a high priestess vengefully sticking pins in his faux body. His newly found grandfather Gio had warned him about playing with fire. And here he thought Charlotte was just a little ember.

Maybe she was calling to yell at him? After the tortured look, Charlotte turned away at his act of betrayal. He wanted to hold her and tell her everything would be fine, but Max needed to stay away until he knew for sure if they were half siblings. Gio contended he was being ridiculous and scared of a commitment to Charlotte. When had it gotten that far? They were childhood nemeses and became friends, at least until he'd received the news that his dad wasn't his biological father. He rushed to the judgment that Judge William P. O'Donohue must be his father. Why had he concluded that? According to Gio, there were two obvious answers…he wanted it to be so, and he was avoiding a relationship with Charlotte. If the former mobster was right, there would be no living with him.

Running his hand through his hair, he realized he had no answers. He'd returned to this city to obtain so many answers. As of today, all he had were more questions. He was adding more and more onto his list. How had Charlotte weaseled her way onto that list and into his every thought? Why?

Charlotte O'Donohue was a pest. He saw her as the little sister who tagged along on summer adventures, didn't he? She was a woman now, and she wasn't his type. Right? She had curves that haunted his dreams. Her nervous habit of biting her lip made him concentrate on her mouth way too many times. He wanted those lips trailing down his chest. He wanted to lavish his own with deep kisses on those lips, those breasts that she always covered. Those eyes of hers bore holes into his very soul. Could she actually read his mind? It seemed as though she had some sort of psychic ability. He disliked her freckles. It made him remember when they were kids. Even in heels she barely came up to his shoulder, and he had to lower his head to whisper in her ear. When she pulled her hair up, all he could think about was nuzzling her lovely neck. Besides, she was the sister of one of his best friends. She was the daughter of a man he respected professionally and personally. She could be his sister. Yes, avoidance was best for now as was the increasing number of cold showers.

A soft knock broke his internal reflection. "Come in."

"Hi boss." Nathaniel "Nate" Beauvoir's smile broke Max's dark thoughts. "I'm here, and I have information." He quickly shut the door and took a seat in the uncluttered chair as his boss sat at his desk with his head in his hands.

"If you recall, you are an investigator. You're paid to obtain information."

Nate nodded. "That is true." He noticed Max's muted, clipped tone. "You're in a foul mood, again. Do we need to hire an escort for you?"

Max's eyes shot fire as he addressed his old friend. "I don't need to hire a woman."

"You're in a nasty mood for some reason, and usually with you it means you haven't–"

"That's enough. We aren't discussing my sex life or lack thereof."

"Is it that Charlotte, Judge O'Donohue's daughter? Maybe she'd be open for a good roll in the hay?"

Max's eyes rolled back into his head. "Who are you? Who says stuff like that these days?"

Nate snickered. "I do. Since I already know you're pissed off at me, I'm suggesting that Charlotte O'Donohue might welcome a good snog. You might be the man to do it, and then you'd be a happy little boss."

Max threw his hands up. "That's enough. No more about Ms. O'Donohue. What do you have for me?"

Nate grimaced. "Fine." He cleared his throat and looked over the notes on his phone. "I'll have a detailed report by tomorrow morning, but to sum it up Judge William O'Donohue is one squeaky clean dude. Do you know that he was considered for the Supreme Court?"

Max tapped on his desk. "No, I didn't." He continued tapping.

Nate knew the familiar cadence. "In Morse Code you're telling me that the woman is making you crazy?"

Max flattened his hand on the desk. "I wasn't telling you that. I was telling myself that. She's not my type. She has short legs and freckles. She looks like a little sister rather than a debutante. By the way, after all of the years we've known each other, why do you still call me the boss?"

Max's friend smiled, leaned back, and stretched his legs comfortably out in front of him. "I've always called you the boss since the first time you flew off of an aircraft carrier. You always called me Chief."

"Because you were. So, Judge O'Donohue is clean. Did you discover anything that would lead you to believe that he had any sort of relationship on the side with any woman?"

Nate lifted his hands behind his head. "Nope. There's not even a rumor. He was a hard ass, but he was fair. His kids are all adults, and there's hardly any scandal concerning them, except for the youngest two. You already have me looking into Conor's death. So far, I found nothing."

"Okay," Max muttered. He suspected that Conor's death and Charlotte's disciplining of a man who had betrayed her would be the only stories his prying friend could unearth.

"Boss, there's this great photo from the newspaper you should see. Charlotte decked this guy in a bar after she'd thrown a beer on him. Even though you don't want anything to do with her, we should see if she'd like a couple rounds of drinks with us. Maybe that would change your sour disposition?"

"We aren't in the Navy anymore, Chief. Besides, she's a nice girl. You don't mess around with women like that."

"Yuk, nice. I hate nice girls, and here I thought she might help with your affliction. I like the naughty ones, and you used to too before we all moved here."

Max shook his head. Nice girls were trouble. They invade your thoughts and worm their way into a closed heart. They were also very needy, wanting you to be faithful, reliable, and husbandly. Your thoughts turned to possibilities like a home with two children and a dog, and Christmas with her family. They wanted you to be marriage material. Where did those thoughts come from? "I'll read the report tomorrow. I'm heading home."

Nate straightened up. "Do you want to hit a happy hour somewhere?"

"No, I need to go home. I need to work on the house."

"You're becoming a stick in the mud, Boss."

"I do my best thinking when I'm working on tile or cutting pipe."

Former Navy Chief Nate Beauvoir stood and opened the office door. Something was going on with his friend. He knew there was a threat hanging over Max's head, and he knew that this assignment was so much more than just this office. "You sound like you're becoming domesticated. That's a nasty habit to begin, Boss. Think about how you want to live your life while you're cutting that pipe. Enjoy."

"I will." Max reached for his cell phone and gathered his items from the chair. As he walked past his assistant's desk, he waved. "I'm heading home to think. Why don't you do the same?" Max's question was directed to his closest confidant in the office.

The woman blinked twice. "Are you kidding?" Carolyn Westen had been personally asked by Max Shaw to transfer to Kansas City. After discussing it over with her recently retired husband, she was surprised when he announced he was ready for a change. "Max, are you feeling well? You've been acting a little unusual."

Max turned and flashed a smile that showed off the endearing dimples he'd used to get away with so many things when he was a child. "I am not kidding, and I'm great. I've been acting like…it's not important. It's a beautiful day, and we've been working hard. I'll see you in the morning."

He didn't wait to be thanked but headed to the elevator quickly. It was then he remembered his car was parked at a nearby hotel. He ate an early breakfast there with the mayor and left his car behind when he walked to a nearby attorney's office.

Carolyn shook her head. She wondered if his up and down moods had anything to do with the constant calling by that Charlotte person.

As Max exited through the building's glass doors, he thought the walk to the hotel might clear his head, especially on a beautiful early summer day like this one. He was stepping onto the sidewalk when she appeared at his side.

"I've been trying to speak with you, Mr. Shaw."

Damn, it was Charlotte. Max continued to walk, but she met him stride for stride. "Charlotte, what is it? I've had a long day."

"I've been calling you."

"I've been busy."

"Max, look at me." Charlotte grabbed his arm and stopped him in his tracks. They both looked at her petite hand on his sleeve. Each had their own thoughts from the physical connection. "I have to talk to you."

"Take your hand off of me," Max commanded in a quiet, halting voice. Her touch made him very uncomfortable, warmer if possible. It was as though there was an electrical connection between the two of them. Charlotte's hand was removed immediately. "What is it?"

"Dad is making me do this. I need to do this for him. He wants, well, he wants–"

"Charlotte, just spit it out." Max almost smiled at another of her endearing traits…her babbling when she was nervous.

"He wants us to be friends so you can still come over to his house. Geez, this sounds like something we would have said when we were kids."

"On that we can agree." Max began to take another step, but Charlotte blocked his movement.

"What did I do? Well, I know what I did. I kissed you, and I'm sorry, but then you asked me out, but you acted like you didn't want to be with me–"

Max placed his hand over Charlotte's lips. Just touching her was a mistake, but he needed to silence her. There weren't many other ways to do that to the woman in front of him. "Stop. Just stop. What will make you stop with this ridiculous conversation? You're an intelligent woman. Tell me what you want."

Charlotte stomped her foot. Max removed his hand before she bit him. "If you think I'm a child, I'll act like one. Just tell me what is going on with you. Dad is worried, and I don't like seeing him upset. I won't be a part of it or the reason. If I've done something to anger your highness, just tell me. You make me do stupid things."

If Max could've sat down on the warm concrete to throw a fit, he would've at that very moment. Charlotte was unrelenting, and he knew deep down she wouldn't stop until he told her something, anything. He would tell her and hope for the best. His shoulders dropped in surrender.

"For what it matters, you make me do stupid things too. I just need to take a step back. I have a lot of work to do, besides, when I met you again after all of these years, I thought you were involved in that real estate scheme the Martins had going on."

Charlotte threw up her hands. "I knew it! You're going to hold my innocent involvement against me. That's ridiculous!"

Max stood firm. His back straightened as if he were at attention. "I hadn't seen you since you were a child. You could've been a Russian spy for all I knew. You were found with a dead body."

Charlotte felt her face flushing. "Oh, my dear Lord! You are an idiot and perhaps, a coward. Tell me the truth. I know you're lying. You wouldn't have asked me out if you thought all that was true."

How could she possibly know? Max eyed her with suspicion. Charlotte did have some sixth sense that could run a secret mission into his thoughts. "If I tell you the real reason, will you go away?"

Charlotte nodded then curtsied. "I will happily depart your highness' presence, never to return. I'm the one who doesn't want to be here anyway. Despite what you might think, I am a big girl, and I can take the truth. Just say it." She was expecting to hear all about the beautiful woman and his new relationship with said woman, and how he'd enjoyed his examination of her tonsils at the event the other night.

"Charlotte, I received some disturbing news the day of our date. It affected how I looked at you, how I thought of you. That's why the night out was an epic fail."

"Now we're getting somewhere. What happened?"

"I discovered Edward Shaw isn't my biological father."

Charlotte placed her hands over her mouth in shock. Max was a grown man. He'd lived a life without knowing he wasn't one man's son? "That's unbelievable. You even look like your dad. Don't they call that imprinting?"

He did look like Edward Shaw, in fact he had more facial similarities with his father than with his mother. Hell, he looked more like his recently discovered grandfather Gio. "That's why things didn't go well with you and me."

So, it wasn't the woman? "We could've rescheduled, or you could've told me, Max. I understand that must have been a shock. Who is your father?"

Max drew in a breath. "That's the real problem."

"Oh no." The concern on Max's face shook Charlotte to her core. "Did you put him in prison? Is that why you look like you lost your best friend?"

Max grinned uncomfortably at Charlotte's perception. Their conversation was calming down, but his next truth might escalate it once more. "Possibly. I think my father could be your father."

Instead of screams, Charlotte's laughter filled the air. "Are you high or drunk?"

"I'm not mentally impaired in any way."

Charlotte's laughs brought tears to her eyes until she realized the man in front of her was completely serious. "We can debate about the impairment, but you aren't kidding! You really think my father is your biological father? How?"

Max raised his eyes to the sky. "The usual way, Charlotte. When two people fall in love–"

Charlotte's smile vanished. "Don't be obtuse, you sanctimonious devil. My father would never–"

"But I have my suspicions. I'm fifty percent Irish, and your father has always welcomed me into your home. He even got along with my mother, and no one does that. Judge O treats me like a son, and we have become more than just friends."

"He likes you. He respects you. He said he treats you like a son, not that you are his son."

"I just have this feeling–"

"Maxwell," Charlotte said, but stopped. "What is your middle name so I can yell at you properly?"

"Edward."

"Maxwell Edward Shaw, you sir, are an idiot."

Max made a move around Charlotte and began to walk away. He wasn't going to allow his life and secrets to play out on a city sidewalk. "I was a sanctimonious devil just a second ago."

Charlotte continued doggedly at his side. "You can be two things at the same time. What does Gio say?"

"He says I'm being ridiculous." There was no way he'd tell her about Gio's suspicions that he was afraid of Charlotte, of commitment. Yes, he was using this as an obstacle to keep them separated.

"There you go. The former mobster, your own grandfather, has more sense than a federal prosecutor. That's America for you."

"You're taking this very well," Max said sarcastically.

"Because I know there's no way my father is your father."

"How can you be so certain? Maybe he's not your father."

Charlotte tugged at his sleeve to stop his motion. "Again, you're an idiot. Max, look at me." With her other hand she held off the sunglasses he was about to raise to his eyes. "Don't you dare put those on."

Finally stopping, he looked into her eyes. It was dangerous to look at Charlotte's face. Those full pouty lips were sensual but were in direct contrast to her barely covered freckles below her eyes. Then there were those large, wide eyes that seemed to know his soul…what he had left of it. He took a deep breath to steel himself from the intimacy. "I'm looking."

"Good. Listen to me. Judge William P. O'Donohue has been in love with one woman, my mother. My father's first love and only lover has been and still remains Rosemarie Theresa. I know for sure because I heard the stories from each one of them. They used their love story to discourage all of their children from sleeping with someone on the first date. In my case, I was encouraged to never sleep with any man unless there was a ring on my finger and a wedding license located on the table beside the bed. Neither one of them ever made love with anyone else. One and done. And it wasn't just a story to dissuade us from having sloppy sex in the backseat of a car."

"Seriously? That's crazy."

Charlotte hit him hard on his arm. "That's romantic. That's the way it should be. They were perfect for each other."

"Did you have sex in the backseat in spite of them?"

Charlotte lowered her head at Max's pointed question. "It wasn't sloppy sex in a car. I was recently engaged, and I thought we were in love. I thought we were going to get married. I thought I'd waited long enough, but I guess I hadn't. I should've waited a little longer."

Max wanted to throttle Charlotte's ex. She deserved so much more, so much better. "I'm sorry for what your ex did. Back to your dad, Gio did say he didn't think the judge would ever have cheated on your mother."

"Don't you remember what it was like in our house when we were all children?"

Max fondly recalled every hour he spent there. When the judge hit the door in the evening, he couldn't walk three feet into the house without having at least three kids hanging on him. He was undaunted by the appendages until he found his wife and kissed her soundly on the mouth. Max remembered Judge O'Donohue always asked her how her day was and how he could help her that night. He was a man in love...with his wife.

"Max, my parents loved each other so much. It was so pure. I don't like to think about them doing it, but there were six of us! If you want to know who your father is, why not ask your mother? She was the one there."

Max winced. Fear coursed through his body. "You're right."

Charlotte noticed his surrender. She pulled out her phone and hit a number. "But first, we are going to settle one part of your puzzle."

"Who are you calling?"

Charlotte patted his sleeve and held up one finger to silence him. "Dad, I have a very weird question, but I need an answer. I'm here with Max, and if you want peace in your house, you just need to answer me."

Max hung his head down in embarrassment. How could she just call her father and ask him such a delicate question? But that's what that large obnoxious Irish family did. They talked, argued, and above all they loved.

"Dad, is there any way you could be Max's biological father?"

Max heard the tremendous timbre of Judge O's laughter. Charlotte hit the speaker button so he could listen. When the laughter subsided, the judge finally answered.

"Max, I wish you were my son. I wanted an entire team of children, but I was vetoed by my wife. Edward isn't your father?"

"No," Max answered quickly.

"Dad, he took some DNA test, and he discovered he was half Irish. Now he assumes that any dad of a large Irish family is his father." Charlotte winked at the very uncomfortable Shaw. "Max is having a life crisis. First, he discovers a retired mobster is his real grandfather, and now this."

"Max, I'll be happy to take a DNA test if that will make you feel better, but I think it's time you speak to your mother," the judge suggested.

"I know," he answered. He did know, but discussing even simple matters like the weather usually blew up into an argument of some kind. Looking back, his mother and he could never agree on anything. He refused to go to the preppy boarding school she selected for him. His father sided with him. She forbade him to join the Navy after high school. He went to the Naval Academy and flew jets. She wanted him to join a very well-established law firm making six figures. He was a JAG attorney and eventually chose another path in public service.

"Max, I didn't know your mother until your family moved to Kansas City, remember? I think you were in grade school."

Max shut his eyes. Of course, the judge was correct. Why hadn't he remembered that? Maybe he was blinded by his fear of commitment? "I was, but I thought you knew my father before we moved here."

"I did. He was one of the FBI agents on a case I was pulled into, but your mother, sister, and you were in New York at the time. In fact, I think my wife knew your mother before I did. I'll have to think about that one. Maybe Jane will remember."

Charlotte knew another way to know the truth about the women's meeting, but she'd have to wait until later. Max didn't need to know she could speak to her deceased mother or with his dead grandmother who haunted the mansion he was remodeling. The man in front of her seemed to be on his last thread. "Dad, I'll let you go. I'll drop by in a while." Charlotte ended the call and stared at Max. "Well?"

"Do you want to go back to my house and have a drink?"

Charlotte smiled. She'd missed just talking to Max, but she needed to protect her heart. "Um, we can just go to a bar." Neutral ground would be best with this man.

"With the news coverage, I really don't want to be out in public right now."

"As we stand on a sidewalk arguing?" Charlotte's wider smile was met with his. "Sure," she conceded. "I'll meet you at your place. By the way, where are you heading?"

"My car is at the hotel on Grand. Where are you parked?"

Charlotte pointed in the opposite direction. "I'll meet you at the house." As she turned, she patted her friend on his back. "Everything will work out, Max. Don't dwell on this."

Max shook his head affirmatively. Charlotte was right. He should just go on with his life and career, but not knowing the truth left a bad taste in his mouth. At every turn in the last few months, he was met with unearthed secrets since his arrival in Kansas City. The life he thought he knew was in shambles, and he was realizing he'd been lying to himself about the woman in front of him.

Yes, he needed to ask his mother, but he wasn't ready just yet. As soon as she heard of his investigation, she would call his father. Then there would be a call from him. Max wasn't ready for that now or maybe ever.

Chapter Three

"Dad, I won't be over. Max wants me to drop by the house for a drink. He's in a real state over this."

"Of course he is, honey. When you grow up knowing one truth and discover that it was a lie, that's hard to swallow for anyone, but Max's family isn't just any family. If this gets out, there could be more ramifications for him than he's aware."

Charlotte chuckled. "Well, if his secret father doesn't create a scandal, when the press hears about his mobster grandfather all hell could break loose."

"There is that. I'm not sure if Max has any political ambitions, but if he does, he needs to know about every skeleton in his family's closets. Go be a friend and give me a call when you get home."

"Yes, Father. You really need to stop worrying about me."

"Charlotte, I'll never stop worrying about any of my kids."

It was always comforting hearing my father say that. He meant it too. When Paddy caught a bad cold a few years ago, Dad was there every day with homemade chicken soup and his password for the western movie channel. "Dad, I'll try to find out about Mom's meeting with Mrs. Shaw when I get home, but you know sometimes my spirits just won't answer me."

"I figured you would at least try. Take care of Max and call me when you get home."

"I will. Dad, I saw fear in his eyes. I suspect there's more to this than Max jumping in with both feet and determining that you are his father."

"What would he be afraid of, Charlotte?"

I really couldn't fathom what or who would make Max Shaw quake in his high-priced shoes. As soon as he relaxed, that kiss me smile of his was pasted on his lips.

"Dad, it has to be something very big. I'll call you later. I'm here." I pulled into the parking lot of the Taylor Home. I stood outside of my car and looked around at the property. When the house had been a private club, the parking lot had been considered too small, but for a residence it was immense. With a dumpster on the north side of the building and stacks of wood on the lawn, it looked more like a construction zone than a home.

I shook my head and chuckled as I thought about Max's accusation. It was laughable that my father would have an affair with Max's mother because he wouldn't do that with any woman. I was the one pushing him into the arms of the neighbors. And as for Max and me, I was beginning to think that we really didn't have chemistry. Our relationship was more like a huge math problem that was actually as simple as one plus one equal two, but we couldn't see past the elaborate warning on the quiz. Simply, maybe it was just lust? I'd been jealous of the intimate kiss he gave his date. I wanted to be her. I wanted his kiss, his lips on mine creating a frenzy I had never felt even with the one who would always remain nameless.

As I began my walk up to the front door, I caught movement on the second story. Maybe there was a curtain blowing? I saw a shadow float by the window. My eyes weren't deceiving me. I knew for certain there was more life in that house than just Max's human body and even his grandmother's spirit. Once during a tour of the house, I felt a different energy on the second floor, but I couldn't explain it. Whatever or whomever it was wasn't ready to come out of the darkness and into the light of discovery. That would be for another day, or maybe never.

Before I could knock on the door, Max opened it wide. We stared at each other briefly, followed by uncomfortable smiles. His white shirt was open three buttons down showing off a tanned chest and just a touch of hair peeking out. Obviously, he didn't just run for exercise with those pecs. The tailor fit shirt was melted onto him like skin on a snake. His broad shoulders and chest narrowed to a slender waist. I could do push up after push up and never get rid of my midsection. Mom always called it the German-Irish potato waist.

I needed to look away, but my eyes followed down below his waist band. The same tailor must've fitted his suit pants. I looked up quickly. "I forgot to ask if you had air conditioning in this place."

"Just last week I had new units installed. Come on in. I pulled a couple of steaks out for dinner."

"I thought we were just having drinks."

Max shrugged as I passed by him and entered into the foyer. "I figure I owe you a more pleasant dinner than the last one we had."

"Ah, yes. You do owe me." I surveyed some of the work he had accomplished. I knew Dad and Gio had been helping out on certain projects including the staircase. "You have really been doing a great job."

"You won't say that when you see the kitchen. Come on. I have the grill out back."

As I made my way back to what looked like a bomb site rather than a kitchen, I felt a cool breeze pass by my face. It wasn't the air conditioning. I knew what and who it was. I saw one large hole in a side wall.

"Did you have a temper tantrum?" I pointed at the gaping wound in the drywall.

Max smiled uncomfortably. "I threw a hammer through it."

"Do I dare ask why?"

"No. Suffice it to say I was frustrated."

And we were uncomfortable with each other once again. Did he have his tantrum when he discovered his father wasn't his father? But Edward Shaw was an amazing man. As the current director of the FBI, he had returned integrity back to an agency that had its ups and downs. He was hated by some politicians, loved by others, but respected by everyone who knew him, including my own father. Or was his frustration with a woman? I smiled hoping it was because of the absence of any women. Poor guy. Right.

"Are you okay with garlic?"

I looked away from the hole and wondered why he'd ask that. "I haven't turned into a vampire yet. I haven't been bit. Yes, on garlic."

"You haven't been bit yet," Max muttered. He sprinkled the seasoning on each steak and winked when he looked up at me. His makeshift kitchen prep area was a utility cart next to the refrigerator. "Do you want beer or wine? I have both."

"A cold beer please."

He pulled a bottle from a small cooler under the cart and handed it to me. "I'll get these on the grill."

As he shot outside, I opened my bottle and took a large cold drink. The cool breeze came up my back. I heard my name spoken softly.

"Yes? Rose, is that you?"

"Yes, Rose."

I glanced out the back door at Max and walked quickly into what used to be the proper dining room, complete with built in cabinets for china and crystal. "Rose, do you know who Max's father is?"

"Yes."

"Could you give me a name?"

No answer was returned. Damn ghosts. You could never trust their consistency. Obviously, there must be rules on the other side, but I hadn't figured out their game plan yet, nor had I found any manual to solve the confusion. "Rose, I just need a name."

"His mother."

I hung my head down. "Yes, he needs to talk to her. Max needs your help. You need to watch over him."

"Family."

"Yes, he is your family."

"Yours, Charlotte. Come to him. Challenge him."

Ah, there it was again. Max was mine? How was I supposed to challenge him, and why would I do that? I really wasn't as sure in that assumption as the spirits that surrounded me. "I wish I knew that for certain. He's very difficult, and I'm not sure he is a project I want to take on. I'm not into renovating. Does that make sense?"

"Yours, Charlotte. Trust."

"Okay. For now, I will just trust you all. Be patient with him. He really wants to restore the house to its old glory."

"Home."

"Yes, your home."

"Your home."

Damn, this was frustrating. "My home? No, it was yours, and now it is Max's."

"Who are you talking to?"

I jiggled my bottle as Max came up behind me. "Just myself. I was thinking about some projects around the house I need to do. I'm selling my house."

"Really? Why would you do that?"

I smiled and pretended to admire the lead crystal design on the corner cabinet. "Because I'm changing careers, and I need to downsize."

Max had pushed up his shirt sleeves, his tanned forearms showing. I was a sucker for arms like that. I followed his left arm as if it was a fine piece of machinery to admire as he raised the beer bottle to his mouth and drew a long drink. "Real estate will be on the back burner?"

"I won't be returning to the agency. I'll be practicing family law. I'll be a bloodsucking vampire too but a nice one." His face showed no sign of dismissal or approval. He didn't even smile at my joke.

"Are you moving into a smaller space?"

"Dad's house."

Max began to choke on his beer. He wiped his mouth with the back of his hand. "You are moving back in with your father?"

"Thus, the reason why he wanted us to make peace."

"Now, I completely understand. You're moving back into your little pink bedroom?"

I shook my head. "It hasn't been pink since I turned sixteen. It's a light sage color that matches one of my stuffed animals, and I think I had a dress in the same shade."

Max's snicker was annoying. "At your age, don't you think it'll be uncomfortable to live with your father?"

"At your age, don't you think it will be uncomfortable to have your grandfather move in with you?" My brow rose in superiority.

Max held his beer in a toast to me. "Gio will be living in a suite on the first floor. My master bedroom will be on the second level. We're both single men and need our privacy." His eyes seared through me as if he was taunting me to return a witty remark.

"I had a reporter come up to me the other day and ask me if you and I were romantically involved," I said flatly as if I could care less. "I told her we were old family friends, and that was all." I didn't look up from my continued examination of the lovely woodwork. Max said nothing in response as I ran my hand slowly over the magnificent dining table that was still standing in the middle of the room. I caressed the edge and smirked when I realized Max's eyes were following my every move. "You are keeping this, aren't you? Rose picked this out many years ago."

"How do you know?"

I looked up quickly and met his eyes. Could I lie to Max? We were just about to find out. "I'm sure Gio said something."

"Ah, yes, Gio. I'm keeping it, but this wall over here is coming down." Max pointed to the area shared with the kitchen.

"But you'll lose the built-ins. You can't do that."

Max took another drink of his beer. "I can, and I will."

"But you shouldn't." I stepped over to the soon-to-be destroyed cabinets

and formed a line down the fine wood with my touch. "Look at this work. I've seen many of the old homes in this city, and this is one of the finest. They made everything with care and with the best materials available at the time. By the time you are finished, this house will be worth millions."

"Charlotte, I can't save every single thing in this house."

I continued to study the work of art. "But you could try. You don't always have to tear down and throw away. Some things can be saved."

When I looked up, Max stood next to me. I could feel the material of his shirt against my bare arm. "Are we still talking about the wood or us?"

I felt the cool breeze run against my neck. "I'm not sure."

My voice unexpectedly quivered. When Max took my bottle from me and placed both of them on the dining table, my body trembled. He returned even nearer than before. I could feel his body heat and smell the soap he used. As he looked down at me, I became completely lost in those caramel eyes. Surely, he wasn't my brother. Dad wouldn't lie. Please, Lord, he can't be my brother. I've never felt like this with Sean or Tom, or even Paddy or Conor. This is biblically bad.

"What is it about you?" Max asked as he tenderly touched the side of my head and brushed his fingers through a few strands of hair.

"I have no clue."

"Well, there's something. I'm not thinking of you as a little sister right now. Your friendship means everything to me. I can be my true self, good or bad, when I'm with you." His face lowered. I shut my eyes. "I know you've said it before, but you called me the devil to my face, didn't you?"

I rocked back and took a step away from his body. When my eyes opened, I giggled. "I called you a sanctimonious devil. I've also called you an idiot, selfish, and domineering. But I like you."

"The funny thing is—" Max hesitated. "Never mind."

"What?" I could see real anguish on his face. Was it that difficult for him to share with another person? Was that the fear I saw? "Tell me."

Max chuckled nervously. "You must have a sixth sense. My call sign when I was in the Navy was Satan. You nailed the devil analogy."

Sixth sense? You have no idea, buddy. "You have got to be kidding?" He shrugged. "You're not kidding. That's very unusual."

"Satan Shaw, just a little alliteration from my buddies."

"If those were your friends, what do your enemies call you?"

"Ironically for my current situation, they call me an arrogant sonofabitch."

"Max, don't you think you should check those steaks?" I was beginning to see another side to the man I thought I knew. He might be put together in expensive suits on the outside, but internally he was a trainwreck. I didn't want to be caught in an accident at this railroad crossing.

"I have them marinating. I haven't even put them on the grill yet."

The curtain still hanging on the large bay window began to float in the air. Max would only think it was the air conditioning, but I knew better. "Let's get them on the fire. I'm beginning to get hungry."

"Yes, ma'am," Max said as he saluted and left me alone in the room.

"How can he possibly tear out these cabinets? He's an idiot."

"Yes, but our idiot." Rose's answer made me laugh.

"I'll talk him out of it. He is very hardheaded. Are you sure he's really related to you?"

"Family."

"Fine. I understand. I have a family like that too. In fact, all of my family acts like Max, even my sister. Rose, I'll talk to you soon." I thought I saw a reflection from outside, but the sun was beginning its descent in the west, flooding the dining room with shards of light.

"Danger, Max."

"I agree, Rose. I hate to talk about your grandson, but sometimes the way he looks at me, like tonight, is very dangerous for what little of my virtue I have intact." I chuckled, but there was no answer from beyond except two words once more.

"Danger, Max." I headed to the small back patio to find Max placing the steaks on the grill alongside strips of vegetables.

"What are your plans for here?" I asked as I looked around the area. In the early days of this lovely structure, the back area was used by staff to come and go unnoticed by the family. There were two small pads of concrete at different entrances, one by this door and the other by the basement where we had escaped from only months ago.

"I'll tear all of this out and put in a fantastic patio, maybe a pool over there?" My host pointed to the south side of the back garden. "I'll demolish part of that parking lot and add grass. Gio will have access out of his suite."

"Do you know how much this is all going to cost?"

Max turned both steaks. "Probably my entire trust fund, but I don't care."

"You can always sell it."

"No, not now. I like the old girl."

"So why is the house female?" The trainwreck's thought processes were on a track of their own. I was realizing the more I was around him, the more I didn't know this Max at all.

Max looked up toward the top of the structure. "Look at her. She's stunning."

"She is that." As I looked up, I shielded my eyes. I saw a curtain flutter on the third floor. How could I get up there? What lie would I have to tell? "Yes, she's a little under the weather right now, but she just needs a little tender loving care. She has a good foundation and with a little makeup she'll be photo worthy. That sounds like me," I quipped. I was rewarded with Max's soft smile. He was extremely handsome, and as I studied his facial structure while he paid attention to the two caramelizing steaks, I saw so much of Gio in him. His strong nose and lovely full lips were a little softer but chiseled like a Roman statue's face.

As Max lifted the plate proudly to admire his work, we heard the squeal of tires rounding the corner on the quiet residential road behind the property. Max placed the steaks onto his side worktable and watched the scene unfold. With our attention drawn toward the street, we only heard a snap from one of the bushes near the parking area. Max grabbed my arm as he turned.

"Drop, Charlotte," he yelled as he threw our bodies into the grassy hill near the steps. I could feel his hand behind my head. His other arm was around the back of my body. We landed together, shots firing simultaneously from the lot and the street. Max's over six feet frame covered my body completely. There wasn't one inch between us; the fear was palpable.

"We're sitting ducks out here. Just lay still," Max commanded. He threw a tarp over me and crawled toward the door. In what seemed an eternity, I was alone. I continued to hear shooting, but now the sounds of police sirens added to the reverberations in my ears. I sensed Max next to my body, and he began to return fire while kneeling next to me. In a matter of minutes, his gun was the only one firing.

With sirens closing in on the property, Max put the gun down on the small table and found my hand. Just seconds ago, I had removed the tarp to watch him in action. Now, he pulled me up to a seated position and into his arms. His large hand stroked through my hair.

"Charlotte, are you okay? If you're hurt, your father and your brothers will kill me." His eyes searched my face, arms, and body for any damage.

I held onto his neck as though he was the only thing keeping me alive. "They may still kill you, but I'm okay. How about you? You have a gun?"

"I'm fine, and I have a gun. I learned years ago that lawyers need a little extra protection."

Before any other words could be spoken, we were surrounded by police. I only hoped that my detective brother wasn't in charge of this cavalry. I prayed that Sean, my other law enforcement sibling, had the night off. When I saw Sean hurdle over the short rock wall, I knew God wasn't listening to my prayers.

"For the love of God, what the hell, Max? Are you trying to kill my sister?"

Max was busy brushing grass and leaves off of me. "I had no control over this, Sean. We were being shot at. We had a shooter from the parking lot and then a car on this backstreet. Maybe you good guys should go after them."

Sean grabbed Max by his collar. "You ass. You don't put my sister in danger. You've already done it once with that woman who attempted to burn you both alive."

I quickly jumped in between the two men and shoved Sean back. "Stop it, Sean. I'm fine. Max protected me as much as he could. It's not his fault."

"The hell it isn't. He's a federal attorney. He's always in danger. You've had threats, right?"

Max was busy handing his firearm off to another officer. "I always have threats, Sergeant O'Donohue. That's why I have a gun. I'll up my security."

Sean smirked. "Good for you. My sister won't be around here for a long time, like never."

That was it. I had watched two grown men talk over me since my brother's arrival. "That's enough, Sean. Max did the best he could."

"You tell that to Dad when he gets here."

My mouth dropped open. "How could Dad possibly know?"

"Because I saw the address, knew Max was involved, and called the old man."

"You always were an outrageous snitch," Max muttered as he looked over the shredded skin on his forearms. He had caught the brunt of the impact from the edge of the patio.

Sean began to reach over me to assault Max. "What did you say, you preppy spoiled rich boy?"

Two other officers managed to grab my brother before he struck a federal prosecutor. I looked over to Max and shrugged with embarrassment. He offered me a slight smile. My focus turned to his bleeding arms.

"Max, your arms. We need to get something on that." My hand held his as I examined the cuts.

"Sir, there's an EMT unit in the parking lot. Let's get you out there." The officer extended a hand out. "Miss, you should be checked out too."

I was checked for a concussion, but my eyes followed the light correctly, I knew the date and year, and who the president was. I was deemed satisfactory. Of course, my father didn't see it that way. He arrived while a paramedic cleaned Max's wounds and removed small bits of loose concrete from his injuries.

The judge didn't ask any questions or make any accusations. He just held me in his arms and reached for Max, patting him on his back. "I'm just relieved to see the two of you standing. What the heck happened?"

"It was a well-orchestrated attack," Max answered. "I'm sorry that Charlotte was involved."

"It wasn't your fault." I felt my father's gaze. He was attempting to gauge my feelings and Max's as well. He had his judge face on, and that was never very good, especially if you were the recipient of said look.

"As soon as you two are released from the police, I'm taking you both back to the house."

Ah, he had returned a judgment. He would be the one to keep us safe. Both of us.

"I'll be fine here," Max answered.

Dad shook his head. "No. There is no negotiation in this matter. You'll grab a bag, and you'll spend the night with me."

"There's no use in sparring with him. He won't take no for an answer when he gets this way." My words seemed to soften Max's resolve. He surrendered and nodded affirmatively. Dad would be taking his children home.

Chapter Four

By the time we reached the house, I was tired of being treated like a China doll that might crack at the slightest touch. I even sat in the backseat of my father's car, while my vehicle remained parked at Max's house. The FBI wanted to check it from top to bottom.

While the two men in the front seat thought I should be treated like a child, I decided to act like a petulant one. As soon as I entered my parents' home, I headed straight to my room. My stomach rumbled. I hadn't eaten since sometime around eleven in the morning. Maybe I had a leftover chocolate bar in my old room?

"Charlotte, I'll have sandwiches ready in a minute," my father called after me.

"Sure. I'll be down in a bit." I needed time away…away from my dad, but definitely away from Max. The smell of his aftershave or whatever cologne he wore was transferred on my shirt and on my face. His five o'clock shadow had rubbed my skin, and I desperately wanted the feeling scrubbed off. As soon as I reached the top of the stairs, I headed into the bathroom and splashed water on my cheeks and chin. Looking up into the mirror, tears began to flow down my cheeks.

My hands began to shake as I grabbed a towel. Get it together.

Charlotte, what have you gotten yourself into now?

My mother's voice was clear as if she was standing only inches behind me. "I'm okay. We had a situation."

Charlotte, don't lie to your mother!

I smiled as I looked into the mirror. I brought my right hand up to smooth my hair. It continued to shake violently. "Mom, I'm scared of so many things."

Fear can be good, dear. Be careful with your heart.

I was trying to do that, but Max and I were almost literally being thrown together at every turn. As I exited the bathroom, my body slammed right into one of the men I was unsuccessfully evading. Max's hands automatically grabbed both of my upper arms.

"Are you okay?" His eyes focused on my face, evaluating my condition. His concern brought me to tears.

"I'm in shock," I sobbed. I couldn't hold it together any longer. His arms encircled me, bringing me closer against his chest. "I'll be fine in just a minute." I tried to pull out of his embrace, but he folded me closer.

"Charlotte, you're safe now."

I believed him at this moment. His low murmur shook my heart. I was safe in his arms. This man made me crazy, yet I couldn't imagine not knowing him. I wanted to be in his life. But Mom had just said to be careful with my heart.

"You need to stay away from me," Max whispered.

What did he just say? I didn't move, but he did. His arms relaxed, and he patted my head as if I was Mickey the pet dog.

"I put you in danger."

Tears stopped flowing. In such a short span of time I understood my mother's warning. My heart stopped caring, and I was able to push off from that amazing broad chest. I rushed past him and managed to enter my bedroom. Just for impact, I slammed the door. "Go to hell, Max Shaw."

"Geez, are we back to me being the devil?"

"Back? You always have been. Go away."

"That's what I'm attempting to do. Besides, we still might be brother and sister."

"If you are my brother, I'm never celebrating your birthday. I'll put your name back in the hat if I pull it for Secret Santa gifts. I'll be nice to your kids, but not to you or your wife. Do you understand?"

My declaration went unanswered. Damn, he'd left before he heard the remainder of my speech. I changed into sweatpants and a long shirt and just kept focusing on the door. I couldn't go downstairs, but I was starving. My body had stabilized. I wasn't shaking or crying, but my temper continued to rise.

"Charlotte, honey, I brought you a sandwich and a beer."

My father was truly the best man I knew. I opened the door, and he stood there with a plate in one hand, a beer in the other, and a cautious smile on his lips. "Max told me you might not come down. Apparently, he said the wrong thing?"

"Dad, he seems to always say the wrong thing to me."

"That's how it usually begins," my father whispered.

I took the plate. He'd even included chips, thank God. I took a quick sip of the beer and sat on my bed to eat. "He's infuriating. I was so right when I said he was the devil. Did you know his nickname in the Navy was Satan? How is that for poetic justice?"

Dad raised his shoulders. "Charlotte, you'll feel better in the morning. Being shot at always affects you."

"You make that sound like it's a natural thing."

"I've been shot at three times over the years. I couldn't sleep for days after the first time. Finally, your mother helped me out of my shock. You and Max will make up tomorrow."

I glared as I filled my mouth. My father held a pipedream that Max and I would end up as a couple, that we were in love with each other. If I loved anything about Maxwell Shaw, it was that he constantly proved to me that I was right about him. He was the wrong man for me.

My father assured me that all would be good in the morning. When I woke up the next day, the sun was shining and birds were singing. I peeked my head out of my room to check the hallway for sightings of Satan. The bathroom door was open and the second story seemed vacant. As I ran into the hallway, I heard male voices downstairs.

"He's still here," I said out loud.

"Of course he is, dear."

"Mom, Max makes me–"

"Afraid, Charlotte. Stop it. Your heart is so large, and you are brave."

"No, I'm not."

"Stop being so fearful. I raised you better than that. Be my Charlotte."

Being rebuked by someone from the great beyond was always unsettling, but this time my mother had hit the target. I was afraid, and she did raise me better than how I was acting, especially when anything involved Max Shaw.

After a brush through my hair, water splashed on my face, and putting on a casual dress I had hanging in the closet, I took a deep breath and walked slowly down to the first floor. I dreaded this meeting, but as I entered the kitchen everything seemed deceptively normal.

"Good morning." Max and Dad were by the coffeemaker, but the stranger who stood as I walked in was the one whose smile made me feel comfortable and welcome in my own family home.

"Good morning. And you are?"

"Nathaniel Beauvoir, or you can call me Nate."

Max offered me a cup of coffee. "Nate is my investigator and will be my security for the time being. This is Charlotte O'Donohue."

The guest extended his hand out for a shake, and I happily received it. The man was gorgeous with light brown skin glistening in contrast to his perfect white teeth. He was muscular and maybe an inch or two taller than Max. His lilting accent seemed like one I'd heard in the Caribbean.

I avoided eye contact with the devil. Sliding past him, I kissed my father's cheek and grabbed a plate.

"Judge, this is the best omelet I've had in a long time."

"Thanks, Nate. I love cooking now that I'm retired. You should come by for dinner Sunday. Max will be here. I'm making chicken parmesan, and it's a family favorite."

"If Max will be here, I will too." Nate flashed a smile and a wink that made me giggle and Max grimace.

"I didn't know I'd be here," Max commented flatly.

"You will." My father made it sound like a direct command. "Gio will be here too. It's just a family dinner, Max. You'll survive."

I was enjoying this morning's antics. Filling my plate with scrambled eggs, sausage, and a helping of hashbrowns, I sat down across from my new handsome friend. "Nate, where did you meet Max?"

"In the Navy. He was one of the few pilots and JAG officers I liked so I looked him up when I got out. I'm very meticulous, and I can find out the darndest things. I'm also unrelenting so the investigator job is perfect for me."

"And the bodyguard part?"

"Even better. I carry a gun. I've had to save him a few times."

I looked up at Max. "This wasn't the first time he's been shot at?"

"Nah, he's been shot at before, but usually it's only threats." Nate leaned in as if he was telling me a state secret. "There was this time when the daughter of this very well-known evangelist had a hankering for our little Maxie. She showed up at his apartment with chocolate sauce and—"

"That's enough." Max's irritation was on full display.

Nate winked. "I'll tell you Sunday, Charlotte."

Max continued to stand, hovering over us while drinking his coffee. His sour mood delighted me, and Nate entertained me on a morning I thought would go in an entirely different direction.

"Nate, where are you from?"

"Originally, from the Bahamas, and I hail from Jacksonville, Florida. I haven't lived there in years. I visit my mother a couple of times a year in Nassau, but with my job, I go where the Boss goes. He's in Kansas City now so that's home for me until the next move."

My side glance offered me a view of Max and my father leaning against the kitchen counter.

"You didn't lose your accent, Nate?"

The big man leaned back away from the table. "I just visited my mother a few weeks back, and I tend to slip back into the old ways. You have a good ear if you could hear that."

"I'm a good listener, at least that's what I've been told." I looked over at Max directly and smiled sweetly rather than sticking out my tongue. His face was unchanged.

"Nate, we need to get into the office, but first I need my car at the house."

"What about my car?"

Max placed his coffee mug into the sink. "It's been cleared. Your dad will take you over. Nate? We've got to get going. Thanks Judge O for the bed last night and for feeding me. I promise that nothing like last night will happen again."

My father patted Max's back. "You know you can't promise that, but thanks for saying it."

I noticed there was a shared knowing gaze between them. I had the distinct feeling that my father and Max had talked quite a bit without me last night. I'd have to do my own cross examination of the parental unit later.

Nate began his walk out of the kitchen, mentioning we would talk on Sunday. Max awkwardly stood at my side. "Charlotte, I'm sorry for what happened. We'll make every effort to keep you safe. In the meantime, I need to, well to—"

"Stay away from me. You made that very clear. No problem, Max." I took a bite off of my plate.

"Right. I'll see you Sunday." Then he kissed the top of my head, and I was back to China doll status. He metaphorically shoved me into that uncomfortable box that was labeled sibling and sweet little girl. If he knew me, I wasn't always sweet. I might seem to bend, but I didn't break…at least not yet.

As Max vanished into thin air, my father joined me at the table. "How are you?"

"Surprisingly good. Nate seemed nice."

"Yes. What about you and Max?"

"What about us? There is no us. Besides, he could be my brother."

"Jesus, Mary, and Joseph. He is not your brother. I don't know where in the heck he got that idea."

I reached over and touched my father's hand. "Because he desperately wishes it was true. He loves and respects you so much. Apparently, we were the family he wanted. That's why he figured it was you. He wanted it to be you."

"Edward Shaw is a great man. He and Max have a good relationship."

"Dad, I think he's feeling betrayed by his parents right now, both of them. His mother has lied to him all his life, and Mr. Shaw has held a secret from him. And Max is holding his own secrets."

"So now what?"

"Max needs to speak with his mother, but in the meantime, maybe we could do a little investigating on our own. Are you in?"

My father's eyes sparkled. "I'm in, as long as you do one thing for me."

"Anything, Dad."

Dad's other hand landed tenderly over mine. "Trust Max and give him another chance."

"Oh, come on!"

"Charlotte, trust me. I know things."

"And I know things too, Dad." I took a breath and closed my eyes. "There's something going on with him, and it definitely doesn't include a relationship with me."

"Have you talked to your mother?" My eyes opened as I heard the question.

"I tried, but there was nothing this morning. They didn't even wake me up. Maybe there were too many people in the house?" I often wondered why they picked the times they did to speak to me from the great beyond. Were they having an extended breakfast time with God? Did they run into a favorite movie star and had no time for us mere mortals?

"Maybe, and maybe you're not open to reception? Remember when we added foil to the television?" Dad began a full belly laugh. "We made Sean hold the antenna for over thirty minutes just for fun."

"No, Dad, I don't remember. I'm the youngest. A lot happened before me."

Dad sobered up quickly. "Yes, it did, but one thing for damn sure didn't happen. Olivia Shaw and I never touched past a handshake. You can take that to the bank." He stood up quickly as if the discussion ended in more ways than one.

Dad began to mutter something about he wouldn't know what to do with any other woman. He wasn't Max Shaw.

My brothers described the rich boy wonder as a player when he returned to the city, and yet I was uncontrollably placing myself in Max's path over and over. Maybe, if I just had my way with him for one night, all of these yearnings and pent-up feelings would disappear? It wouldn't really change things…we didn't look into each other's eyes honestly now. Nothing would change, but I could say I'd been with the great Max Shaw.

As Dad muttered, I smiled. I wondered…

Chapter Five

"Just put the extra leaf on the table, please." My father's frustration with my brothers was increasing.

"Why does Max have to be at our Sunday dinner?" Sean asked. Actually, my brother sounded like a whiny brat. Max was great as long as he was purchasing the drinks during happy hour or providing baseball tickets. Showing up around our family's table this Sunday was one step too far in the current environment.

"Wait a minute, Max has been a friend for years," Tom's wife Meg admonished. "He's been at this table recently way more than you have, Sean."

Tom lined up a peg and a hole in Mom's dining table and motioned for Sean to do the same. Paddy eyed the alignment and nodded. "Max is and was my friend from school. We all know him. I don't see a problem. Push softly, Sean."

"I can push softly, Thomas." Sean was obviously irritated about more than Max's attendance for a good meal. "I saw Brody the other day. He's a friend of the family. Maybe we should have him for Sunday dinner?"

"Perfect," Paddy commented. "I'm talking about the table, not Brody. He worked for Dad, that's all. I don't have a good feeling about that guy."

Tom stood back as Paddy gave the table an inspection. "Max and I went to school with Brody. He's a nice guy…not much personality, but nice."

Paddy huffed. "I dislike nice guys. Max isn't one. I would usually like that kind of bad boy, but the real reason Max isn't welcome here is he keeps putting our little sister in danger."

"Of losing her heart," Meg whispered as she passed me.

"Oh, do tell," Jane said as she followed.

"You two are so subtle." The women in this family had me falling in love, married, and pregnant with his child before the end of the year. Max's hot and cold routine wasn't enjoyable. It would take a lot more than his handsome face, beautiful body, and witty conversation to make me fall in love or in bed with him. But my thoughts were recurring, always placing me exactly into his arms and under his spell in more ways than one. This was lust, pure and simple. What would Sister Regina Ann say?

"Charlie? Earth to Charlie?"

Sean waved his hand in front of my face. "What?"

"Where were you?"

Briefly, I wondered what all of the men in the room would do if I honestly admitted I was thinking about Max next to me after a night of lovemaking. "I was thinking of something I have to do on Monday. Did I tell you all that Dad and I found a small office in Waldo for me?"

"Wonderful. What else do you need? What about your desk at my office?" Tom's encouragement was heartfelt and much appreciated. This was a big step for me, although I felt like I was taking three or four steps back in time. Selling my home and moving back in with my father seemed like I was failing.

"I have my desk at home. You'll need the other one for a new agent."

My father looked over at me and nodded. Jane and Meg reentered the room with a tablecloth. "Charlotte has something to tell you all."

Paddy's brows furrowed, Tom smiled, and Sean shook his head. "If this is about Max and you, I think I'll puke," Sean said as he put another chair at the table.

"Will you quit with the Max stuff?" I stopped and took a deep breath. "You all know I'm going to begin my family law practice. I'm selling my house to give me a financial cushion to get my business going. I'm moving back in with Dad for a year or so. I hope it will be shorter than that to give me a good start."

"And me some company," Dad added.

Our admission was met with silence. Movement began in the room once more as Jane and Meg placed the tablecloth, and the boys set the remainder of the chairs.

"What? No comment?" I was shocked that the Irish family who always had an opinion about everything from what socks to wear to a sporting event to what Irish band played what song better was mute upon my announcement.

"No, why should there be?" Paddy seemed to be the voice for the entire family. "I'll feel better that you won't be living alone, and Dad needs company. I see it as a win-win. Anyone else have an opinion?"

There were murmurs, but only smiles. Paddy ruled that the arrangement would be a good thing. It was deemed approved by the oldest and no younger sibling would buck him. I thought I saw relief in Dad's eyes. Our idea had been approved, I was heading into a new life, and back to my father's first love of law.

The aroma of the two roasts in the oven wafted through the house. Jane finished the mashed potatoes and gravy, Meg pulled the salad from the refrigerator, and I plated the homemade rolls Dad made before church this morning. The doorbell rang and every muscle in my body tensed. Max was here. Gosh, what was I, sixteen again? And how many times had I asked myself that since the day he reentered our lives?

"The devil has entered the building," I said out loud.

"Charlotte Rose!" My sister's admonition was always said with a first and middle name.

I avoided her daggered look. I heard Gio's boisterous laugh. As Max's newly discovered grandfather, Gio was the genuine article compared to Max's slick demeanor of duplicity. The elderly mobster was suave and charming and never demeaning. Max could learn a lesson or two from him. Nate announced loudly he had brought two bottles of his favorite Irish whiskey, and Max said something about knowing the way. He stood in the kitchen before I had time to evade or dodge.

"Charlotte, I brought the dessert." He held three boxes from my favorite bakery. "They even had the peach tarts you like."

Jane snorted, and Meg clapped her hands. "Charlotte loves those. How did you know?"

"She mentioned how good they were, and I remembered. It's great to see you two." He had directed his attention to my sister and sister-in-law.

Meg took the boxes from his hands and replaced them with the large bowl of mashed potatoes. "These go on the table, Max. Send the judge in while you're at it. He needs to remove the roasts."

Max didn't answer. He just did as he was told. Was that the best way to handle Max Shaw?

By the time Dad checked the meat, and we placed everything on the table, most everyone was seated. Jane sat next to her husband Brad who arrived late from dropping off the kids. Their four children were with their other grandparents at a baseball game. Tom saved a seat next to him for his spouse, and I found the only empty place in-between Max and Gio. How coincidental! My family! Sometimes I wished I checked my DNA and discovered I had a secret bunch of biological benefactors lurking somewhere in the shadows.

After a prayer of thanks by Dad, the passing of food began. Nate was peppered with questions about Max's days in the Navy.

"He did that movie thing when you buzz someone's house. He was showing off for a girl, and he buzzed the wrong house. It was the mayor's! I'm surprised they didn't throw him into the brig."

"They needed me. I shipped out the next morning, remember?" Max's voice was void of the same enthusiasm as his friend's. "I flew missions for four months straight laying cover for SEALS and Marines."

"Max, tell them the story about that doctor in Norfolk. Remember–"

"I remember, Nate, but I'd like to enjoy my meal. Paddy, have you heard anything around headquarters about the car or the shooters from the other night?"

"No, Max. Have you talked to the FBI?"

Max nodded and then filled his mouth with food.

"We're going down to the lake next week," Jane announced. "Brad's parents have invited all of us. Anyone interested?"

"Are your kids coming?" Sean asked as he reached for another roll.

"Of course. The kids would love it if you came," Jane quickly answered.

Sean shook his head. "Nah. If the kids are coming, I'm not. I just want to drink beer and sit in a float on the lake."

"They're your nieces and nephews, you jerk."

Max touched my leg under the table. "Things really never change around here, do they?"

"No, and may I remind you that this is the family you wanted?"

"There is that." He patted my leg and removed his hand quickly.

"So, Charlotte, your father says you're going back to law?" Gio's question broke the moment with Max. I was actually grateful.

"I need to try this. I wasn't ready when I was younger, but this is my shot. I either do it now or never."

"You'll be wonderful," Gio stated calmly. "I just know it. You know I know things."

I smiled at his charming demeanor. "That's funny. My father constantly tells me the same thing."

Gio wiped the side of his mouth with his napkin. "We are living pieces of history. By now, we should almost know everything."

"Speaking of history," Tom interrupted. "Gio, I would love to hear some of the stories of the old days in Kansas City. I know organized crime was big over the years. Were you around when the River Quay area was blown up?"

Dad cleared his throat. "Tom, could you help your wife remove some of the dishes? We can talk later."

As I glanced at Gio, I realized he was sharing a look with my father. Gio seemed to be thanking him. "Was that a bad time?" I whispered so only he could hear.

"Your father knows it was for me, Charlotte. He was saving me from embarrassment."

Now I was the one who patted a leg. Gio's hand landed softly on top of mine. "I've told you before, your father is the best man I've ever known."

I looked at my dad and nodded. How could any man compare to the best man on the face of the earth? Were my standards too high? Was I disillusioned because my heart was broken before? Yet, the man on my left fell into my vision. Max smiled at me. I didn't even know if Max was truly a good man.

After dessert–my peach tart was just as good as ever no matter who brought it and remembered it was my favorite–the dining room was vacated. Sean and Paddy went into the garage to look at Dad's mower. It also offered Paddy the opportunity to call his wife Linda and check in with her. She was staying with her sister in Chicago for a few days. Their two sons were doing whatever they did on a summer day. Tom, Max, Nate, Gio, and Dad headed to the living room to sample the whiskey. The ladies and Brad began the cleanup in the kitchen.

As the youngest, and as just one of several, I felt as though I was invisible for years. No longer the center of attention, I was just one of a team in the kitchen. I was also away from

Max, but occasionally I could hear his voice. It sounded like they were discussing the mansion and a variety of work that needed to be finished. Maybe I could go back with Dad one day when Max was at work? I needed to try to talk to Rose and see what she knew. She had warned of the danger. I thought she was telling me that Max was dangerous, or that one of the eaves was about to drop from the attic. Either answer could realistically be correct.

After all the dishes were back in the cabinets, and pots and pans were hidden away, Meg joined the men, and Jane and her husband said their goodbyes. They needed to pick up those pesky kids. I stood like a mannequin just taking in the view from the hallway. There were a lot of strong men in that living room, and I just wasn't ready to spar in a conversation, or to be asked questions about Max and me. I also didn't want to hear any Navy stories. I needed to know the man he was now. I followed Jane and Brad out onto the porch and waved my goodbye as I sat down on the top step.

Besides Conor's favorite bench at the park, this was always my special place. I would wait here for my siblings to come home from school when I was little. I waited here for Dad to return from work. He would gather me up in his arms despite the file folders and briefcase under his arm. I was struck by Bobby Trimball when an errant throw of the newspaper missed its mark and broke my nose. I thought Paddy would kill the bicyclist that day. Bobby moved away the next year when his dad lost his job. My little place on the earth was the best place to watch the world from until the day I retreated out here after Conor's funeral. I couldn't tolerate the stoic family mourning anymore. I brought the tissue box out as my companion and went through it like it was a package of pasta. And I sat here the evening of Mom's funeral. It was raining, and my tears mingled with drops from the sky. Despite the rough few years, I could still be comfortably invisible in my special place.

I rubbed my hand on the step. "You and I have been through a lot together, and I don't know any more than when I was a kid. But you're still here as a passageway into that house."

"Is this a private party?"

Before I could answer, Max sat down next to me. "Don't kid yourself. You know quite a bit, Charlotte."

"Please call me Charlie. I think it would be better if you did. Charlotte is a little too–"

"Nope. I prefer to call you Charlotte. Charlie was that little obnoxious tag-a-long sister. Charlotte is a very wise, lovely woman."

I stared straight out into the street. "Do you ever do what you're told?"

"No."

I glanced toward him in disbelief at his comments and his invasion. "Just no? You have no extra explanation?"

"No." Max smiled shyly.

"The woman you were with at the charity function the other night is very pretty. She's on one of the news channels, right?"

"Yes, and she's a good friend from Atlanta."

I bobbed my head back and forth. "Is everyone from that city moving up here?"

Max chuckled. "It does seem that way. Despite what you may have seen or thought, she and I are old friends, nothing more than that."

Ah, he knew I needed an answer. Surprisingly, we shared a laugh. "Max, we'll be friends too." I suspected we'd be friends without the benefits of the exploration of my tonsils.

"I need friends. Have you listened to Nate? He'll throw me under the bus at the drop of a hat."

"He does seem to enjoy telling all your secrets." I said the magic word and silence enveloped us. "Max, you need to talk to your mother before this eats you up."

"You mean the deception for my entire life and the secrets kept?"

"I'm sure your mother was trying to protect you, and your father, well, he might not even know."

Max leaned back with his arms behind him. "He's the head of the freaking FBI. He should know."

"But he might not. Maybe he thought you were his. It seems the Taylor women live with their secrets. Maybe your mom was pregnant when they married."

"I find that very hard to believe."

"What? Your parents loved each other once or else they wouldn't have begun a life together."

Max sat up. "Do you know my family? You know Gio and Rose's story. She was married to someone else, but she was in love with Gio. She never stopped loving him. I can see my mother doing the same thing."

You have no idea, Max. I wanted to tell him that Rose continued her love story with Gio despite the years, despite death, but he wouldn't be receptive. I knew by now that my special gift didn't need to be shared with everyone, even those you loved. I didn't even reveal my talent to the front porch step.

"Max, talk to your mother. She may have the answers you need. Then you can have a very honest conversation with your father."

"And then what? I'm a federal prosecutor. What if my biological father is one skeleton that could destroy my career?"

"Then you begin again. Look at me. I'm moving back in with my father."

Max began to chuckle. "I'm moving my grandfather in with me."

I nudged his arm. "What's wrong with us?"

"I sincerely have no clue, but you and I seem to be in this together."

"Then let me help you. I know you have Nate, but Dad and I can help. We can be very stealth-like when we need to be. We can gain information from sources, and they won't even know they told us anything."

"Subtle? Stealth-like? I would never describe any member of the O'Donohue clan as either.

"We can be, Max Shaw. Just let us know what we can do for you, and we'll be there. I hate to bring this up, but do they have any leads on the shooting the other night? Is it about one of your prosecutions?"

"They don't know yet. You heard your brother. I'll meet with the FBI agent in charge tomorrow, but their original assessment was that these people were from out of town. Even Gio has made calls to some of his old cronies. They hadn't heard of any hits on me and neither had the FBI, but no one is sure."

"What do you do?"

Max flashed an insincere smile. "I go to work. I'll go on."

I pointed my finger at him. "And you call your mother."

He grabbed my finger. "Has anyone told you that you are one huge nag?"

"Since the day I began to make noises."

"Well, that explains everything. We better get in there before they all create more stories about us."

We stood and turned to return to the group. Max placed his hand in the small of my back, pushing me into the house. I turned to see Max's attention was drawn to a silver sedan slowly passing by. The two men in the front seat both wore sunglasses shielding their looks. They looked directly at us and smiled.

"Get in the house, Charlotte," Max commanded as he shoved. The men passed, turned, and returned. This time the one in the passenger seat stuck his hand out of the window and pointed, fashioning his hand in the form of a gun. They raced off. There was no license plate.

It seemed as though Rose had been right…Danger, Max.

Chapter Six

The Taylor Mansion

"Liat, this is Max. Is my mother at home?" Dreading this call was the understatement of Max's life. He'd rather fly a jet into a sandstorm than talk to his mother.

"Mr. Max! It is wonderful to hear from you. How are you?"

Liat had been his mother's personal assistant and in charge of all household business since Max turned twenty-one. The woman's husband had passed away, and her children were grown and out of the home the Vietnamese immigrants had made.

"I'm good. My work is what I expected, and I've reconnected with several old friends. Is Mother in?"

"I'm so happy you are happy. You deserve it, Mr. Max."

"Thank you. Liat, is Mother at home?" Max was beginning to lose his nerve.

"Actually, she is on the telephone in the other room. She's breaking up with that polo player from Brazil."

Max searched his memory. What Brazilian polo player? "Is he a newer edition?"

"She was only with him through the season in the south of France. You know how that goes."

"I do indeed. Will she be long or too devastated to speak?"

"He will be the one in tears! Ah, she has just hung up and is begging for the telephone. Take care, Mr. Max."

Before he could say goodbye, Max heard his mother's voice. "Maxwell, what is it? You don't usually call to check in on your mother."

"I'm sorry I called at a bad time."

"It's not a bad time. Did Liat give you that idea? That's silly. The man was boring, and he liked to spend my money like a pour from a generous bartender at the club."

"I see. I did want to check in, but I had something I needed to address regarding the family."

Olivia Shaw sighed. "Maxwell, your trust is safe. I may like to dally, but I'm not an idiot. Do you need more money for that relic of a house? Not that I'll ever come back to that town and see it."

Be careful what you say, Max thought. I came back. "No, I don't need a cent. I've been doing some of the work, and Gio and Judge O'Donohue have been helping me with the woodwork. You remember Judge O'Donohue, right?"

"Yes, he was a lovely man. His wife had all those children. That's what happens with Catholics."

Max gulped back the inclination to scream, not just at his mother, but just because. Dad was Catholic, and he and his sister had received all their sacraments as children. His mother was a judgmental witch, but that's how she had been raised in the Taylor family. "Mother, I've learned that my DNA has a problem."

"Are you ill? Is there a problem with your heart or do you have an immune deficiency? Your maternal grandmother had both. Some said she died of a broken heart, but I think it was plaque buildup. She ate too many rich foods. Maxwell, are you eating properly? Have you been maintaining your runs and weight training? You have to watch the stress level in your job–"

"Mother, enough! My DNA doesn't match my father's!" And so he finally said it out loud. "Who is my biological father? It sure as hell isn't Edward Shaw."

"Edward Shaw is your father."

"Mother, he is not." Each of Max's words were said deliberately measured. "Just tell me. It isn't Judge O'Donohue, is it?"

"Don't be ridiculous. I have nothing more to say to you."

"Mother, I need to know. I have to know. My job is very high profile. If I want to continue into politics–"

"No, you will not get into that mess. Who is putting ideas in your head? Is it your father? Or that judge?"

"Neither. I was approached before I left Atlanta. I wasn't interested in my life becoming a fishbowl, but now I might consider it."

"Maxwell, you need to come home so I can dislodge those thoughts from your mind. Politics is not for you. Period."

Max wondered if she really would hire a surgeon to fix part of his brain. Obviously, she wasn't going to disclose her secret to him. "Mother, we are going to try this one more time. Who is my real father?"

"Maxwell, I don't want to discuss it."

"Mother, damn it. I need to know."

"You do not. It doesn't concern you."

"The hell it does. Were you pregnant when Dad and you married? Is that what happened?"

"Maxwell, I have lunch with Eileen Poole in fifteen minutes and my chauffeur is waiting. We will discuss this another time. Have a good day."

Max stared at his cell phone. "She's hung up on me. Who the heck is she protecting? It's not me." Max hit another number.

"Son, how is my favorite child?"

Max could tell his father was smiling. He always said that, but he always said it to his daughter as well. "Dad, I just talked to Mother, and it wasn't pleasant."

"It very rarely is, Maxie. What's up? You don't sound like you were just checking in with her about her newest man."

"She just dumped the Brazilian polo player."

Edward Shaw's laughter lightened Max's heavy heart just a bit. "I hadn't heard about him. I thought she was still with the actor from Rome. Your mother. She's always looking for something and someone."

"Dad, I'm fine, but I had a regular check up with blood tests, etc. Well, I had my DNA checked."

"Max, you're scaring me."

"Dad, my DNA results concluded that you're not my biological father."

For a man who rarely skipped a beat, Edward Shaw was silent. "Max."

"It's true, isn't it? Did you know? I mean maybe you married Mom and didn't know she was pregnant? I could see her scamming you."

"Stop, Maxie. Your mother didn't hide it from me. We dated before I was deployed. I was smitten, but she wasn't on my level. By the time we began writing back and forth while I was away, I began to fall in love with her. I thought she was the greatest, and back then, she was. She was so loving and considerate. Did you know she stayed with my mother for a summer after my father passed away? I didn't ask her to do that; she just did."

"Well, she changed," Max growled.

"She did over the years. When I came home, she had moved on. She had her father's money, and she was heavily influenced by her grandfather. She lived with the old codger in New York. Their money did all the talking, but she still saw me now and then. I professed my love, and she patted my hand. She told me how nice that was. By then she based a good marriage on stocks, bonds, and social standing. I was deemed as unsuitable by her grandfather."

"Are you kidding me? I wish he could see you sitting in the FBI headquarters right now."

"I wish he could too. Well, I received a call from your mother about six months after I arrived home. She was in tears. She asked me to come to New York City so I took the train up there. Your mother was in great distress. We went to Central Park and while sitting on a bench, she told me she had made a huge mistake. She always loved me, but her grandfather was against it. He set her up with an up-and-coming politician."

"Well, that explains her response when I told her I was thinking about politics."

"That would do it. Well, Max, she'd been on the arm of that guy all summer in Martha's Vineyard. He was supposedly from a very famous family, and to this day, I have never asked her who it was. I have my suspicions. I could've investigated or asked her friends, but I respected her privacy. I think she might have even brought him to Kansas City to meet her mother. You know, Rose Taylor never moved permanently to New York City with old man Taylor and Olivia. Eventually, Mr. Taylor returned to Kansas City for his business, and your mother stayed with her grandfather. Your mother and I made a deal that day on that bench to become a team. She told me she was pregnant. We married as soon as possible, and you were mine. You have always been my son, and you always will be."

Max Shaw blamed Charlotte O'Donohue for the tears that were sliding down his cheeks. Damn her. Why did she have to make me feel? They became a team on a bench in Central Park. Charlotte and he had their own moments on a bench. "I want that so much, but Dad, I have to know."

"Do you really, Max?"

"I do. What if I have a more public career than now, and suddenly this man comes forth during a rally, or when I take the oath for senator?"

"Senator? I can see that. You'd be great, Max. I understand what you're saying. It could crater a career before you even launch one. Even now, you need to protect your job. Family secrets can prove very deadly."

"You don't know half of it."

Edward Shaw chuckled. "I wondered when you were going to tell me that you were the target of a shooting. Do you think my agents in Kansas City don't tell their boss about what happens to a federal prosecutor, much less to his son?"

"I figured they had."

"Judge O'Donohue's daughter was with you?"

"Yes. Charlotte, the youngest one."

"I remember. She had those brown curls, and she seemed to always have one pigtail higher than the other."

"That's the one." Max smiled. He'd forgotten how she used to look. He enjoyed watching her now, her every move. She was frenetic when she relished her work; she was slow and meticulous when she was unsure. Her tongue would stick out of her mouth as she concentrated, sliding slowly over those full lips. When she walked away, her beautiful backside didn't sway, but he could see the outline of her curves…Stop it, Max.

"So, Dad, here we are. I need to discover who it is. Will you help me?"

"I can't Max. I won't do that to your mother. I understand, and on a personal level I'll be here to be your sounding board and aid along the way, but I won't search for the man or pepper your mother. She has never told me all these years, and I won't invade her privacy now. Does that make sense?"

"Yes." Max was disappointed in the answer, but he did understand.

"And Max, I know you'll track him down because I know you. But I'm your Dad. I don't care if you find out his name is Santa Claus. Do you understand?"

Max closed his eyes and nodded. "I understand. I always want you to be my dad."

"Tell Judge O hello for me. I'll call him soon. And Max, I love you."

"I love you too, Dad."

Max ended the call and sat back in the large chair in his bedroom. As he gazed out the window, he noticed Gio walking slowly up to the house. He was followed by Judge O'Donohue who was carrying a small cooler. They were here to work for the day. Max hit the contact on his phone. "Nate, the investigation is on. This has to be completely under the radar. No one, absolutely no one needs to know about this except for you and me. Do what you do best."

Chapter Seven

"What are you two up to?" In the kitchen, my father and Gio were in such an intense discussion they didn't even hear me come in through the front door. Mickey looked up from his place at Dad's feet. He quickly laid his head on Dad's shoe to continue his nap.

"Nothing," they answered together.

I headed to the refrigerator and pulled out a can of diet soda. "That can't be good when you both are covering up something."

"Sit down, Charlotte." My father pointed at the chair across from Gio. "We need to discuss something with you."

"Okay. Now you're worrying me."

"We were working at the house today. Dear Charlotte, we found out that Max called his mother, and she refused to tell him who his father was. Apparently, Edward doesn't know who the man is either." Gio's eyes were soft, but worried.

"What do you think he'll do now?"

My father took a drink from his glass of iced tea and shook his head. "He'll track him down. He's probably planned an operation of sorts with Nate."

"That sounds right." Max wouldn't stop until he was successful. I'd learned that much about him. He was unrelenting and determined to a fault. "What are you two planning?"

"I have some calls out," Gio admitted, "but my daughter was in New York at the time when it happened. I knew a guy that hung out with society. He's still alive, but he doesn't remember much. There were no rumors. Obviously, my daughter is still scared to this day about the entire situation. It frightens me to think Max could be walking into a hornet's nest."

"And I'm calling Edward later tonight. I won't bring it up, but maybe he'll want to talk." My father reached for my hand. "Charlotte, we need you to go undercover."

I nearly choked on my drink. "Dad, I don't think you really meant it that way, did you?"

Gio's laughter filled the room. "Whatever it takes, Charlotte. Take one for the team."

"Hey, we're talking about my daughter, Gio." My father's act of indignation didn't play well. All three of us were laughing at the poor choice of words.

"You want me to spy on your grandson," I nodded toward Gio and then toward my father. "You want me to spy on your friend."

"No, honey. We want you to help him. Don't let him get killed."

"That sounds ominous. What do you two know so far?"

"Max told us that the man is from a very influential political family. His mother ran in some very rich circles even back then. The man must be affluent either on his own, or he's a trust fund child. She led him to believe that it would be dangerous to even search for him. That's someone very powerful, and she may even still socialize in that circle of friends." My father had a list on the table. "Charlotte, I'd say the man is still in New York or in Washington. He has a family by now if he's in politics. That's almost mandatory."

Gio had his own list. "Edward asked Max about getting into politics. The boy is actually thinking about it. Maybe his biological father could be a deterrent to his career? If that's the case, the man knows about Max, but obviously Max doesn't know about him. The man is aware of that. If the man doesn't know that Max is investigating, then that's an advantage for our boy. Charlotte, do you remember that Kansas City had a boss named Pendergast way back when?"

"Yes, he built several projects around town including Brush Creek and Municipal Auditorium, and he ran the town."

"He led a well-oiled political machine, one that could be ruthless. That's the kind of man we could be looking at. I've talked to a few people around town, and when the Shaws lived here, there were a few rumors about my daughter meeting with a man briefly at a club function. They were friendly, but nothing more. Edward wasn't at the event that night. It was some fundraiser. I can't seem to find a lead on who the party honored or what it was for. If I could nail down those details, we could have a good beginning."

"So, I'm supposed to get Max to talk?" I looked over Dad's list. There were a few names and phone numbers. "He won't tell me anything."

"Charlotte, you underestimate yourself," Gio said. He slid his list over to me as well.

"I keep telling her that, Gio."

"You two are outrageous. You should take this act on the road." I looked over the notes. "I'll do my best, but if Max tells me to get lost, I will. I don't want to be that woman who can't seem to take a hint."

"Max won't tell you to leave," Gio insisted. "Charlotte, he likes you very much. I can tell."

"I like him. We're friends." Upon my statement, the two co-conspirators smiled knowingly. But I didn't know whatever they knew. I only knew that Max could hurt me; could hurt my heart. But I'd help. Max and I were friends, and he was hurting. No matter what, I wanted him happy, and he needed answers.

By the time Dad and Gio returned from the grocery store, I was sprawled out on the living room couch looking over the appraisal on my house. Tom thought the house would sell quickly so I needed to be ready to move. I figured I could put some things in storage and donate pieces of furniture that I no longer would need in the future. Most of those items had originally been from Jane when she left her first apartment.

"Gio looks tired. Where is he?"

Dad threw his keys on the coffee table and plopped into his usual chair. "He's worried about Max, and he's making dinner. He wants to cook this family dish for you. He couldn't help Rose or his daughter, but he has a chance to make a difference with his grandson."

"I get it. It's good to know one thing for sure. Max isn't my brother." The undaunted federal attorney had gone as far as to compare blood types with Dad. They were incompatible. Finally, Max realized his error.

My father shook his head. "Where did that boy ever get that idea? For the umpteenth time, I have enough sons, and there can't be any others running around. I swear." He crossed his heart.

I jumped up. "Let me get a bible."

He pointed to the couch. "Sit yourself down. I was thinking, this could be serious stuff."

I plopped down on the couch and set aside the house information. "Dad, I agree. Sunday, Max and I were out on the front porch, and as we came in, there was a very suspicious car passing very slowly in front of the house. It went one way on the street, then turned, and came back. One man pointed his hand in the shape of a gun. Max didn't know I saw, but I could see the fear on his face."

"I'll talk to Paddy to see what we can do. If he has no ideas, I'll discuss it with the police chief. Maybe Max should cool it?"

I looked over my glasses. "Really? Max cool it? This was the boy who had to run one more mile than Tom. He was a fighter pilot. He is one of the youngest federal prosecutors in the country. He's remodeling a haunted house, only he doesn't know about the spirit invasion. He wouldn't know how to cool it if he sat on an iceberg."

"You win Charlotte. By the way, Gio and I were working in the formal sitting room, and I guess he had a nice conversation with Rose. He heard her. She's worried about Max and the renovations on the house."

"Really? Maybe there's some clues hidden in there?"

Dad nodded. "Gio said that Rose did like her puzzles." We both heard a pan fall onto the kitchen floor. "Let's go see what he's doing."

What Gio was doing was creating the most delicious manicotti I'd ever eaten. He also added a salad with a homemade dressing he remembered from his Sicilian grandmother. We sat around the table after dinner, too full to even move our plates away.

"I add a good Italian sausage, and I believe fresh parsley and basil is the key," Gio remarked.

Dad nodded and he rubbed his stomach. "I don't know if that's what makes it so good, but I'm stuffed. This was the best."

I agreed. "Gio, it was amazing. It was such a good meal, but you seem distracted."

My father shook his head to dissuade me, but Gio nodded.

"Charlotte, I'm frustrated. I only hear bits and pieces from Rose right now." Gio hid his face in his hands. His frustration was embarrassing to him.

I reached across the table. "Gio, you still hear her sometimes. So many people would give anything to hear their loved ones after they've passed on. I used to worry that I would forget how a loved one's voice sounded."

There was a brief smile crossing his lips when he removed his hands. "Charlotte, she said something about my daughter's friends. Do you have any ideas?"

"Let me think." I looked down at the men's lists that I'd carried in with me for dinner conversation. It took me a minute before I hit the table with my hand. "Of course! Your daughter had friends! I bet they still have a place here in the city. Now, we just have to track down some of these women."

Both men looked at me as though I had suggested a fate worse than death. "Fine, I'll track down some of these women. Dad, I need Phoebe's phone number."

"Why would you call Phoebe? She retired as my personal assistant when I left."

"Sure, but Phoebe knew everything that went on in this city. Mom said if there was news to know Phoebe Lawton unearthed it. The woman could keep secrets better than a priest."

My father nodded. "That is true. She held every confidence for me, and she never shared any trial news with the press. You're right. Phoebe might know something, but Charlotte that would've been years ago. She wasn't even my assistant, and I wasn't even a federal judge when Edward and his wife came back to Kansas City."

"I'll begin with Phoebe and go from there. It couldn't hurt."

Both men nodded. "Charlotte is right, Judge. It couldn't hurt. She may be onto something. Women in this city know everything."

Rose was onto something. Someone in this city knew about Max's mom. Someone had been at some party and saw the apparent attraction between the woman and the mystery man. As Dad began to clear the dishes, Gio poured another round of wine. I began to write my own list. What type of man would attract Max's mom? Max's father, Edward, was a handsome and powerful man. But he hadn't always been powerful. His family didn't have money. But this man did. He ran in her society circles.

"Here's who we're looking for."

My father turned on the dishwasher. "You know who it is from a list?"

"I don't have a name, but he would've been handsome, intelligent, determined, connected, powerful, driven, intense, playful–"

"Are you describing Max?" Gio's question suddenly sent shivers up my back.

"Of course not–"

"But you are, Charlotte." My father's smile was wicked.

"You two are awful. You keep thinking that Max and I–"

Gio waved his hand to stop me. "Should be together!"

"Let's look at the task at hand. You two are worse than Sean and Paddy trying to concentrate on a board game. Besides, this list of adjectives describes every man I love." I felt my cheek. It was warm. Of course, the judge and the mobster were correct, but that would make sense. Max would be like his father, wouldn't he?

"So, you might love Max?" Gio's impish grin made me laugh. My father bent over to mask his own laughter.

"You two!"

Chapter Eight

I met her at one of our favorite French bakeries near the Plaza.

"Charlotte, your father said you are putting together a family law office. I'm so excited for you, and I know your father is absolutely thrilled."

I nodded. Phoebe Lawton's white hair was precisely pulled back in her signature chignon. I remembered the first day I met her. Mom took me down to Dad's office the first week he became a federal judge, and I wore my favorite Sunday dress. It originally had been my Easter dress white with embroidered lavender roses. When we entered the office, Phoebe stood and welcomed us, even commenting on how pretty my attire was.

Dad was in court that day. Phoebe led us down and snuck us into the back of the room. That was the first day I fell in love with law. My father's authority was palpable. He didn't even sound like my dad. He was menacing and very serious. The man in the judge's seat wouldn't play water balloon baseball with you. I was in awe.

We listened for several minutes as a witness was questioned. At one point, Dad noticed us. He merely blinked, but I felt so special that he could see us. Phoebe shuttled us out a few minutes later. She also took Mom and me to lunch and asked me about school and my friends. She was kind to the daughter of her boss. Over the years, all of us kids learned that she was just kind. It didn't matter that we were Judge O'Donohue's children. When we lost Conor and Mom, Phoebe was there making calls, checking off lists, and making sure we ate. No one wanted to eat, but she threatened to force feed us if necessary. I would've paid big dollars to see her shove a roast beef sandwich down Paddy's throat!

Phoebe ordered us coffee and an assortment of fruit and croissants. I added a little milk to my strong brew as Phoebe talked. "But I know you want to talk about Olivia Shaw. That woman is a real piece of work. She was in school with my sister-in-law when she lived in Kansas City. Before high school, they all moved away leaving that big old house sitting there. I hear her son is restoring it."

"Yes, he is. Actually, Dad is helping. He's taken up woodworking."

Phoebe laughed. "Or course he has. The man can't sit still. I didn't think he'd last this long as a retired man of leisure."

"He's keeping himself busy. He's currently helping me get my practice up and running. Phoebe, Dad told you what I'm looking into."

"He did. I checked with my sister-in-law, and then I did some digging of my own. She attended a country club party after Olivia and Edward came to Kansas City. Olivia was there alone, and supposedly the man we're looking for was there too. But Charlotte, Olivia had friends from here join her in New York City one summer when she originally met him. It may have been after her graduation from college. No one is sure on that one. Well, the Taylor family was invited to a fundraiser cocktail party for an up-and-coming politician. The friends were with her that night. Supposedly, there was an immediate attraction between Olivia and this man. He was a very young politician with high ambitions. It may have been a fundraiser for his congressional race. I can't seem to discover the truth on that one."

"What was his name?"

"No one could remember. Do you believe that one, Charlotte? It's a crock."

One could always count on Phoebe to speak plainly. "I can't believe no one remembered his name."

"I think they've been told to shut up, or maybe have been paid off?"

Phoebe's diabolic mind had to be the result of seeing too many federal conspiracies cross her desk on their way to my father's.

"If no one will talk, then we have a dead end."

Phoebe wagged her finger in my face. "Not necessarily. What does your father always say? Do you remember?"

"Trust your intuition and never give up."

"Exactly. Your gut knows more than your head," she answered enthusiastically. "I did a little research. During that period of time, there was a midterm election in November. I made a list of the congressional races in that area. Then, I did a little more digging, and looked up which of them had a connection or a house on Martha's Vineyard. I came up with three names." Phoebe handed me a letter sized piece of paper.

I looked over the names and flushed. "You have got to be kidding."

"Olivia lives in a world we only dream of or watch on television, but I wouldn't want to be her. Her mother was miserable living with that awful man, and then the grandfather took over as the official jail keeper."

I touched each name. "These men are insanely rich and very powerful. This one here is in the news constantly with a tech company. Another one's brother was in congress until he was killed in a tragic car crash, and the third is a billionaire."

"So, you are going to have to be very careful. No wonder Max and you were shot at."

Shock replaced my blush. "You know about that?"

"Of course. I still like to listen to the police chatter on my scanner. Besides, your father filled me in on all the details, and why it's so important to discover who this man is. The secret is safe with me." She crossed her heart.

"I know. Our family has trusted you with so much. I'm so happy you're on the side for good."

We shared a laugh, but Phoebe became deadly serious. "Charlotte, any one of these men may not want a son to just pop up. Do you understand what I'm saying?"

"They wouldn't kill their own son, would they?"

"Each of them is ruthless, as powerful men usually can be. Not one of them will admit to anything. The closest you'll get to them will be their communications director."

"You're right. I could think up a few stories to get my toe in the door, or to get Max into an office, but all they have to do is deny it, and Max would be ruined."

"But you can narrow down the list, Charlotte." Phoebe winked.

"And how would I do that, Mrs. Lawton?"

"You could visit Marcia Blaine Comstock. I have her address at the bottom of that sheet. She'll be expecting a call from you. Marcia was at that cocktail party here in Kansas City when Olivia moved back with her family, and she also accompanied her to Martha's Vineyard where they would've all met. If anyone would crack under cross examination, it would be Marcia. Take a good chardonnay with you."

"Way to bury the lead, but I love you!"

Phoebe smiled. "Charlotte, better yet, I have an idea. Let's just drop over there now."

"That's fine with me. We can stop and get the wine along the way, and I'll order some French pastries to go."

Phoebe lifted her coffee mug. "Now, that's a plan. Let's go take a deposition, Ms. O'Donohue."

Chapter Nine

"Phoebe, I can't believe you're here. How many times have I invited you over?"

"Millions," Phoebe answered as we entered the very large house off of Ward Parkway. "My sister-in-law sends her regards. Did you hear that her husband had a stint put in a couple of months ago?"

The homeowner led us from the hallway through the house to the outside patio near the pool. We called right after we picked up the wine, and Marcia had managed to set up a lovely table with artisan bread and a large salad set in the middle. "I did. I sent a card. I thought you both might enjoy a lovely light lunch by the pool." She spotted the wine and removed it from my hand.

"I'm Charlotte O'Donohue, Mrs. Comstock. I'm a very big fan of your column you have in the social newspaper."

"Thank you, dear. I know who you are. I once met your mother at the children's hospital. She was a lovely woman."

I nodded. Without words, I stuck out the box of treats. "We brought dessert."

"Ooh, I love this bakery. Please, both of you, sit. Let's enjoy it."

We shared a lovely meal filled with reminiscing. The information I was compiling on various members of good standing in our city was massive. I only attended a couple of charity events a year, but I knew the names of the influential people in this city. But these two women were connected, and so many secrets were exposed until Phoebe asked the question about that party nearly four decades ago.

Marcia looked down and gazed out at her perfect swimming pool. "That was a long time ago. I don't remember who that event was honoring."

"It was a congressman," I interjected hoping to jog her memory.

"I don't remember, and I can't–"

Phoebe and I looked at each other knowingly. She couldn't. Did they all sign a blood pact?

"You can't or you won't?" I found myself asking. I was like a bulldog with a bone. This was all for Max, and that scared me to the core that I was willing to go this distance for a man who was a friend. And nothing more.

"Ladies, I can't."

"So, Olivia has gotten to you." Phoebe's eyes had hardened. She was totally invested in this investigation. "What is wrong with all of you? Olivia Taylor Shaw is just a woman, and this gentleman, and I say that loosely, is just a guy who messed around with her."

"You don't understand, Phoebe. I promised. I signed–"

"Oh, my sweet Jesus! You were required to sign a non-disclosure that doesn't allow information out after all of these years? Why on earth would you do that?" My voice was high pitched with disdain.

"Ms. O'Donohue, I just met you. We were young. His family could ruin us. Now that's all I'm saying, and if you are friends with Olivia's son, you'll drop this."

As Marcia stood up, I did as well. "This is for him. He deserves to know who he is. This could haunt him for years one way or another."

"Understand this, both of you. This man can ruin all of us. Olivia's son could pay for this in so many ways. He's a federal prosecutor, right? Well, if this sees the light of day, by Friday he would lose his job and end up being a defense attorney in Peculiar, Missouri. I'm sorry. Please show yourselves out."

Marcia walked away from the table and disappeared into the house.

"Well, that went well."

I was incredulous. "Phoebe, how can you say that?"

"She confirmed we're on the right track. We have three names, Charlotte. We can narrow this down, but you need to go back to the judge and plot our next move. I can be over at the house by ten tomorrow morning."

My father tried a few cases of conspiracy against the United States government. The least he could do was plot one of his own against just one person, or maybe three no matter how powerful these men were.

But when Phoebe arrived the next morning with donuts in hand and searching for the coffee maker in the kitchen, my father was still ranting.

"What in hell are you two thinking? First, you're telling me there's non-disclosure statements involved in a relationship that happened nearly forty years ago. Secondly, these are powerful, wealthy men who could snuff you out like that." Dad snapped his fingers for emphasis. "Third, you and Max have already been shot at. Maybe it's not a case of his, but rather this man's friends scaring Max off. Fourth, I have my card game today."

"You can still make your old cronies' card game, Judge,' Phoebe said as she plated the breakfast items. "You need to make the coffee. I'm thinking we just need an hour of your time."

Dad shifted over to the counter and began to do as he was instructed. "Phoebe, I thought you had more common sense than this."

"Oh, please. These people are nuts. All Olivia Shaw needs to do is to tell Max who his baby daddy is. She tells him to keep his clap shut, and all go on with their lives. Judge, you're the one that involved Charlotte in this search. What do you know that we don't?"

My father banged on the counter and ignored Phoebe's question. "Damn it, you two don't know what you're getting into."

"But I do." Gio had unexpectedly walked into the kitchen. "This is my kind of work. You nice people shouldn't get your hands dirty. I'll be damned if I'll allow them to shoot at dear Charlotte and my grandson now that I have him in my life."

Gio's hands tenderly touched my shoulders. "Judge, I've never seen you this afraid."

Dad pointed at the file folder in the middle of the table. "Take a look at these suspects, and I think you'll change your mind."

Gio pulled out the chair next to me and put his glasses on to look at the sheet at the front of the file. Phoebe stood in awe. She obviously knew who Gio was. It seemed as though what she was having a problem with was why the man walked innocently into our home.

"Here's something. This man here was in Europe at the time. That summer he was driving drunk on the Riviera and killed a young man."

"You're certain he wasn't in Martha's Vineyard?" I asked.

"Absolutely. The young man he killed was the son of Vincente Palma. He was a chef for one of my contacts."

"And?" I poked.

"And he's still paying the family until this day. It was either that or my contact would've broken every bone in his body and disposed of him in Lake Como."

Dad shook his head. "I don't want to hear this. I can't hear this."

"Then don't listen, goody two shoes. I, on the other hand, am fascinated," Phoebe directed. She sat down in awe of the former mobster. "Please, go on."

My father murmured Phoebe's name and continued to make the coffee.

Gio reviewed the next name. "This one here is a narcissist. He could be a contender. I could see Olivia being with him. The third one has a powerful family. They once took out a Mafia leader during the early fifties, and I'm not talking about having him over for dinner. The patriarch was ruthless and highly successful. He had his own syndicate of sorts." Gio's eyes peeked over his glasses. "Now, we are down to two. That's manageable. Here's my plan–"

"No, no planning. I signed on to investigate, yes. But Max needs to be aware of what this Scooby squad is doing," I demanded.

"Gio called me last night." Max entered. I thought Phoebe's mouth couldn't gape any wider, but I was incorrect.

"Wow," she muttered. Phoebe winked at me and pretended to whistle silently.

"And now the leader of the pack has arrived. Did you bring your psychedelic van?" Dad asked sarcastically. "Seriously, Max, I know this is important, but I've been talking to the police chief. Those shooters were ghosts. They came in from out of town, and they have nothing to do with your cases. At least that's what they think. They were paid killers."

"I know." Max introduced himself to Phoebe, and she was immediately smitten. He had that effect on women. Even on a bad day, and apparently it was, Max Shaw was movie-star handsome. Today, he wore faded jeans with a tee that showed off his broad chest. He hadn't met a razor in a few days, and he needed to have those luscious brown locks cut.

"Here, kid. Take a look at these names." Gio slid the folder to him. "We've already eliminated the first one. He was in Europe that summer, and I know that for sure."

"That leaves us with a billionaire and a political dynastic family," Max said dryly. His lack of passion probably had something to do with his red eyes. He looked like he hadn't slept in days.

"Both would have the money and the manpower to set up a hit," Dad concluded as he passed out the coffee.

Max looked up at him. "We all have decided that was a hit on Charlotte and me?"

Dad's heavy sigh brought our focus on him. "Yes. The police are pretty sure these guys were from out of the region. False names were used on a rental car receipt and at a hotel up by the airport. Paddy even looked over some of the threats from your prosecutions. Most of them are currently serving time. You're very good at your job, Max."

"Thank you, Judge."

"Now what?" Phoebe asked as she reached for a donut. "Do you give up?"

"No, but I've made some decisions. I need to slow this down. Gio, all of you, stop investigating. I appreciate what you've done, but this is my search. I'll eventually visit my mother. I will find out. So, thank you."

"What? You're going to just give up?" I couldn't believe my ears. This wasn't the Max I knew and cared so much about.

"I'm not giving up, Charlotte. I'm just going to take my time. I have a lot of decisions to make in my career and in my life. I'm becoming more comfortable in my job. I have that case involving your former clients. I have the restoration of the house, and I need to get my act together. I want us all safe."

He looked directly at me. I folded my arms across my chest and began to sulk.

"And you, Charlotte, have a practice to establish. For you to be safe, you need to stay away from me. Thank you for doing all of this, but it's over, Charlotte."

I wondered immediately if he secretly was telling me that we were over. Not that there was a **we**. His caramel eyes were almost black. As his glance met mine, my heart slowed with that recognition. I wanted to cry, but I would not. I wouldn't give him that.

"It is indeed."

"Have a donut, Charlotte." Phoebe pushed the plate toward me, and I selected one of my favorites. I took a large bite and glared at Max Shaw.

Gio was quiet, as was Phoebe, and my father was humming.

Humming? I realized that Judge O had convinced Max to cool it. That's what he wanted, and he wanted to keep his daughter safe. Mom always said there was more to our father than we all saw. I assumed she'd been talking about what happened behind their bedroom door.

As I read the room, I was beginning to see something, and I didn't need a spirit from beyond to frame my final conclusion. Phoebe thought she knew the city; Gio thought he knew his criminal contacts, and I just thought I was perceptive. We had been played by two masters of the courtroom.

Max continually avoided my deadly dagger stares, and my father was smiling. There wasn't anything to smile about, was there? After some light conversation and more coffee, Dad suggested Phoebe drop Gio off at the community center where he volunteered. Dad knew I was finishing up paperwork for Tom on my last sale. As the three of us left the house I nudged Gio.

"I know you think my father and Max walk on water, but have you noticed the very quick surrender as soon as we got closer?"

Phoebe heard me. "I know. They both have conspired against us. You would think the judge knew us better than that, right? Well, how do you want to play this, Charlotte? They seem to be concerned about your safety."

"Charlotte, I think we should stand back and watch them for a bit. You have a practice to start up, and that is very important for your future. Your career should be your priority." Gio's common sense was genuine and made out of his own concern. The little mobster had wormed his way into my heart.

"We agree that we will **allow** them to do their little mission for now. I'll keep an eye on them."

"I'll check in on your father now and then, and if I run into anyone who might know something, I'll still ask my questions," Phoebe admitted. "Your father could never handle me."

"And I'll watch over Max," Gio volunteered. "I worry about him. It seems like he's been on his own way too long."

"I agree. I'll get my life back in gear, and we'll just keep each other in the loop…for now."

We all became a team that day against **them**.

Chapter Ten

"Is your house ready for an open house?" Tom asked over the phone.

Laying on my own couch in my own house for one of the last times, I balanced a large bowl of popcorn on my stomach. "Yes, what else do I have to do on Saturday nights besides clean? I figured we could list it Monday?"

"Yes, that would be perfect. Maybe we'll sell it before the open house."

"Sure, why not."

Tom laughed. "No, I'm serious. Do you remember Brody? He was one of Dad's clerks."

I popped a kernel into my mouth. "Yeah. He was really nice when Conor and Mom died. Why are we talking about him?"

"Well, he was driving by your place when I was fixing that one piece of guttering. He says he might be interested in purchasing your home."

That was a little weird, and yet I could use a quick sale. "That's nice. How is he?"

"He asked about you. I think he's always secretly liked you. He says he tried to get your attention during the St. Patrick's

Day parade, but you didn't hear him. Brody would get your mind off you know who."

I scoffed. No one would have gained my attention that day. Before the infamous kiss, I was planning my attack, and after the dismal outcome of an unresponsive Max I was searching for a place to hide. "I have no idea who you're talking about."

"Charlotte, maybe you should move on."

Tom's advice was received even though it was unrequited. "Brody is really the brotherly type, besides, he's short compared to all of you, and he's always smiling. You know I like the dark, tall, and brooding type."

I waited. There was an abundance of silence on the other end of the phone. Tom was thinking about his next response.

"Charlotte, as for moving on, are you sure about this law thing?"

"Yes, Tom."

"And you're sure about moving in with Dad?"

"Yes, Tom."

"Charlie, what's going on?"

"I'm watching a soft porn movie on one of the streaming stations."

"Charlotte Rose, tell me. I'm worried about you."

"Tom, I'm fine. I'm at a crossroad in my life. I'm moving back into my family's house to live with my retired father and his neurotic dog. I'm spending money without any income coming in, and I'm sitting home on a Saturday night again."

"And you're heartbroken again."

"I'm fine."

"Charlotte, Max is Max. He's been a good friend for years. I love him like a brother, and because of that I know his faults intimately. He's dangerous, ill tempered, and frankly he wants what he wants when he wants it. I suspect he clouds the definitions of sex and love blending those words for his needs. You'll never be first with him, even if you two were to become involved. He'd tell you the same thing."

"He has Tommy, in his own way. I didn't like it the first time I heard it, and I really don't need to hear it a second time from you. He and I are friends. God, I hate that word."

"Okay, so you two are buddies. That's good. We can all still get together."

"Yep. I just love being friends with men."

"Ah, geez. I can't catch a break with you. I'll let you get back to your soft porn movie."

"Thank you. I figure this is going to be the closest I get to a man's naked butt so I might as well enjoy it." I began to crunch on the popcorn.

"Enjoy."

I placed my phone on the coffee table and hit rewind to see the butt again. It was a nice one. The actor was completely tanned. That sent my mind wondering. When it wondered, its path led me to a tall, handsome U.S. Attorney who made my heart quicken, and my temperature rise in all the wrong places. Well, at least it was all the bad areas according to my seventh-grade teacher, Sister Regina Ann. I couldn't watch this anymore. Max was a cause for sin. Damn it.

I clicked off the streaming network. The local news was on, and appearing on the screen on cue was the devil. Max was at a live event for a very large city charity. The reporter was interviewing him about an upcoming case. I didn't hear them though. I noticed the gorgeous and very tall blonde wrapped on his arm. This wasn't his same friend from Atlanta.

"Are you friends with her too?" I bet she was going to see a man's naked butt tonight. I threw a cluster of popcorn in the direction of the television. I needed a cold shower. Besides, tomorrow was Sunday. I'd meet up with Dad for Mass in the morning and would enjoy the weekly family dinner. Perhaps I'd see my good friend Max there?

But come Sunday afternoon, there was no Max in attendance. Actually, I'd prayed for that miracle. It made it so much easier. I had things to do, and I had a career to carve out. I had already wasted enough time.

"Did you see that woman Max was with last night?" I heard Tom ask Sean. They thought I couldn't hear, but the funny thing about this house's corners, if you whispered, you could hear every little word. I believe that's how Mom always knew what our secrets were.

"She's a former beauty queen."

"She flew in from Atlanta to see him," Tom answered.

"Do you think they're serious? I mean, wouldn't he have said something to you before he was flirting with our sister?" Sean's question to Tom was met with silence. Finally, he answered.

"I just had lunch with him the other day, and he didn't say anything about a girlfriend. Besides, he wouldn't do that to Charlotte. I'll kill him if I discover that's what he was doing, just playing."

"Hell, we'll all kill him. I thought he was the one."

"Sean, I won't tell her, but we all thought he was the one. But as Mom always said–"

I invaded their perimeter. "Whatever is for the best, right? What will happen will?"

"Hey, Charlie," Sean greeted me nervously. "How's the practice? Do we need to move anything else over to your office or into storage?"

"You two are wrong." I ignored his question. He knew darn well we had the office set up. Tom and Paddy had helped me. "Max Shaw and I are nothing more, not like that. He made that very clear, and I have agreed with him."

"Okay, Charlotte," Tom murmured.

"Yes, Thomas. We discussed this last night," I snapped back. "Everyone in this family has made an assumption on a relationship that doesn't exist. It hasn't and won't."

"What hasn't and won't?" Paddy passed by, stopping behind me to balance his chin on my left shoulder.

"Charlotte and Max," Sean answered quickly.

"If you ever get with that arrogant ass, I'll spank you."

I smiled smugly at my other idiot brothers. "See? Paddy knows." I affectionately patted his arm.

"Now, if he marries you properly, we will welcome him and his trust fund with open arms." Paddy quickly pecked me on the cheek and took the full force of my fist in his side with good humor. Sean and Tom laughed at my expense.

"Are you telling me dear brother that I can't sleep with him, but I can marry him?"

"It's not the sleeping part I'm concerned with. You don't need to be screwing around–"

"Watch your language." My father entered the mix. "That is such an ugly, cheap word. What happened to calling it making love?"

I rolled my eyes. I really didn't want to discuss anyone's love life or sex life in the proximity of my father, much less with my three overprotective brothers.

"Nothing, Dad," I answered. "That would be preferable terminology. I'm thinking if Max is that good maybe I should get some experience." I knew this would end the focused discussion on my lack of a love life.

"I'm not listening to this." Dad's exit was followed by Paddy's.

"Do what you're going to do," Sean commented and walked away, but Tom remained.

"Charlotte, you're my little sister, and I love you." Tom bent down so his eyes were even with mine. "If you do want that experience then just know you could get hurt. And for the love of everything that is holy, please use protection. We don't need any little Maxies running around here."

We shared a laugh as his forehead touched mine. "I promise. No little Maxies. Besides, I'm not sure I could be intimate with Max without laughing. The man thought he could be our brother."

"He wanted that badly," Tom whispered. "He just wants a family who is normal. I told him he had it wrong with us."

"That's for sure. We better join the others before they start up another discussion about Max and me having sex."

Tom pulled away. "Stop saying that. I end up with a visual in my mind. My food hasn't completely digested yet."

"But Paddy is willing to sell me off for Max's money," I answered with a playful slug. We joined the others, including all six of Dad's grandchildren in the living room arm in arm. Our family packed this room, and I wouldn't have it any other way, no matter how obnoxious they all could be. Family was all you had during a tragedy. None of us were perfect in those days, but when the sun came out, and we could all finally smile, that's when family was the only thing I had. Besides, as the baby, I learned years ago to tolerate and take my time to plan retribution. No matter how long it took me.

Chapter Eleven

I was the last car to pull away from the house. When I was two blocks away, I realized I had forgotten to grab Tom's notes on a few things I needed to fix on my house. I circled back to see my father's vehicle backing out of the driveway. I began to follow. Where was he going on a beautiful summer Sunday night?

Dropping back a block, I followed. I soon realized where he was headed. I parked down the street to watch him pull into the Taylor Mansion's lot. Edging slowly up to the gate, I could see my father.

Max greeted him on the sidewalk, and the two walked into the house arm in arm.

"Damn them." I hit the steering wheel. Once the front door shut, I drove into the lot and parked. Slowly, I made my way up the sidewalk and closer to the front door. Dropping down below the windows, I maintained my stealth-like invisibility.

I turned the doorknob and stepped through. I couldn't hear any voices so I made my way into the hallway. When I peeked around the wall heading into the formal dining room, neither one of them was there. I softly walked into Rose's sitting room. I glanced into the backyard to see them sitting casually in two chairs with beer bottles in their hands.

"Charlotte."

It was Rose. "Yes. I have to whisper. I don't want them to hear me."

"Charlotte."

I clenched my jaw. Sometimes the spirits could be obtuse. "Yes, Rose."

"Danger, Max."

"I know. You told me that."

I dropped my guard, and it appeared that my friend Max noticed me. I went on the offensive walking briskly through the nearly completed kitchen and out to join them.

"You two!"

"Honey, what's wrong?" My father seemed genuinely concerned.

"You two!"

"Well, Judge, I think it's us," Max answered. He winked at my father which made me even more irritated. His dimples deepened when he acted cute.

"She seems upset," my father added.

"I bet it's something I did or didn't do. I seem to irritate her," Max added.

I stamped both feet creating a short hop. "You two are just alike!" Oh, my dear Lord! Max is like my father. What is wrong with me?

They watched me, and I watched them. It was a ridiculous standoff. "Say something," I yelled.

"Charlotte, what do you want us to say? Am I not allowed to visit my friend?" Dad asked.

"Of course, but him? Can't you find someone your own age?"

"Why not me? We have a lot of shared likes and experiences, and age shouldn't matter," Max said quietly. He was always in control, or at least he wanted to be. "We both love law and beer."

"Yes, we do love beer." Dad's additional comment made light of the situation.

Max continued, "We both love this old house and Sunday nights on the patio–"

"And we both love you," my father added quickly.

I blinked in shock. Max didn't deny the accusation.

I had to deflect. "You two played Phoebe, Gio, and me. That's inexcusable." My temper was heading into overdrive.

Max stood up making his way to my side. "It was necessary. I think you need a beer."

As Max left, I looked toward my dad. "Why on earth are you collaborating with the devil?"

"To keep you, Phoebe, and Gio safe. This is a dangerous situation, and I didn't need my daughter and two old friends playing amateur detectives around the city. You three had amassed some tremendous information in a short time, but

Max thought it best if his man took over."

Max handed me a cold bottle. "Nate?"

"Nate," he answered plainly. He pulled over another chair for me. "Sit and please listen."

I sat down and took a quick drink from the bottle. "Dad, you and I were going to look into Max's problem."

"I know, honey, but the deeper we got into this, I knew a professional should handle it, someone with complete discretion and authority. Nate is Max's investigator and is sanctioned by the court. This entire thing has national implications. I was fearful that I'd ruin your life."

"Dad, you could never ruin my life." My certainty made my father smile.

"But I could," Max volunteered. "I don't want you paying for my family's indiscretions, Charlotte. I respect your father and you–"

"Don't say that. It sounds like I'm going into the nunnery or something when you say you respect me."

Max's side glance was one of confusion. My father shared it. "Honey, what are you saying?"

"I don't know anymore. You two make me so angry. I don't even care who your father is. It could be the tooth fairy or a movie star for all I care."

"Or," Max muttered. He took a swig of his beer. "He could be a man in the running for the presidency." He saluted me with his bottle.

"Jesus, Mary, and Joseph." I stared blankly at him. "Are you serious?"

"Deadly serious."

"But he wouldn't have someone shoot at you, would he? By the way, which one of them is it? There's several in the running. According to our list though–"

"We can talk about that later, Charlotte. Let's just enjoy this beautiful night," my father suggested. His attempt to keep me out of the loop wasn't working. I could be unrelenting when I was angry.

"I was shot at too, remember? Don't I have a right to know? I mean, if the man does win the presidency, I need to prepare to leave the country, or at least make sure my tax statements are immaculate."

My father began to make some grand statement of explanation when I heard Rose again.

"Charlotte, danger now. Gun. Door. Charlotte. Now."

I stood up. "Max, there's someone at the door with a gun. Now. Do something."

"How do you know?"

"I just know. Max, do something," I screamed. Max ran over to his cell phone and opened the toolbox near it. He removed a gun while calling for help. Dad held me in his arms.

"Charlotte, are you sure?"

"Rose told me. She's frantic."

My father picked up a shovel, and I looked around for

any implement that could be used as a weapon. Max held up a finger to his mouth. He slowly opened the back door and leaned against the exterior wall of the house. I could hear Rose.

"Danger. Danger."

There was a crash within the house followed by glass breaking. Max crept inside followed by my father with his shovel. I held my bottle.

Once inside, the three of us could hear movement in the dining room. No wonder Rose was yelling. The invader was destroying her beloved built-in cabinets. If Max didn't shoot the criminal, I might choke him. You couldn't purchase glass like that anymore.

Max neared the room and waved Dad and I off. With his gun in his hand, he seemed to take a deep breath and rushed into the room. "Drop it."

Dad and I followed in quickly to see one man. He wore a classic suit, and his tie alone was over two hundred dollars.

The man dropped his gun slowly on the floor. Dad retrieved it and stepped back.

"Who are you?" Max never allowed his gun to lower.

"You don't know me."

"I'll look through his pockets," Dad suggested.

"What are you looking for, and who do you work for? You certainly don't look like the breaking and entering kind of guy."

"He's not." My father studied the man's driver's license. "He's from New York. This is Burton Lawrence Richley." He passed the card to Max.

"Get his cell phone," Max ordered. As my father removed the phone in the man's jacket pocket, I looked over Max's shoulder to see the license.

What was a guy in a suit from New York City doing breaking into a home in Kansas City?

My father handed the phone to me. "You'll be better at this than me."

Luckily, there was no passcode. I looked over his text messages first. Obviously, he was working for someone. I turned my attention to his recent calls. Several were lengthy in nature, and those calls were from the same number. I hit his contacts and put a name to the number. My mouth gaped open.

"Max." I showed him my find.

"I know. It's him."

"Him, him?"

Max's solid features softened when he glanced at me. "Yes, Charlotte. Him."

"Holy Mother of God."

"Exactly. I said something a little more colorful when I figured it all out," Max admitted.

"Mr. Richley, the police will be here in a couple of minutes. You have broken into the house and brandished a firearm toward a U.S. Attorney. You can explain before they get here, or we can air this out in front of the police and reporters." My father's voice resonated throughout the under-construction home.

"We don't need the police, do we?"

"You little squirrel," Dad colorfully responded. "You've done damage here. What were you looking for?"

"Nothing."

"Those reporters are going to love this story," Max said quietly. "Future presidential hopeful has a love child who just happens to be a federal prosecutor. That presidential hopeful and current senator doesn't do a damn thing for said love child, until the child grows up and begins poking around. Then presidential hopeful attempts to kill the love child and the daughter of a retired federal judge."

"He didn't order that," Mr. Richley yelled.

My father grabbed the man's lapels of his suit jacket. "He didn't order it, but he sure as hell knew about it, didn't he?"

"No, not until–."

My father pulled harder on the material, winding it within his fingers. "But he didn't reach out or stop those men from scaring my daughter at our home. He didn't warn Max, now did he?"

"The senator can't possibly acknowledge–"

"That's enough," Max shouted. "I hear the sirens."

The door opened, and Nate rushed in. "I'm sorry, Boss. What did I miss?"

My father released his new friend. "We have confirmation of our suspicions, Nate."

Nate smiled widely. "I love being right." He looked over at me and waved. "Hi Charlotte."

I waved back. The police were rounding the corner of the street.

"Nate, this is going to be a circus. I'll meet them. You keep your gun on him." Nate's gun became visible, and Max reached around to place his own firearm into his waistband.

"Why on earth did they send you?" Dad continued to look at the man.

"I was sent to offer a monetary solution, a settlement of sorts."

"Then why damage these cabinets?" I asked directly.

"I had orders."

"For what?"

He didn't answer, instead I heard Rose.

"Charlotte, the secret."

"Oh." My father and Nate looked at me weirdly. "Nothing. Sorry. I was just thinking out loud."

"I didn't answer you." Our invader was confused by me. This guy wasn't a fixer, at least not of the violent kind. He reminded me of a political operative, the kind who appeared on television to explain how his candidate would save the republic single-handedly. Oh, and bring world peace to all while taking dollars from lobbyists.

We all looked over at the large figure entering the room in a dramatic fashion. My brother Paddy sauntered in and looked the man up and down. I automatically handed the cell phone to him. "Detective."

"Thank you." He already held the driver's license. "Mr. Richley, we're going to take you down and book you for vandalism, breaking and entering, and whatever else I can think of at the moment. You could also be charged with several attempts of murder. The FBI and the U.S. Marshals will be notified since you have threatened a federal attorney and a federal judge."

"I just brought the gun for protection," the intruder admitted.

"You brandished a gun," Paddy said in his detective tone. He motioned for the two policemen waiting in the hallway. "Mr. Shaw, we will hold him overnight if you want to come down in the morning."

"No, I'll follow you now. Call Agent Almonte of the FBI. He knows about all of this. I'll call the Director."

"Very good. Dad, Charlotte, we can get statements from you in the morning. I'll drop by the house by nine."

"Dad? You're Judge O'Donohue's son?" Mr. Richley asked, his voice cracking as he asked.

I almost felt sorry for the man, but it was too funny.

Paddy didn't answer. "We'll have someone here tomorrow to photograph the damage."

My imposing brother swept out as quickly as he had swept in. I began to carefully walk over by one of the cabinets. Glass shards carpeted the floor.

"Charlotte, don't. You could get hurt, and we don't want anything disturbed." Max's voice was comforting.

Nate and Max were shaking hands as if they had succeeded in…they flushed the man out! Max had undeniable proof of who his biological father was. But what secret was somewhere in this house? Why was it so important to Max's biological father? Was it another piece of proof that could be devastating to his career? And Mr. Richley saw the cars outside. Did he intend on being caught?

"Judge, I'll talk to you tomorrow. Could you lock up here?" Max grabbed his car keys.

"Of course. I'll have Charlotte stay at my house tonight."

"Ah, Charlotte." I heard my name and looked up. Max smiled at me, a genuine smile. "Charlotte, I'm sorry we shut you all out, but as you can see, we knew it would become dangerous. We could still hit some rocky waters."

"I understand, but I'm still mad at both of you." My matter-of-fact tone caused both of them to laugh. Nate just shook his head.

"I'll wait for you outside, Max. Good seeing you, Charlotte."

"You too, Nate. Next time let's do it over burgers and beers."

"Sure, but this was entertaining." Nate left the house.

My father headed for the back door to lock up. Max looked over at me.

"Well, friend, you can't say things are ever boring here."

Max, you have no idea. If you could hear your grandmother the way I can…

"No, you sure do know how to show a girl a good time."

"Max, I'm going to check the windows upstairs and turn on a light," my father suggested.

Max and I were alone, at least briefly. He came over and looked past me at the cabinets. "I will fix these. I know you love them."

"I hate to see anything of value broken," I murmured slowly. "I hope you'll be okay, Max. That's all I want for you."

"Thank you. You've been such a great friend."

Every muscle in my body tensed. "At least now you know with certainty we aren't siblings. Can you imagine having to get a Secret Santa gift for Paddy?"

Max chuckled. "Your brother frightens me."

"He frightens all of us. It's his big head."

Max seemed mesmerized by my mouth. I wasn't sure if I had a piece of food in my teeth or a smudge of chocolate on my lips from today's dessert.

"It's his big everything. Charlotte–"

"Yes, Max?"

Max bridged the two feet between us and grabbed my face with his hands. "Hell, Charlotte, I'm so happy you're not my sister. Thank God." His lips found mine, and he kissed me with such heat I knew I was sweating. The man could kiss. I know my brothers warned me off of Max, but at that moment I really didn't care. His reputation was proving to be an advantage for me as I reaped the benefits of his experience. Thank God indeed.

I heard my father clearing his throat, and Max stepped back very quickly, almost falling over a chair at the dining room table. He looked around me at my father.

"I'll see you both tomorrow." He waved as he left the house. "Friends, huh?"

I heard my father. I stood still relishing in the taste of Max Shaw. Every inch of me tingled. I was smiling; my eyes were smiling, and I even thought my ankles were smiling. "Yes, friends." Perhaps the benefits would be even better.

"And I won't tell your brothers or your sister. Let's get out of here."

"I'm a big girl. I'll take care."

My father nodded. "But you're my little girl. You'll need to take care if you're going to get involved with Max. I love him like a son, but this won't be easy for any of us. Do you understand?"

"Just keep the wine chilled. When my heart gets hurt, and it will, we'll need lots and lots of wine."

My dad chuckled as he locked the front door, and we headed to our cars. "You make it a pitcher of margaritas, and I'll make tacos."

"Sounds like a deal, Dad. By the way, I'm hungry. What do you have at the house that aren't dinner leftovers?"

"I can whip up a chili cheese dip with chips," Dad offered.

"Do you still have beer in the fridge?"

"Always."

"See you at home." I looked up at Rose's house. "Home." I was thinking of a lot more than food right now. I touched my lips. Max Shaw, we are most certainly not friends. I wasn't sure what we were, but I was beginning to enjoy the uncertainty. He offered a good dose of excitement. That was something that had been missing in my life. I wasn't sure what else he was offering, and I was okay with that for now.

Chapter Twelve

"Charlotte, he's here. Wake up."

I pulled the pillow over my head and sunk deeper into my mattress to insulate myself.

"Charlotte!"

I flung the pillow across the room. "Conor, I heard Mom. Please stop."

Grabbing my head, I passively watched the ceiling fan in my old room. So many thoughts flowed through my brain, and then it hit me. Max was here. I began to leave the bed quickly, but abruptly stopped, grabbing my head once more. I needed to remember that I would never drink beer and whiskey together again. Why did I keep trying different combinations of liquor with him? My father was a professional at it, and I wasn't even a minor leaguer. It made me wonder about my Irish heritage. Maybe I was adopted?

"That's a laugh. There's no doubt I'm his child." I looked around my room. There was no rhyme or reason to how or why I heard some dead people. I just did. There were times when I'd talk out loud, and no one answered. Then there were those quiet times when I could hear their words, warnings, and musings. Conor missed talking about baseball. Mom sang her favorite songs on rainy days. I selfishly never wanted the voices to stop.

"Mom, what do I do with Max? He's so hot and cold. I can't take the thermostat whiplash, but I want to be with him, and I'm not just talking about being in the same room. Maybe it's because of my age. I'm older now and clocks are ticking. I've got to get a grip on this thing before it gets out of hand. Mom?"

No response was disappointing, but not unexpected. I made my way to the bathroom and cleaned myself up. I threw on a pair of shorts and one of my old college shirts, and headed downstairs. I might as well get this over. It was time to see each other after that kiss.

Barefooted, I trod into the kitchen. I saw Max's back as he sat at the kitchen table. He had paper and pen and seemed to be actually working. Dad looked up from his own notes.

"I wondered how late you were going to sleep in. How's your head?"

Max looked up at me and smiled. "What happened? Did you hurt yourself later last night?"

"No. I drank with him." I pointed my finger at my father, the culprit.

Max shook his head. "By now you should know better than to do that. I thought you learned your lesson when we all drank wine."

I grabbed a coffee cup and poured the much-needed liquid in. "It was a weak moment."

I sat down in the chair usually reserved for my father and sipped my coffee. Dad slid a piece of toast over to me. He knew me well; that was the only thing I would eat right now.

"We can go down to give our statements," Dad said.

"No, I believe the FBI will contact you. They may even come here. I turned it all over to them, and I think Paddy is butting in to make sure things get rolling."

Max's phone buzzed. He looked down at the message. "Sorry, I need to make a call." He left the kitchen.

"Well, that was uneventful."

Dad removed his glasses and looked at me. "He talked to you."

"Dad, we aren't in seventh grade. We're grown adults. I'm not sure what I thought would happen. Maybe I need to pass him a note?"

"Max has a lot on his mind right now."

I stuck my tongue out at my father. "Whose side are you on?"

Luckily for me, Dad laughed. "Both. I want both of you to be happy. If that means you end up together, even better. If that means you find a nice guy from church, and Max marries some cheerleader then fine."

"Dad, she's apparently a former beauty queen."

"Who is a former beauty queen?" Max's question startled me.

I was an adult. I would play by adult rules. Heck, I wouldn't even play.

"The gorgeous woman, another one, you were with at that charity event. Sean and Tom were drooling over her."

"Oh." With that he grabbed his coffee cup and went to the counter to refill it. I turned in my chair and watched him.

"Just oh?"

When he turned back around, Max directed his attention only to me. "Yes, just oh. I knew her in Atlanta too. It was over. She didn't realize how serious I was about everything ending. She now completely understands. Besides, it wasn't serious in any way."

"But she thought so."

"Some women get the wrong idea."

I began to reply and then shut my mouth. Maybe I had gotten the wrong idea last night? I closed my eyes and shook my head. I grabbed Dad's other piece of toast and stood up to leave. "Sometimes, women get the wrong idea because men give them the wrong idea, Max." I took a big bite out of my toast as I passed by him. With crumbs falling, I retreated to my bedroom.

A few minutes later there was a light knock at my door. I figured it was Dad coming up to smooth things over for his prized friend. "You can come in, but I don't want to talk about it."

I was surprised to see Max enter and close the door. I sat up quickly on my bed and pushed the breadcrumbs onto the floor. "Nice. I like the green color here."

"What do you want, Max?"

"Charlotte, I figure we're even now. You kissed me on the float, and I kissed you last night."

"What?"

"You heard me. We're even now."

What was he talking about? For someone who was supposed to be this brainiac, I was hearing gibberish fall from his mouth. "Is that why you did it? You wanted to even the kiss score?"

Max seemed uncomfortable, shifting back and forth. His hands were stuck in his pockets, and he suddenly appeared child-like. "It wasn't that way. I know you care, but lots of people over the years have cared–"

"Wait! You won't dismiss me as one of the others. Look, people care about your power, your money, even your looks. My father and Gio care about you. I care about you. And while I'm ranting because my head still hurts, have you ever been friends with a woman?" I didn't wait for him to answer as I continued. "No, of course not. You're incapable of being friends with a woman. You want–"

His hands came out of his pocket as he took a few steps closer to me. "Can I please get a word in? I came up to say that maybe we could try that date again. But this is dangerous for you and me. I've asked before, but I'll ask again. What if we crash and burn?"

I unlocked my arms that had been clenched in front of my chest. "Then we do. We'll try to walk away, and I'll be your first female friend ever."

"Okay. Look, I have to be honest with you. My life before I came back to this city was very different. I was a loner. I had a great home with a concierge and a driver–"

"And any woman you wanted?"

"Yes, that too. Now, I'm working with your father and Gio on a house that's becoming a real home. That place has a heart and a soul. I don't even call that big structure a mansion; it's my home. I came here to search for answers and to discover the secret I thought my family had. Well, I found a doozy!"

"I think there's more secrets in that house," I answered flatly.

"How do you know that?"

Okay, Charlotte, what are you going to tell him? "Well–"

Max's phone rang right on cue, and I was literally saved by the bell. He looked at the number. "It's my father. I need to take this. Don't go anywhere."

I looked around. "It's my bedroom. I'll be here when you're ready."

"Right." Max flashed an impish grin deliberately done to make my heart melt. "Hey, Dad, what's up?" He closed the door behind him.

I heard his voice, but it was muffled. I went closer to the door and began to hear his raised voice. As I opened it slowly, I saw Max pacing the hallway.

"You have got to be kidding? I'm calling him immediately. We can't have someone breaking and entering illegally and pulling a gun on a federal attorney. I don't care who the man works for…wait that's what this is all about. The Attorney General was probably swayed by a certain senator. That's it, isn't it?"

Max began to string along words of profanity. It was quite brilliant, actually. I was in awe. I'd heard Paddy combine obscene phrases, but nothing like this. Max's agitation concerned me. Something was very wrong. He hung up suddenly, and I shut the door. A light knock came again. I opened the door slowly and managed a look of concern.

"Max, what is it?"

He leaned against the doorframe. "I can't talk about it right now. I promise we will later, but right now I'm going downtown. I hope you lose your headache. I'm sorry, Charlotte."

I touched his arm. "Max, it's okay. I'll be here. Call if you need Dad or me."

He just shook his head and walked away. Despondency wasn't a good look on a self-assured man like Max.

I was walking down the stairs when Max's car pulled away from our home. Dad stood at the front door. "Charlotte, what's going on?"

"I'm not sure. His father called, and Max said something about the Attorney General being swayed by a certain senator?"

"Oh, Lord. I was afraid of this." My father's head dropped. When he looked up at me, I was frightened.

"Dad, what?"

"We probably won't have the FBI asking us any questions about last night. I bet they're dropping the charges. That guy works for that certain senator."

"I get that, and I think that the man was looking for something in that house. Dad, Rose has secrets. That house has secrets in it. I'm beginning to think that some family secrets do need to stay hidden."

My father reached over and gathered me in his arms. "Honey, this man is very powerful. Max is going to need all of us more than ever, and he'll need you. He's going to soon realize that all of his success and fame may have begun because of his biological father."

I pulled out of the embrace. "What are you saying?"

"Max may have been given his job with a huge push from a certain senator."

"Nah, you said Max is brilliant. He received the position on merit, right?"

"Yes, but Max will think differently now, and he may be correct. What if this senator has been watching over his son all these years? Max will think he's done nothing on his own. I'm not sure any man, not even the high and mighty Max Shaw, can survive those doubts. I'll call Edward."

I patted Dad's arm. "Dad, he'll need us. We're good in a crisis."

My father kissed me on the head. "You and Max are good in a crisis."

I shook my head dismissively. "And what will we be when the dust settles? When it's just a normal day with no lies or secrets?"

Dad held me closer. "Then, daughter dear, you two will be even better. I need to call Edward, and what are you doing?"

"I'm going to church." I had my own secrets to discover at Taylor Mansion, but first I needed to pray. Praying in a church always cleared my mind and offered me the direction I needed in a difficult time.

When I arrived at our local parish, I sat in the back pew. I watched as one of the church ladies helped a suited gentleman move around assorted flower arrangements and plants. When I knelt down, the pew creaked, and they looked up to notice me. The lady walked off the altar area and slowly down the long aisle. She smiled as she approached.

"Hello. I just want you to know we'll be having a funeral here in an hour."

"I won't be that long. I just needed a little quiet time to pray. Thank you."

The woman looked up and flinched. "Oh my. Now, don't be alarmed, but they're bringing in the casket early for the visitation." She patted my arm as she gave directions to the additional funeral home assistants.

All I wanted was a little peace to talk to God and to ask for guidance. My mind was whirling. I was thinking about secrets and even about the danger that could be ahead. Primarily, I was asking God His thoughts about a certain man. Had that just been a kiss? Hadn't he mentioned that he was happy I wasn't his sister? Was this all in my head? Lord, what should I do?

"This is fortuitous." A woman in a lovely purple dress sat down in the pew in front of me. She turned and smiled as the casket made its way down the aisle. *"You're Judge O'Donohue's little girl, aren't you?"*

There would be no peace today. "Yes, I am," I whispered.

"I wasn't sure what this would be like, so it is good to see the face of someone friendly when I arrive. Oh, and there's no need to speak. I can hear you, dear. I heard your concerns about a certain man."

I blinked. She was still there, her smile so tender and loving that I had no fear. It was her casket and funeral. I continued to study her. She was pure love.

"I knew your mother and father, and I knew Rose Taylor too. Dear, you should know that Rose loved her puzzles. She told me once that she had puzzle boxes all over that house. I had no idea what she meant, but maybe you'll know. Her grandson understands. He knew about the secret panel, didn't he? He protected you, didn't he?"

I nodded slowly. Maybe there was something in that corner cabinet? The intruder was focused on that area of the house.

"Yes, that's exactly where it is. You'll know it. Dear Charlotte, you'll be just fine. We are all rooting for you. When

you finally realize who or what you need and want, go after it. Rose certainly did even back then. Women today have so many choices, but I suspect you've already made your choice, haven't you? Now, all you have to do is decide if he is worth it all."

My thoughts raced in an entirely different direction. I heard several people murmuring at the back of the church. One woman, holding the hands of two teenagers, entered. As they saw the front of the church, they each began to cry.

"That's my youngest daughter and her two children. They were all so very kind to me, much like your family was to your lovely mother. This is the hardest thing I'll do, isn't it?"

I nodded. "Remember it's all about love," I whispered.

"Ah, and now you have your answer, sweet Charlotte Rose." The woman stood up and walked behind her family. She stopped briefly and turned toward me one final time. *"Charlotte, give that boy a good run for his money. He has enough of it to spare, but only you can offer him the family he never thought he'd have."*

I sat down in the pew. My entire body was shaking. Every experience was different, yet the same. I had answers to nearly all my questions. It was all in my hands. "Thank you, Lord," I whispered.

I nearly raced back to Dad's house. "Dad? Where are you? You're going to be late."

The door opened from Dad's office, and he appeared. "What on earth is wrong? Are you okay? I thought you were just going to church to pray?"

"I did. I'm fine, but you need to change. You have a funeral to go to in an hour. In fact, you're missing the visitation right now."

My father looked at me as if I'd finally lost my mind. He was thinking. After a brief reflection, he hit his forehead softly. "Oh, my heavens! It's Mary Flanaghan's services today. I forgot all about it after last night. I have to get changed. Your mother would never forgive me if I forgot one of her best friends' funerals."

Dad hurried past me but stopped at the bottom of the stairs. "Do I want to know how you knew?"

I bit my lip before responding. "I had it firsthand, and no you probably don't want to know. Go. In fact, I'll throw on that dress I have in the closet and go with you. I need to talk a little more with the man up above."

Dad smiled as he began his climb. "And I suspect a few others."

Chapter Thirteen

Dad gave me his key to Max's house, and as I entered, I truly had no clue what I would find in my search. From what Mary had suggested, I figured I would know it when I saw it. I entered the dining room and saw that the broken shards of glass that had covered the floor had been pushed to one side in a corner away from the cabinets. My hand swept across the lovely wood of the dining table.

"Rose, it's Charlotte. I know there's a secret bookcase, but I suspect there are more secrets in this house."

"There has to be."

I nearly jumped out of my skin as I turned around to see a smiling Gio. "Don't ever do that again! For a man of an older age you sure are light on your feet."

"Occupational hazard. You didn't last too long as a fixer if they heard you coming."

"That makes sense. Did Dad tell you I was here?"

Gio removed his hat and placed it on the table. "No. I came on my own. I figured that guy smashed these cabinets for a reason. He was looking for something, but he sure was sloppy. Answer me this, Charlotte. He saw the cars in the parking lot, right? He knew Max was here and was entertaining guests. Why do it then?"

I shook my head. "Perhaps he was running out of time?"

"Or someone else thought **he** was running out of time and that someone wanted to send a very clear message."

I nodded. "The senator."

"Give that woman a prize. That guy is on the senator's payroll, or maybe he's a staffer. One thing is for sure, Max has found a hornet's nest. I'm not sure his mother or his father can protect him."

I headed over to the broken cabinet and pulled out my gloves. "Then we'll have to do it." I opened the cabinet door. "We need to search every inch of these cabinets. He targeted the upper shelves."

Gio searched the other destroyed built-in. After a few minutes of running my hand across each shelf and into every corner, I found nothing. I glanced at Gio, and he was having the same bad luck.

"Gio, I have to be alone with Rose. I'll be right back."

Before he could answer, I entered Rose's sitting room and sat on the window bench where I had once found the old front door key. "Rose, Max is not in a good place, and I'm afraid that it will become more dangerous for him in so many ways. I need your help. Max needs your help. He's found his father, but that man could be his undoing. He sent a man to find something in those cabinets in the dining room. Help Gio and me. Please."

I heard absolutely nothing. I never did understand. The headaches and the nauseousness I felt so many times before hearing the dead seemed to be my sacrifice. But the frustration I felt when I was helpless like now was more debilitating than any physical ailment.

"Rose, please. I have feelings for your grandson. I haven't figured them all out yet, but I think I could be falling in love with him. He's a good man, and I think he can be an even better one. Help me, please." Tears fell down my cheeks. "Damn you, Max Shaw. You make me cry, and then my nose gets stuffy. I don't even have a tissue." I wiped my nose on the bottom of my shirt.

"Charlotte!"

Rose yelled at me. *"Yes?"*

"Not on your shirt."

"I'm sorry. It wasn't very ladylike. Rose, help us."

"Max, yours."

"I'm not sure about that yet, and he certainly isn't despite what you all apparently think. What was the man looking for in the cabinet?"

"Secret."

"Where? We've searched every shelf, and Mary said you liked your puzzles."

"Bookcase. Remember. Sweet Mary.

I nodded. Yes, Mary was very sweet. I stopped thinking. Well, that was stupid. "Yes, I remember the hidden opening behind the bookcase." Could it really be that easy?

"Same. China."

I blinked. Same. China. "Rose, could you be more specific?"

"Same way."

"Same way. Oh, got it." I jumped up. *"Thank you."*

As I ran into the dining room, Gio was continuing the search. "Gio, Rose said that there's a hidden compartment of some kind in one of these cabinets. It's like the hidden bookcase that Max knew about that saved our lives. The same one you used to get out of the house for years."

Gio hit the top of his head. "Of course! This house has a lot of quirks. Rose used to play games, and loved puzzles, and even magic. She installed secret compartments all over to hide things from her husband."

We both began a renewed search hitting on this shelf or pulling on that knob. Finally, I leaned against one of the wooden structures to rest. I heard a click. Gio heard it too and clapped his hands together. Looking back at the cabinet, a small drawer popped out on the lowest shelf.

Gio hovered over me as I removed the drawer. Inside was an envelope. Opening it slowly, my hands shook. There was just one piece of paper held within, but that was enough. It was Max's original birth certificate naming the senator as the father. I handed it quickly to Gio.

"This changes everything. He can't deny this."

Gio shook the paper in the air. "And the ass knew it was in one of these cabinets. How did he know? What is he all about? Does he hate Max for some reason?"

"I don't understand," I murmured. Gio and I heard the front door open.

"It's just me."

"Oh, Dad, we need you." I rushed into my father's arms for some reason. I was scared and confused of what all of this spy nonsense meant.

"What is it? Gio?"

"Judge, you should keep this somewhere safe. You'd be the best one to have possession."

I stepped away from my father as his eyes traveled over the certificate. "Well, this changes everything. I bet Max has another one with Edward's name on it, but his mother or someone had this one completed first. This is becoming stranger by the day. Is this what that minion was searching for?"

"It seems like it. Dad, this house…what else is hidden?"

"Charlotte, it's not just the house. It seems like secrets were in the DNA of this family." Gio's lament was sad and not one bit consoling. "Judge, you're not going to like what I'm going to say, but I need a gun."

My father's jaw muscles clenched. "Gio, I thought about that, but you know you can't. What someone could do would be to leave a firearm here in the house just in case something happened. This someone could say he left the gun here because his daughter was dating the U.S. Attorney, and he was worried."

My father winked at me. "Dad, we're not dating, but I like where you're going with this. I could even point the gun and fire." Even though two of my brothers were in law enforcement, and all three of them had been in the military, I abhorred guns. I didn't like their design and menacing nature. My view was probably skewed by Conor's murder, but I understood their need in certain situations. This one was obviously a time when a gun could be the only protection Gio or I had against an intruder. Of course, I had my own additional warning system with Rose.

"Okay then." Dad opened his jacket, exposing a shoulder holster. He removed the gun. "Here's the safety, Charlotte. It's just like the one Sean carries on the force. It is loaded. This is just for prevention. Heck, you can throw the thing if you have to, but be careful. I'll hide it…" Dad began to look around. "Where isn't Max going to destroy?"

"The sitting room," Gio and I responded together. My father nodded, and together we entered the other room.

"I know." Gio headed to the fireplace. "Rose had a secret compartment here on the side of the mantle." His fingers traveled over the wall and side of the fireplace. "I know it's here." Finally, his thumb hit on a spot and the entire side panel of the area opened.

"Another hidden bookcase?" I questioned.

"Hiding things amused her and was for her protection," Gio answered. Dad pushed away a book and placed the gun inside."

"It's in there whenever we need it." My father's statement lingered in the air like a heavy cloud of danger.

"Gio, what books does she have in there?" There were several stored in secret all these years.

"Charlotte, that's for another day."

I stretched my neck to see the covers of a couple. They were children's books, but the one that had been shoved aside seemed to be a journal. Obviously, Gio wasn't interested in those items seeing the light of day. I decided I would come back another time, or even show Max. It was way past time for some of these secrets to see daylight.

"Is this a party that anyone can join?" Max stood behind us with his arms crossed and a scowl on his face. His caramel eyes were light and red. He seemed more disheveled than he did earlier this morning, and his three o'clock shadow was now more of a seven o'clock one. "Especially since this is my house, technically."

We all had the smiles of children caught with their hands in the proverbial cookie jar. Gio and my father stood silent. Oh, for heaven's sake! "We came over here to look around at the damage, and to find whatever that little idiot was looking for, okay?"

Max's arms dropped. "Okay. I was going to do that later. Did you find anything?"

I nudged my father. "Dad."

My father held out the envelope and handed it to Max. "We figured I should put this in a safe place. Max, this is bigger than just finding your biological father."

"I agree," Max answered before he even opened the envelope. He read over the paper and looked up. "This is–"

"Devastating for a man who is looking at a presidential run," my father quickly added.

Max's eyes darkened suddenly. "That's what this is all about, isn't it? He's going to make a run, and he has sent out people to shut this down."

"Max, I think the first bunch may not have been on orders from him, but the little guy was definitely a political operative or staffer."

"Judge, you're on the right track. He was a staffer from the Washington office. For your information, he's been released."

Gio shook his head. "He came into your house uninvited, and he threatened you. How is this possible?"

I touched the old man's arm. "It's politics. The senator made a call to the right person."

"What about Edward? Is he going to continue the FBI investigation?" Dad asked.

Max smiled. "He's been ordered to have them stand down. I'm on my own."

"No, you're not!" Gio yelled. "You have us. We won't allow you to go through this alone."

I thought I saw a tear in Max's left eye. He appeared uncomfortable with the realization that he wasn't alone. He was part of a weirdly formed family whether he appreciated it or not.

"Thank you." His soft voice melted my heart again. Endorphins were obviously ruling my body and my thoughts. I was definitely not feeling very sisterly toward Max Shaw.

"So, what's the plan now?" I asked the question we all were asking silently.

"I'm not sure, Charlotte," Max answered slowly.

"I have an idea." My father took the envelope and the certificate out of Max's hands. "I'm putting this in a safe place, and only Tom will know where it is. You know he'll tell Meg, and she'll tell her sister in Phoenix. Those are the only ones who will know where it is under pain of death. All they'll know is that it's an important document that either one of us may ask for in the future. That birth certificate is your life insurance, Max. Now, we are all going over to our home, and I'm grilling these great steaks and fixing a fantastic dinner. We'll have a few drinks and come up with a brilliant plan."

Gio placed his arm around his grandson. "Max, it'll be good. We've got you."

"I know," Max murmured. He wiped at his eyes, removing any evidence of any tears. "I'm not used to being part of a group effort."

"You'll get used to it," I admitted. "When you're the youngest in a large family, privacy is very overrated."

One of Max's arms was wrapped around Gio, the other came around my waist and pulled me closer. He glanced back at my father. "Let's get those steaks on the grill."

"Now, that's a plan." Dad's face beamed. But I knew my father. He had his doubts. This was a circumstance that belonged in a movie plot, not in our lives. Dad had seen a lot as a judge, Paddy and Sean had their stories, and even Tom had his war tales, but the enemy we were facing was an unknown entity. There was no playbook when you were facing down a man who had been cornered, or at least thought he had been threatened by someone who just wanted to know who he was.

"You all go, and I'll be there as soon as I do a couple of things here," Max said as he stepped away from Gio and me. My narrowed eyes stared him down.

"You aren't coming, are you?"

Max's thin smile was a giveaway, but he shook his head. "I really will, but I need to change and do a couple of chores before I can relax, if that's remotely possible with all of this hanging over me."

As Max swept his gaze around the room, I realized the renovation of this house, and the secrets that kept popping up to the surface of discovery were becoming overwhelming.

"We will see you in about an hour?"

I accepted his nod. Max headed up the stairs to change as Dad and I made our way to the door.

"You two go on. I'll wait for the boy." Gio opened the door for our exit.

Dad waved as he headed to his car. "An hour will give me a chance to get things on the grill."

As I followed behind my father, I was almost in my car when I noticed my purse was missing. "Dad, I need to get my purse. I'll be right behind you."

Dad gave me a thumbs up, and I walked back up to the front door. Before I could enter, Gio appeared. "Is everything okay, Charlotte?"

"I am losing my mind. I forgot my purse. I set it down in–"

That's when a torrid of water streamed down on me from the second floor. The shock of the coldness and the unexpected rain mixed with my screams. I stepped away from the entry and looked up. Gio's mouth was wide open, yet he was speechless.

"Shit."

Max was above me, leaning out of the window. "You can say that again."

"I'm so sorry. I'll bring a towel down."

"What the hell, Max? First, it's gold glitter and now water? Why?"

Gio reached for me. "Get in here. We'll get you dried off."

I brushed off streams of water from my sleeves. "This damn blouse is dry clean only. I never buy a piece of clothing like this, but it was on sale, and it's my favorite designer." My screams had stopped, but now I was whining, and I had every right to do it. I wiped off a ball of liquid hanging on the edge of my nose and looked up to see Max almost flying down the stairs with towels. "You!" I pointed at him. "Why do you keep doing this to me?"

"I'm so sorry. Here, let me help you."

I shook my head and water sprayed from my hair as though I was a dog shaking off an afternoon rain. I grabbed at the towel and jerked it from his hands. "Don't you dare touch me. You've done enough. What the hell were you thinking?"

Max looked from me to Gio as though he was pleading for his life. "I thought you'd left."

"I forgot my purse. I was so busy thinking about your situation, I forgot it." I attempted to wipe off with the large towel as I continued to drip in the foyer. Gio took the other towel in Max's hands and wrapped it around my hair.

"I'm so sorry. There was a backup, maybe a leak in the bathroom, and I had a bucket–"

My shoulders rose as I cringed. "Please tell me this water wasn't from the toilet. Please, even if you have to lie."

Max ran his hand through his hair nervously. "Oh God, no. It was more like a leak in the shower, and I placed a bucket there this morning. It was full. I figured out where the leak is located."

I sniffed. "Oh goody. I'm so happy for you." I removed the towel from my hair. I could only imagine what I looked like. Gio began to chuckle, and I had my answer. "Max, could you possibly find my purse in the dining room? I need to get into some other clothes."

"Sure." Max fled. He had no idea he was saving his own life at this very moment.

Gio hugged me. "You have to admit, it is funny. First glitter and now this."

"We seem to be like oil and water, Max and me."

"I wouldn't say that. You two are just finding your way with each other. Love is like that. Sometimes it is messy."

"The word is loathe. Loathing is like this, and it seems to only be messy for one of us." I removed the other towel to reveal a very wet blouse which seemed to be shrinking by the minute.

Max appeared with my purse. He smiled, and his eyes lowered below my neck. He stretched his arm out with the purse as if it was a prize in his hand. "Um, Charlotte, you should keep the towel around you for the ride home."

"I'll be fine. If you don't stop fussing, I swear I'll be getting free health care in prison because I will kill you!" Retrieving my purse, I searched his face. "What is wrong with you?"

"You're wet." Max seemed to be the ultimate fox in the chicken coup. What was wrong with him?

"Duh, Max. Of course, I'm wet. I suppose I should be grateful I'm not glowing this time, but–" I made a face at him. "What are you looking at?"

Max stepped closer, grabbed the towel, and wrapped it forcefully around my shoulders. "Your shirt is wet, very wet, and I'm sure you're cold. In fact, I know you are." He pointed at my chest.

"Of course, I'm wet and cold. Oh my Lord, Gio. I think your grandson isn't as smart as everyone says he is. You're very perceptive to notice I'm cold, and yes, my shirt is probably clinging–" I whipped off the towel and turned to leave. I caught a view of my disheveled mermaid act in the beveled glass mirror to the right of the entrance. My beautiful blouse, my beautiful white designer blouse, was almost translucent. As I turned, the revelation was embarrassing. My lace bra was completely visible. Since we had already concluded I was cold, my nipples stuck out like two sore thumbs. I reached out for the towel and plastered it against my front. "Max, we will never, ever talk about this. All you had to do was tell me rather than stammering like a teenager who hadn't ever seen a pair of breasts." I felt my blood pressure rising. "You are such a–"

"Charlotte, be nice."

Rose's interruption wasn't helpful. I hit Max with my purse. *"Poop Head. See you both in a few at Dad's house."* I stalked out before any more could be said.

Chapter Fourteen

When I arrived, Dad wondered, and I told him to not ask. Fearing for his life, he didn't. Max and Gio arrived and pretended that nothing had happened. Avoiding eye contact became a professional sport.

The steaks were fantastic, the plan for Max's preservation and dealing with his new-found identity was going nowhere. After dinner and several ideas—Gio insisted he could find someone to whack the senator—Dad and the retired mobster were cleaning up in the kitchen and talking about the good old days. Mickey had warmed up to all of us, but he wasn't in with his owner. Instead, I looked in the living room to find Max on the floor petting the spoiled dog.

"You're a good boy, aren't you?"

Neither one of them heard me as I entered and sat down beside the weary prosecutor. I wanted to throttle him, instead I would be an adult. "I would say a penny for your thoughts, but yours might be worth a million."

Max shoved me with his arm. "More than a million. I'm so sorry for earlier, Charlie."

I winced. "Oh wow, we're back to Charlie?"

"You've been one of the guys all night. I thought it might be appropriate." His wink lightened the mood. "But, given the earlier situation, I am convinced you aren't just one of the boys. Again, I'm so sorry. I'll pay for the dry cleaning, the blouse–"

"Forget about it, please. I'm just going to be more careful around you. I did feel like one of the guys tonight. They're still in there sharing stories of the old days. I've heard most of them, but Gio was describing the night he went dancing with a certain stripper. He's very interesting."

"Do you know he never married? He loved only one woman."

"He loves. He still loves her so much."

"I guess so."

"I know so."

"You're a hopeless romantic, aren't you?" Max continued to scratch behind Mickey's ear. We both laughed at the dog's shaking leg.

When Max spoke such pretty words about me, my hardened heart cracked. Sitting like this, next to him was romantic. I wanted nights like this with the man I loved in our own home, playing with our pet, and dreaming of what our future would be like. In a form of defense, I moved an inch away from Max's body. "No, I'm a realist and a hopeful romantic. Gio loves Rose to this day. There's a love that does last forever even after death." And I knew that her love for him hadn't died when Rose took her last breath.

"Speaking of the Taylor women, I spoke with my mother again."

"And what did she have to say this time?"

"She was furious, and she told me to back off. Now that I know who my biological father is, I need to move on. She even threatened to have my father come visit me. She's so angry she'd actually call Edward Shaw."

Mickey began to snore. "I'm taking it that they still don't get along?"

"They do when it suits her. Unceremoniously, they've been separated for all this time." Max leaned back against the chair and splayed his hand across his forehead. "One day they were just not together. We were still in Kansas City when Dad headed to Washington. Mom was here now and then, but in my senior year of high school I was pretty much on my own. Dad went his way, and Mother cocooned herself in New York with all her little friends."

"And where did that leave you?"

"Thankfully, I finished high school here with my friends, and then I was living with Dad in Alexandria, Virginia before I went to Annapolis. My life really didn't change except Mom insisted I come to New York City every Thanksgiving so she could show me off to her groupies. My sister lived with her. They are very much alike."

"Really?" Dad contended that Jane wasn't as much like Mom as I was. He said I had her temperament. I didn't recognize it, but occasionally Sean would call me Mom.

Max lowered his hand and grabbed mine. His touch was all-consuming. I looked down at our hands. "You should understand by now how important my time was with your family. I looked forward to returning to the city just because of the O'Donohues."

"That's nice. I'm sure it's good to have Tom back in your life as your best friend."

"Charlotte, you're not going to like what I'm going to say," Max whispered. "You are my best friend right now. I trust you more than people I've known all my life, well in my upside-down life."

I swapped my sincere smile for my fake smile and gulped. Oh Lord, I was afraid of this. I knew this was my fate with this man. Why did I get my hopes up? I knew, but some dead people thought they knew better. What did they know?

"Thanks?" I finally wondered out loud.

"I told you. I can see it on your face. Please don't cry because I don't need to cry anymore today."

"Friends don't hold hands, Max." I pulled my hand out of his hold. "I appreciate that you appreciate me."

Max's eyes narrowed. "What is wrong with you? Surely, you're not going to argue any cases speaking like that?"

"I won't be arguing cases."

Max chuckled. "You will. Divorces, custody trials, abuse–"

"Yes, but not like you do."

"You aren't cutthroat like I am. You're nice."

My shoulders rose. This was truly a cringe worthy moment. "And now you're calling me nice. You really know how to deflate my confidence. You can be an incredible nuisance while still being charming. I won't forget you have thrown glitter and water on me, and you ogled–" As I began to lift my body up off of the floor, Max pulled me down again. I nearly landed in his lap.

"You think I'm charming?"

I managed to maintain my offense despite that smile of his. "That's what you got out of that rant?"

"You know, I didn't believe it when Tom and Sean said you were a brat, but you can be one, can't you?"

"I was a little girl."

Max pursed his lips. His eyes seemed to burn through me. There was that damnable heat again. "And now you're a big girl. I owe you a date. You owe me a chance, and you said we would remain friends even if we crashed and burned. That's what you said."

"Do you memorize everything I say? You've said that too." I couldn't turn away from his gaze. I was going to stand my ground.

"I listen to you. I see you. Charlotte–" He stopped talking as he took my face into his hands and pulled me closer. We were just about to touch our lips when…

"Max, I was telling Judge O that we could–"

Gio stopped in his tracks as he stood over us. "Sorry, you two."

I pulled back quickly and stood up. "What were you telling Dad?"

Gio cleared his throat and began again. "I was telling the judge that maybe we should go on the offensive. Maybe we should keep up our research and get a bead on what makes the senator tick. We know he's powerful, but we don't know anything about his private life, his staff, or his mistakes."

"So, we profile him?" I looked down at Max. "Gio has a point. At least we'd be prepared going forward. It won't hurt to do it, and it'll give me practice. I'll have to profile my clients and their relationships. You can continue being the brilliant man that you are, and we'll do our thing. It won't be dangerous to do a little digging."

Max put both arms up in the air. "I surrender. You all win. Okay, detectives, I'll do my job, and you all do what you're going to do."

Gio clapped, and I jumped up and down in celebration. We were so happy with the approval from the lord himself that I leaned down and kissed him on the cheek. "I can't believe I just did that." I could feel my face redden instantly.

Max's caramel eyes held their sparkle for the first time in a couple of days. "I'm glad you did."

"What are we celebrating?" Dad asked as he entered the room.

"Charlotte just kissed Max," Gio gleefully answered. "Now, if we can only get him to stop throwing things on her."

Dad's brow rose in confusion and surprise, Max and Gio shared a laugh, and I hit a retired mobster on the arm.

It was dark before Max pushed Gio out of our house. Dad followed them out with Mickey for a short walk down the street. I waved from the front porch as Max's car reversed down the driveway. Then he drove forward. What on earth?

Max parked the car, exited it, and ran up to me. "After the bucket fiasco earlier, Gio says I should do this."

"Okay? What did he think of now? I refuse to send the senator a message with any dead animals."

"I won't let him do that, but he did say something about a poison pen letter, a real one. No, he said to do this. He said I needed to do this."

Max tenderly took my face in his hands again and came closer. "I should kiss you on the forehead, but I can't when I see those lips–"

And then he didn't. His lips touched mine briefly, and he withdrew. He stood back and studied me, but this time I didn't flinch or feel one iota of embarrassment. I liked the way Max looked at me. He smiled at my face, but as his eyes lowered to take in my body, his eyes darkened. I could tell he was thinking. I didn't feel inferior or lacking in any way. Instead, I squared my shoulders and stood up with every particle of pride I could round up within me. At that very moment, I knew I was in this for the duration and for the battle. Max Shaw wouldn't get the best of me. Yet, he would. In a brief second, his mouth returned to mine, and the tender touch of lips to lips was brief but all consuming. I stood there like a board not knowing what to do with my hands, my body. I wanted to wrap myself within him.

Max steadied me with his hands on my shoulders, and he smiled. "Goodnight, friend."

He ran back to the car and disappeared into the night. "Damn you, Max Shaw. Now I have to take another cold shower."

Chapter Fifteen

"You should see my office," I suggested to Max as we walked around the corner from the ice cream shop. "This is so good." Max surprised me with a visit. He'd pulled up as I was getting out of my car in front of the building. I was returning from an elderly client who needed an addendum on her will.

Max relished his chocolate chocolate chip ice cream cone. "I don't want to take you away from your work for too long."

"You aren't. Did I tell you about the couple the other day? I really tried to see if there were any options where they could stay together. They should have had counseling. He found someone else, but she's keeping the house, and I settled an amicable child custody arrangement. They have three kids under the age of twelve. I did suggest the children receive counseling."

"You're going to have a terrible track record if you try to get every couple back together. Some people aren't meant to be. Take my father and mother. They are both better apart. I remember my father becoming miserable when my mother began all her antics. He's happy now. Still single, but happy."

We arrived at my office door. "My name is on the door.

Aren't you impressed?" I did my best television hostess act to present the perfect lettering on the entrance.

"Why does it say C.R.?"

"Because that's my name, and I thought the initials looked more professional," I answered adamantly. "I want you to meet my office manager, assistant, clerk, etc."

Max finished off his cone and followed me. He looked around the corner to greet my office mate. "Phoebe Lawton?"

"Max Shaw," she replied as she stood up. "Wow, since when are we lowly litigators visited by the great U.S. Attorney?"

"Since there's an ice cream place around the corner. Since when does a federal judge's legal assistant come out of retirement to set up a family law practice?"

"She gave me a nice salary, and I was completely bored out of my mind. Charlotte is very open to working around my vacation schedules too."

Max began his tour of my three-room office. He peeked his head into my conference room that also served as my library. "Nice. You'll need more law books. I might have a few you could have."

"I'd appreciate it. I'm working on a larger collection as the budget allows. By the way, did you finish the prosecution of the man who defrauded the energy department?"

Max looked over my law degree on the wall. "We negotiated an outcome. It won't be in the news anytime soon because there were some higher up lobbyists in Washington involved too. The Attorney General will indict that part, but I did my job." He continued his surveying, looking inside my office. "Your desk is very organized."

"Oh, it wasn't this morning," Phoebe volunteered.

"We don't need to share that information with the highly acclaimed prosecutor, do we Phoebe?"

"No, we do not, Ms. O'Donohue. By the way, Mrs. Paglia called to tell you that they want to schedule for next week about the will. She's bringing her husband. I put them on the calendar for Monday morning."

Max looked down at his watch. "It sounds like you're in business. You may be able to move out of your dad's house sooner than you thought."

"I hope," I admitted. "I love Dad, but Mickey and he have their own routine, and sometimes it doesn't coincide with my schedule. The man and the dog refuse to sleep in on a Saturday morning."

"I understand that." Max looked at his watch again. "I can't seem to sleep past six in the morning even on the weekends."

"You need to figure that one out. There's nothing more wonderful than sleeping in late on a Saturday, especially when it's raining or snowing. I just lay in bed, even if I just stare at the ceiling."

Max's arched brow sent a thrill through me. "Really? Is that what you do in bed?"

"Stop teasing, it's not attractive." Max and Phoebe gave me funny looks. "Seriously, he's just trying to make me feel uncomfortable, and I refuse to do it. To do it would prove that he'd gotten to me, and–"

"Counselor, you're babbling." Max had proved his point, and he seemed very satisfied with himself. "What are you doing after work?"

"Nothing. I was going to have the house to myself. Dad and Mickey are going to the next-door neighbor's house for dinner and cards."

"Drop by the house. I want to show you the finished kitchen, and Gio made lasagna. I'll warm it up."

"If you throw in a glass of wine, I'm there."

"You're easy. I'll have dinner ready at six. See you then. Good to see you, Phoebe." Max pointed at me. "Take care of this one."

As Max departed, I looked over my messages on Phoebe's desk. I could feel her eyes on me. "What?"

"Damn, he is good looking. Why haven't you taken advantage of him, or have you?"

"Phoebe, we're friends."

"Ha! Keep telling yourself that one. His eyes...he's drawing up a plan to devour you. Lasagna may be the main course, but you my dear, are definitely dessert. What a way to go. Max Shaw is one fine man."

My temperature was rising. When I looked outside the window, he was waving at me. "Yes, he is. Seriously, I'm not his type." If he was going to devour me, it really didn't matter which course I was to be.

Later, I dropped by Dad's and changed before heading to Max's. In my mind, it was no longer the Taylor Club or Mansion, it was Max's home. He was settling in and spending a bushel full of money on the renovations. Restoring the house to its former glory was an undertaking, but once it was completed it would be a jewel that Rose would be proud of wholeheartedly.

I knocked on the front door, but there was no response. I turned the knob and yelled hello. "Max? Are you here?"

"Sorry, I didn't hear you," Max said as he walked down the staircase. He was buttoning his shirt, tucking it into his jeans. "I just finished replacing a light fixture in my bedroom. Did I tell you that the master suite is completed? The bathroom is amazing. You'll have to come up and see it."

"Okay." My answer was shaky. I needed to get a grip. Since when did the mention of a bathroom become sexy? Probably when it was connected to Max's bedroom.

"Dinner is almost ready. Take a look at the dining room."

I walked through to see that the dining and kitchen were now completely open with a door cut out on the north side of the house. I almost cried when I didn't see the cabinets. "Max?"

He held his hands out to stop me. "Hear me out. Look, we moved them to the west side of the room for the living area bump-out. The two that were shattered by the minion have been moved into the sitting room. I hired a wood specialist.

I didn't even know they existed. He was meticulous in every detail. Seriously, go look in the other room."

I bit my lip so I wouldn't cry. You'd think this was my grandmother's house the way I was acting. I was emotionally attached to pieces of wood. I shuffled into Rose's room, my sneakers squeaking on the recently polished wood floor. My heart lightened as I viewed the setting. "Oh, Max. This is gorgeous."

"Do you like it? Gio drew out from memory the way Rose used to have this room set up. He remembered the chairs and the fabric. I'm still waiting on a small writing desk to come. He thinks it will be similar to hers. She used to write countless letters right in that corner with the sun streaming in from the window. How do you like the curtains?"

I ran my hand over the two Queen Anne chairs in one corner, and I admired the pristine clean mirror over the mantle. "You didn't touch the fireplace at all, did you?"

"No, but I did have it inspected and cleaned. If I hadn't become an attorney, I think chimney sweep would've been a very profitable profession. It cost me a fortune to have all five fireplaces in this place repaired, plus there'll be an additional one in the living area."

I pretended to be nonchalant, but I focused on the side where the gun was hidden. Max eyed me suspiciously.

"And if you're wondering if we discovered the gun in the secret compartment, that would be a yes. Gio informed me it was your father's idea."

"He wanted us safe if something happened again."

Max pointed at me. "He wanted you safe."

"Yes, I suppose so, but the way you're looking at me, I have a feeling I'm in more danger from you."

With his eyes narrowing, Max shook his head. "That could be a distinct possibility, but probably not in the way you're thinking."

What way was he thinking? The devil had done his job. I slowly made my way to the curtains draped over the large window, Rose's window, to avoid Max's heated gazes that set my body on fire. The tapestry was a marvel and a beautiful distraction. "Where did you get these?"

"France. They're custom made. When I found a discarded photo in one of the upstairs closets of Rose, I noticed the chair she was sitting in was stunning. The pattern is as close as I could find."

"You have honored her." I felt a cool breeze across the back of my neck that soothed my warm body. Rose's voice was softer than usual.

"Charlotte. Love."

Of course, I couldn't answer her or ask a needed question. I still didn't know how Max would accept the fact that his grandmother haunted his house, or that his friend and grandfather could hear her.

"Charlotte. Proud."

I understood completely. "Max, Rose would be so proud of what you're doing."

"Do you think so?" He pushed his hands deep into his pockets. I loved it when he looked like a little boy and less like a menacing rake from olden days. When he was unsure, he was so much more relatable and less dangerous.

"I know so. The lasagna smells amazing."

"The lasagna. I need to get it out of the oven."

Once he was gone, I whispered out loud. "Rose, he really is trying. He wants a home here. He hasn't said that, but he's changing."

"Yours. Charlotte."

"I don't know about that."

"Love him."

I giggled. "You are very pushy."

"I know things."

I gasped. "My mom used to say–"

Max was calling out to me. I wiped away my tears and pretended I was hungry. I needed my mother so badly. I wanted her to hold me in her arms again and tell me everything would be okay. She'd always say, "I know things. Trust me."

Gio could cook. The lasagna was perfect, the salad and bread were wonderful, and the wine was cool with hints of pear. Our dinner conversation was a discussion about law. I was used to that from the years at the O'Donohue dinner table. I loved working with people, and each day I understood more that I had made the correct decision for my life. Max's job had a stress level that would put me six feet under in less than a year. He had perfected ways to overcome the pressure with running and quiet time. He admitted that Rose's sitting room would be the perfect place to sip an Irish whiskey and read a good book.

Max threw the towel on the counter as he finished the last pan. "How do you like the waterfall edge on the island?"

"It's amazing." My voice trailed off while I looked over the pot filler faucet on the stove. "But I love this. It's the little things that make me so happy. I want one of these."

"You really don't ask for much, do you?"

I fiddled with the faucet and moved onto the professional refrigerator. "Nah, I'm very low maintenance. I could learn to be high strung, but why? Who needs all that?"

"Not the cars, the clothes, the parties, Charlie?"

"Nope. I'm good with an old movie on a Saturday night and a great pizza. A beer or two is good if I'm not trying to lose weight. I always have these persistent twenty pounds that go up and down like an elevator."

I turned to see Max leaning on the counter watching me. "Charlotte, I hadn't noticed."

"You are very kind. It's an Irish thing. My grandmother had hips that birthed twelve children. I have them honestly. Damn DNA." I suddenly realized I had mentioned a very sore subject. "I'm so sorry. I didn't mean to bring that up."

"No problem. I'm becoming numb. With twelve children, are all the cousins here in the city?"

"Most. Being part of a very large Irish family doesn't make it easy to date."

Max thought for a second about my unusual disposition. "I never thought about that. What do you do?"

"You date and marry someone from college or you're an old maid. There's an Irish saying I know Dad also said wrong, but it was something like marry and you marry the entire family. We're a large extended family so there's only those two choices for a good Catholic Irish girl, right? I suppose you could always move out of town–"

Max remained silent. It may have been the first time I saw the man without a funny or smart retort. I lessened his pain by changing the subject.

"I'm surprised you don't have Nate hanging around."

"I'm tired of living in fear. I can protect myself. Besides, Nate can be a bit much."

"No. Really?" I smiled.

Max pushed away from the counter. "Hey, come see the master suite. I want to see what you think."

"What kind of faucets do you have in the bathroom? If there's one that spouts wine, I'm in." Again, what was wrong with my mouth tonight? But Max seemed to take it in stride. I followed him up the grand staircase that Dad and Gio had worked on. Any flaws were corrected and unseen. I'd only been on the second floor during one tour before we'd listed the mansion. To the left, the long hallway was the corridor to at least six different rooms, including what used to be a billiard parlor. I followed Max to the right of the stairs.

"I enlarged the master suite so that this side of the house is separated with only three bedrooms across the hall." He opened the French doors, and a light automatically bathed the room brilliantly.

"Oh my." The large bay window was in front of us with a distant view of The Plaza. The bench below it was padded and accented with several pillows of different shapes and sizes. There was a comfortable sitting area with chairs and a couple of side tables. To the right of the room was a stylish king-size bed and a lovely bench at its foot, a set of tables and lamps on either side. "This is absolutely stunning, yet it's comfortable."

"I think so. It's Modern and European. Check out the bathroom." Max led me past the bed and through another set of French doors. On either side were two large closets. Both had an island of drawers in the middle. Before me was the most beautiful bathroom I'd ever seen.

My eyes were drawn to the mix of modern and romance. A mirror rimmed in a silver metal hung above the double sink and counter. There was enough space to hold every woman's dream allotment of makeup. But my attention quickly turned to the double shower with two rainforest shower heads and a large square one in the middle. There were built-in seats. I always wanted to sit and shave my legs. This was like looking into heaven's secrets.

"You haven't seen the tub."

"I'm in love with the shower." I turned and followed his lead. There it was on the other side of the room like a shining beacon in the darkness. The very modern square on the edges but rounded tub was framed by tile. Behind it was a very chic gas rectangular fireplace cut into the wall. Plum and gray towels hung on the built-in rack with a shelf parallel which would be a perfect place for a wine bottle and two glasses. I could live in that tub for the rest of my days.

"I actually did the tile work over here." Max was on the other side of the room, pointing at his handy work, but I remained behind salivating over a pristine standalone bathtub. I thought I could hear angels singing, and not a pesky ghost contending that I belonged with this man. Here and now, I was in love with this porcelain beauty. I would name the thing, and we would date. Of course, wine would be involved and the occasional mango pineapple scrub. Bubbles would be essential.

"Charlotte, are you okay?"

I looked up quickly. I was squatting on the side of the tub, laying my head on the side. "Yes, sorry. I've never seen anything so beautiful. I don't have much time by myself, and this tub is unbelievable. I could think of so many things to do in it."

"So could I." Max's voice changed. Three little words held so much passion and promise, I nearly lost my balance. I stood up quickly, but my legs wobbled. While I pretended to admire the artwork on the wall, I could hear Max chuckle. The devil knew what he had done to me, but I wouldn't and couldn't face him until the color went down in my cheeks.

"This place is unbelievable. The bathroom takes my breath away."

"I noticed." Again, his voice rumbled, sending a fire rushing through my body. I could feel him standing close behind me. I could feel his warm breath. If he touched me, I might lose my mind and babble complete nonsense. It would be nice to be held, to be kissed, to be…wanted. It had been a long time.

I looked at my watch. "Wow, look at the time. I should go. I love the gray and plum towels. Is it plum? It sure is pretty." I kept on rambling and turned to leave the most amazing bathroom ever but was stopped by two hands on my arms.

Max turned my body until I stood before him. "Stop. I'm not going to do anything you don't want me to do."

He tipped my face up to look into his eyes. I spoke first in an effort to outline our parameters. "You've made our relationship very clear."

"I also told you that I'm looking at my life in a different way now."

My lower lip quivered. "But what if you think this is what you want, and then you don't? Maybe in a few months you'll be hitting the bars and clubs again and wanting the beauty queen."

"Charlotte, she's gone. I made it very clear to her this time." Max lowered his face down to mine, but I pushed him away.

"We've had a great night. Don't mess it up. Let's take our time. I need to be sure, Max. More importantly, you need to be sure."

"We can't get to know each other better and just have a little fun?"

I sighed and then laughed. "Oh, you are very good. So this is what pro league seduction sounds and feels like?"

Knowing he was caught; he began his endearing child act. "It's what I do very well."

"Ah, and I recognize blarney," I joked. I reached up and took the hand that was holding my face into mine. "Come on. I know you have dessert in that kitchen."

"Do you want to hear what I would normally say to a woman?"

"Sure. I might as well experience the entire scene."

He stopped and pulled me into his arms. "I would hold you like this and gaze into your eyes. I would say that you were supposed to be the dessert. How's that?"

I had no words. His eyes could melt a nuclear reactor or the coldest iceberg. His arms held me as though he was the only safety net between me and falling to my death from a ferris wheel. His voice was low, sending chills down my spine. Did I want to be dessert? No, not tonight. I wasn't ready to just have a little fun. I had to pretend I was unphased, but I had a suspicion he knew better. "It was okay. I still need dessert."

"Wow, you're a tough audience."

I pulled him along behind him. "I grew up with brothers, remember?"

"I remember. They're the ones who will kill me if I ever hurt you."

"You have met them! Now, do you have ice cream, pie, cake…what?"

"I picked up your favorite cupcakes from the Brookside bakery."

"Pasta, bread, and my cupcakes! You really were trying to seduce me. What should a girl do?"

Chapter Sixteen

Taylor House, Sunday Afternoon

"Gio, who are you talking to?" Max thought he heard his grandfather. He'd just turned on the dishwasher and grabbed a beer. He'd heard talking. Maybe Charlotte or the judge had dropped by? But when he entered Rose's sitting room, Gio was speaking out loud to no one.

"Rose."

"Ah, you pretend to talk with her? That's sweet."

"No, Max. I converse with Rose."

The suspicious grandson sat next to him on the window seat. "There's perfectly comfortable chairs in this room right over there."

"But this is my place, Max." He touched Max's hand and patted. "Max, listen to me. I talk to her, and she talks to me."

"Okay." Max took a drink from the bottle. "I'm going to cut you off from your wine. You probably shouldn't be drinking with your meds anyway."

Gio stood up and walked toward the portrait of his beloved Rose that hung on the opposite wall. He blew a kiss toward the painting. "You would've been her sidekick. I think you would've been pals."

"Are you feeling okay? You're making me feel uncomfortable." Max joined him.

"Feelings make you uncomfortable, don't they?" Gio's question took his grandson by surprise. "You have begun to feel, and that's messing with all that you know is true."

"I feel."

Gio laughed. "When it serves your needs. What's with you and Charlotte?"

Max sat down in one of the large chairs. Why use a window seat when you could sit in a three-thousand-dollar chair? "We're friends."

"Give me a break. You showed her your bathroom."

Max chuckled. "I did, but what is that supposed to mean? She likes houses and furniture, remember? She used to sell real estate."

"You don't just take a woman up to see your bathroom which happens to be in your master suite, Mr. Fancy Pants."

Gio was about as subtle as a truck. "I thought she might like to look at what I've done in the house."

"Did you show her your office upstairs? No, you did not. That room was at the top of the stairs, and you passed it on your way to the bedroom. Did you discuss what the living area will look like? No, you did not. Don't toy with me, boy. And don't you dare mess with Charlotte O'Donohue. You and I both know damn well that she's marriage material, if you'd get your act together and stop acting like you're someone you're not."

Max adjusted his position, straightening his posture to compensate for the euphemistic nerve the elderly man had hit. "Gio, you are overstepping. You really have no idea who I am."

"I do, Max." Gio shuffled over to the other chair. He touched the fabric arm. "Take this chair. You didn't need to spend thousands on a chair like this. But you have enough of your mother in you that you are trying to impress even when no one is here to see it. I know about your life in New York City, Washington, and Atlanta. Hell, I saw you on television when you were dating that actress. Max, that's not you. You need to know who you are. I worry about you. I worry you'll have all of your shiny and expensive things, and you'll be alone in this big house. You'll be held captive by who you think you should be."

Max shot up out of his chair. "Enough. That is enough. I know damn well who I am. I'm a U.S. Attorney. Who says I want Charlotte? She really isn't in my league anyway."

Gio smiled. "You are right, boy. Her league is majors, and you're still in the minors. Max, I've known amazing people over my lifetime. I've known bums, criminals, killers, and I've known the best ones like Judge O, Rose, and Charlotte. Figure it out, but don't take too long. Someone else will see her value and snatch her up. I've seen that Brody guy hanging around the judge. He likes her, and he'd fit in perfectly with her family."

Max's left hand balled into a fist. He took another drink and glared at Gio, but the man smiled.

"Max, sit down." He pointed toward the other chair. "Sit down."

Max slumped into the chair. "What else have I done wrong?"

"Listen to me now. Rose is worried about you."

"Gio, stop. I'm worried about you. You're talking to dead people, and relaying messages?"

"Max, she is still here in this house. She loves you and is worried about you. She is your family, and yes, we talk. That's what I was doing here the day of that murder. That's why I come and work here while you're at the office. Judge O knows. Char–"

Max's attention was piqued. "Charlotte, what?"

"She'll kill me. Fine, I need to be honest if I'm expecting you to do the same. Charlotte knows about it because she can hear Rose too."

Max's eyes crossed. "Charlotte can hear dead people like my grandmother. Right."

"She heard her the night that the senator's staffer came into the house. You didn't hear anyone, did you? Charlotte told you there was danger."

"She heard the guy."

"She did not. Rose told her. Rose told her about the dead body she found here in the sitting room. Rose has told her many things. Charlotte hears other dead people too."

"You aren't making the case for me to do anything with Charlotte O'Donohue except keep my distance and run away from crazy. She will remain on the friend list." Max shook his head as if he were shaking off Gio's comments. The elderly man was certainly losing his faculties.

"Fine. You're going to do what you're going to do. You make excuses for what you're feeling." Gio threw his hands up in surrender. "I'm done with my gospel now. It's your life, but Rose wants you to have her car. She just told me."

Max decided to placate the delusion. "And exactly where is this car? It's quite a few decades old by now."

"She says it is in the storage shed on the edge of the property. She says you tried to open the door a few months ago, but you gave up. You looked inside, but the windows are too dirty."

"Okay. Fine. Yes, I've checked every storage structure and shed on this property. Good guess, Gio."

Gio looked up in disgust. "Rosie, he's not believing me. Where's the key?"

Entertained by the act, Max remained riveted by Gio's actions. "Can you see her? Is she thinner now?"

Gio's features hardened. He turned to face Max and propelled a threatening finger in his direction. "You spoiled little rich kid. If you keep this up, I won't tell you where the key to the lock is, or where the car key is. Now, pretend to be open minded. I'd like to see her car again."

Max sobered up at the threat. "I'm sorry. You really do believe you can talk with her, don't you?"

"Because I can," Gio yelled as he stood. He headed to the window seat. "Have your structural engineers messed with this wall at all?"

"No, we bumped the house out for your suite down this hallway and past the sunroom." That was before Max thought Gio was off of his game.

"Good." He sat on the bench, bent over, and began to move his hand up and down on the wall. Slowly, he rose up. "I can't do this. Max, will you look over in this corner by the bench, please."

Max decided it was better to indulge him. "Sure, why not? How many more hiding places are in this place?"

"I'm not sure. Her husband was a brute, so she had to have her hiding places. I shouldn't tell you this, but what are you going to do, put me in prison?"

As Max knelt on the floor, he looked up awkwardly. "I could. What did you do?"

"I didn't do it, but I had it all planned out to kill your grandfather, Rose's husband. She made me cancel the operation. It was a good plan. No one would've tracked it back to me, but I was afraid they might have thought Rose had done it. Some have speculated he was murdered."

"I'll remember to come to you if I ever need anyone whacked." Max searched around the bottom of the seat where it met the floor. "Exactly what am I looking for?"

"Wait." Gio listened to Rose's voice. "She says to keep your left hand where it is. Now, with your right hand, pop the wood where it meets the wall."

Max listened intently. He steadied his left hand in place. Near the wall, he saw the wood plank. There didn't seem to be a nail in that one slender piece. He hit it as if he was nailing it down. Instead, the plank slowly sprung up, revealing a pocket. Reaching in, Max unearthed a small tin. He handed it up to Gio.

"She's watching us?" Max asked nervously. "She knew where my hand was?"

"Yes." Gio opened the tin and within was a small pouch housing two keys. He handed them to Max. "Here you go, boy."

"Holy Jesus."

"Yes. I wet my pants the first time she talked to me," Gio shyly admitted. "I was scared to death, and then I took advantage of the situation. Every time I'm allowed a visit, I feel blessed. I'm not sure how long it will last. Charlotte says there must be guidelines and restrictions. Her mother and brother wake her up in the morning when she's late, but they won't tell her the lotto numbers."

Max leaned against the wall, mesmerized by the two keys. "Charlotte hears her mother and Conor?" His voice broke as he asked. "This is unbelievable."

Gio stood and clapped. "Let's go get that car, Max."

Max's legs were weak, and his mind was addled. As he struggled to stand, Gio offered a hand. "Conor? Unbelievable."

"But, ghosts won't help you win at the casino. Let's go." Gio led the way out of the back of the house and down the north pathway. The storage shed was larger than a garden shed, but smaller than a garage. He remembered the area used to house the caretaker's tractor. Sometimes, Rose would hide from her husband in the structure.

Max didn't know what to think. The keys in his hand were physical evidence of a metaphysical experience of some kind. One key was definitely for an automobile; the other had to be for the lock. His hands shook as the key fit and the lock, after a little tugging, could be pulled apart.

With a door that hadn't been opened in decades, Max put his weight into the endeavor. Once it opened a bit, Gio helped to shove it open. There it was. A tarp that was in shredded pieces from years of temperature fluctuations covered what looked to be a vehicle. Gio carefully walked toward the front of the car. He lifted the cover and saw the license plate.

"This is it!"

Max continued to throw off the decaying tarp until the car was displayed. "I really don't believe what I'm seeing." Max picked up one side of the cloth convertible top. It disintegrated in his hands. The interior's leather was cracked and warped. Dirt covered most of the instrument gauges. He came around to the front to stand by Gio. He placed his hands around the old man's shoulders.

"It's her car, Gio. It's a beautiful Jag Roadster. A baby blue antique wonder."

"It was her only freedom. You and she love Jags." Gio tugged out of Max's physical contact and turned away. He didn't want him to see his tears. But Max could hear. He could see Gio's shoulders shiver as he wept.

Max came from behind and placed his hands on his grandfather's shoulders to comfort him. "You gave her freedom too, and you gave her the love she deserved. You also gave her a beautiful baby girl, my mother. You gave her everything that was good in her world."

"And yet I was a bad man. I played with fire, and I was burned. Her husband had me put away." Gio cleaned up his face with his handkerchief and faced his grandson. "Don't get me wrong, I did everything I was convicted of, but he set it up that I couldn't be there to save her."

"Gio, this spoiled brat has learned one thing. You can't go back in history and fix things. You can only do better and live in the moment, and even for the future." Max returned his arm over the man's shoulders and looked lovingly at Rose's car. "We are going to get your suite finished as soon as humanly possible, and we are going to restore this old girl. You and I will drive down Ward Parkway in a baby blue sports car, the mobster and the attorney. Can you see it?"

Gio nodded. "I'd like that very much, but you know I have my apartment until the end of the year."

"I know, but you could move early. You'll just give the landlord a bonus."

"No, I paid for it through the end of the year."

Max heaved a heavy sigh. "You know, I know a lawyer who could get you out of that, right?"

"Who?"

Max shook his head in dismay. "Oh, I don't know, maybe some rich kid, or maybe a family lawyer who could say you're ill and negotiate a few bucks back for you, or maybe even a retired judge…I need a drink, and I want to hear more about Charlotte and her ghosts."

"She's going to kill me, Max. She wanted to tell you."

Max shoved the door and locked their treasure up. "I'll deal with Charlotte in my own way, but I want intel."

"And the car?"

Max smiled. "Nate knows a guy. He was in the Navy with us, and now he owns an auto company. He is in Kansas City this coming week for the race in Kansas. We'll go talk to him. Now, how about that drink?"

"I'd like that. I could whip up a little pasta. Do you have any clams?"

"Sorry, just a can of them. I did buy that fresh garlic and parsley you asked for last week."

"And I know you have white wine, so we have dinner."

Arm in arm they walked back to the house. These uniquely different men would talk for hours about a woman that Max had never known but knew now that she loved him very much and wanted to protect him. They also talked about a woman whom they both knew was fiercely independent and demanding. One man adored her like a granddaughter, and the other wondered what he was feeling for the very first time in his life.

Chapter Seventeen

As I walked up the sidewalk to the house, I noticed Gio standing outside at the front door. "Hello you! Where's Max?"

"He's working in his office. Second floor at the top of the stairs. You can't miss it, the master's office."

"At least I'm safe so far from glitter or water." Gio didn't laugh at my joke but kept looking at his old watch. The black band was worn, and I bet he still had to wind it each day. "You seem a little anxious. Is everything okay?"

"I'm waiting for a friend. This is very important."

He continued to look out into the street. "I'll go see Max."

"Yes, do that."

I looked back. I'd never seen Gio this way. It must be one important friend. "Hello Rose." I always said hello even if I didn't receive an answer. "You better check on Gio before he has a coronary out there." I headed upstairs and saw the large office, its door open to the hallway.

"Max?" I called out as I entered.

The chair spun around to reveal the star prosecutor. I was stunned by the glasses on his nose. "Glasses?"

"Readers. No need to tell the world. What's up?"

"Vain, you are, Max Shaw. You said I could drop by with my client's petition for full custody. This is his second attempt, and I don't want any mistakes."

Max's hand extended out. "Gimmee. You seem to abhor mistakes. Have you dotted all the i's? Have you proofed and double proofed, checked all information, and reliable sources? Have you–"

"Yes," I interrupted. "I've done everything humanly possible. No, I don't like mistakes especially when lives are on the line."

Max looked over the document. "Humanly? Any other sources?"

"No." I wondered where he was going with this. I looked around the office while he read the straightforward petition. One wall held photos from his life and career. There was an amazing one of his father when he became the head of the FBI. To the side of it was a photo of his sister playing at a baby grand.

"Have you attached statements from the grandparents?"

"Yes. Both sets are backing him. His ex has been abusive to their daughter, and now she's married to a gentleman, and I say that loosely, who has a questionable reputation."

"Why was it denied the first time?"

I came to his side and stood over him, reaching out to have him focus on page twenty. "It's here with all of the social service's reports. I am arguing that social services are overworked and forgave several missed appointments."

Max leaned back, removing his glasses. "I would word it a little differently. The judge isn't going to appreciate blaming a department."

"But I'm not. I'm offering them an out."

"By the way, have they assigned a judge? Do I know him?"

I grimaced. "Well, we'll probably get Judge Roberta McAllister. She's been grabbing custody hearings recently."

"I take it from your face she's not that forgiving?"

I sat on the edge of his desk. "She's considered a hardass."

Max feigned shock. "Charlotte O'Donohue, language. I should wash your mouth out with soap."

"Try it and die. Brothers, remember?"

"How can I possibly forget? You keep reminding me every chance you get." Max scanned the next few pages. "May I keep it overnight and drop it by your office in the morning on my way to work?"

"Yes, please. I wanted to file it by Thursday."

"Where's the child currently residing?" Max placed my hard work in the middle of his very organized desk.

"She's with a foster family and is thriving. Her grades are up, and she's happier. She wants to be with her father though. She's a lovely little girl." My focus was taken by a man walking up the walkway. Gio greeted him with open arms and a kiss on each cheek. "You have company, rather Gio has company."

Max turned his chair. "Who is that?"

"Should we find out?"

"I believe we should."

By the time we reached the foyer, Gio was sitting at the dining room table with his friend. Both men stood as we entered. "Max, I want to meet my very good friend, Bobby Mack. Bobby, this is Max Shaw."

The man rounded the table and grabbed Max's hand with both of his mammoth paws. "It is an honor to meet such a famous man, and this must be the little wife."

"Or not. I'm Charlotte. I'm just a friend."

"She's the judge's daughter," Gio added. "You remember Judge O'Donohue, right?"

"Oh, yeah. He sentenced me to five years for that little job I did for Guido—"

Gio cleared his throat and acted as though he was choking. That stopped Bobby Mack's rather interesting dialogue.

"Gio, we'll let you visit. Sorry for the interruption," Max said politely and began to guide me away.

"No, Max. He's here for you," Gio warmly answered. "Bobby Mack is our new security guy."

Max leaned in. "Excuse me?"

"Who better to protect you than a former enforcer? He has credentials."

"My bonafides are good, Mr. Max. I used to work for Sal the Tuna in Jersey, Gordo Fiortino, Mr. Manne in Vegas…"

As he continued, I covered my mouth. The man deserved respect, but right now all I could do was stifle a laugh. Max's face was priceless. His wide eyes matched his open mouth. He turned to me and grabbed my arm.

Leaning down, he whispered. "My life is a freaking streaming mob soap opera."

"I must admit, it's never dull over here."

"Help me. What am I going to do?"

I felt sorry for him but just a little. It was gratifying seeing the great Max Shaw squirm. "Um, Gio, could we talk to you in the kitchen? Mr. Mack, may I get you something to drink?"

"Water is good. I've been in AA for twenty years now."

"Congratulations." I wiggled my finger at Gio. "Come with us."

We all huddled in the kitchen around the massive marble island.

"Gio, what were you thinking?" Max asked.

Gio shrugged. "I thought he'd be the perfect man. He's retired, but he needs the money. His daughter doesn't want him around anymore. With his record, it's difficult for him to apply for gainful employment."

Max turned around. "There's a reason for that." I watched both of his hands develop into fists. When he faced us again, he seemed a bit calmer. "Where's he going to stay, and don't say here."

Gio opened his mouth and closed it quickly.

"Oh, Gio," I pleaded. "What were you thinking?"

"I want to protect Max. Rosie is still saying there's danger, Charlotte, so I have to do everything to protect our boy."

What was Gio thinking mentioning Rose? My eyes focused on Max. He didn't seem surprised by Gio's statement. What did he know? How did he know? Had he heard Rose? "I understand that you want to help. Max has Nate, and he is obviously very capable of protecting himself. He's also installed an excellent security system for the house. By the time he's finished, this place will be a fortress."

"Or a prison," Max added quickly. "Okay, so if he works here, where is he staying? How much is he being paid, wait, what am I paying him?"

I grabbed a glass from the cabinet and headed to the refrigerator to get Bobby Mack's water while Gio and Max negotiated.

"I was thinking we could put two bedrooms in that suite downstairs. We'd have our own kitchen, bathroom, and living area. I really don't mind sharing. It'll still be more room than a cell. It'll be a palace for the two of us. As for pay, well, anything you can spare. He won't need much. Frankly, he probably has some savings stashed somewhere."

"Like under a mattress or in the Caymans?" Max asked.

Max could actually be a standup comedian if his federal gig didn't work out. His serious face coupled with sarcastic humor amused me more than I would ever admit to him.

"I'm taking him his water. You two finish here." I hastened my escape before one of them could stop me. "Here's your water, Mr. Mack."

"Bobby, please. So, you're the judge's daughter? You're the youngest one?"

"Yes, that's me. I hope you don't think badly of me because of who my father is."

Bobby flashed a smile. "On the contrary. Your dad is one of the greatest men I've ever met. Sadly, the first time I saw him was not under such good conditions."

"I see. Bobby, why can't you live with your daughter anymore?"

"She has a new husband. He don't like me much. All I was doing was teaching her son how to count cards. It's a very valuable skill, Miss."

Dad would laugh so hard tonight when I told the tale of Bobby Mack's visit. "Well, you never know about people, do you?"

"Not true, Miss. I can tell you're good people. Gio is the best, and he said the federal attorney is a standup guy."

"That he is," I agreed. "Are you on parole?"

"Nah, not anymore. I've served my time, and I did everything they told me once I was on the outside." As he took a drink, he looked around the room. "Nice place. It'll be better when it's all done." He noticed something in one of the windows. "That's not finished right."

"What is it?"

"That glass sensor isn't good enough. If you just slam a door, the alarm will go off. I could improve that real easy."

My eyes widened. "Bobby, are you self-educated?"

"Yes, Miss, but I got two degrees while I was in prison. I have my electrical engineering degree, and I have another one in environmental engineering. I could do some good work here. We have to take care of the soil and how we develop our community, you know?"

"Wow, that's amazing." Just when I thought it couldn't become more entertaining, a very happy Gio and a very confused Max returned.

"Bobby, when do you have to vacate your daughter's house?" Max asked as if he was interviewing a new employee.

"I left last week. I have a room at a hotel with enough money for the end of the month, but I can start immediately. I have a cot in my car." He looked around. "I could set it up here by the window."

Gio stepped in. "No, you'll stay with me until we have our lodging ready at the house. In the meantime, we'll get you acquainted with the security system. Won't we, Max?"

"Sure. That's fine. We'll work something out." Max had completely surrendered.

"Bobby was commenting that the window sensors are installed incorrectly." I thought Max needed to know that this might be to his advantage.

"No, the company is the best in the city and Nate supervised." Max wasn't giving one inch now.

"Sorry to disagree, but if you check your mother panel, you'll see that it isn't functioning correctly, and it never will. I was telling the judge's daughter that you could just slam a door, and the alarm would go off. In fact, if someone does break the glass it might not warn you. Also, we need to move that camera outside this window. You might consider installing an additional motherboard if you haven't already. Gio and I were discussing the installation of a new fence with a security gate. You could run it with the flip of a switch by the front door or via WiFi."

I passed Max on my way to grab my bag on the kitchen island. "Bobby has two degrees in electrical and environmental engineering. Boom."

"I'm pretty sure I'm breaking some Rico statute somehow," Max whispered. "Two mobsters living with a U.S. Attorney?" Max shook his head then turned to the two men. "Bobby, we'll work something out. Don't worry."

The hardened criminal shook Max's hand rapidly. "You won't regret this. Thank you, sir."

"Max."

"Sure, thank you Sir Max."

My knight in shining armor.

Chapter Eighteen

It was almost the end of the summer despite Kansas City's oppressive heat and humidity. Today, there was a cooler breeze that gave me the promise that I wouldn't have to shower every night when I arrived home from work. As roomies, Dad and I were doing well. As friends, Max and I were faltering. It was difficult to maintain my distance from him. I saw him at Sunday dinners, and we shared the occasional lunch downtown or near my office, but we were never alone. It was better that way for both of us. As much as we said we were friends, I wondered if we were convincing ourselves or denying our relationship every time we spoke or were in close physical proximity to each other.

Max remained busy, and my practice was growing. There remained a weird gravitational pull between us. Our tug of war was different. Neither one of us wanted to pull the other over the line, but we didn't want to give up our hold on each other either. During a night when I couldn't sleep, I admitted to myself that Max scared me. I was afraid of falling deeply in love when I looked into those caramel eyes. His strong shoulders could be a soft place to lean my head, but what would the price be if I used him as a pillow of protection?

In the hours of darkness that sleepless night, I was enlightened. I needed to concentrate on myself and my career and back away from the dream, or nightmare that was Max Shaw. If I changed my mind, I knew deep down that my heart and soul would be lost to Satan Shaw.

As I grabbed the mail on a Saturday afternoon, I heard an unusual car horn. Two men were waving at me from a light blue sports car. They were two men I knew very well. "Dad, you have to see this."

The judge arrived on the porch just in time to see the convertible enter our drive. "Would you look at that? That's Rose's car."

"Really? It is amazing."

"Max had it restored. Gio has been telling me about the money spent, the hours of detail work. I think Max and Nate even did some of it."

Gio was struggling to remove his body from the car as we greeted them.

"Wow, just wow." Max looked every bit the playboy as he sat behind the wheel.

"Get in, and I'll take you for a ride," he invited.

"Yes, Charlotte, get in. I'm done for now. My backside can't take that thing for very long. You kids have fun."

I gave him a quick kiss on the cheek. "I love it when you think I'm still a kid." I jumped into the passenger seat while Gio shut the door. With just a lap seat belt, I settled in. The smell of new leather permeated the interior despite the top down. "Max, this is so pretty."

"She's not just pretty, she's fast. Hold on." Max backed out onto the street, and we were off.

We didn't talk until we sat at lights, but we smiled at each other and laughed like we were kids again. Max reminded me more of the boy who used to take my hand and help me cross the street, than he did the hardened prosecutor I knew he was. But not today. Today, he was just Max. My Max?

Once we hit Ward Parkway, Max increased his speed. As we entered the Plaza area, people pointed at the car and whistled. "Let's head to the highway." I nodded my approval at Max's suggestion.

Over an hour later, we returned to the house. "I'm going to have a headache later from the wind, but I don't care. That was the best time I've had in a long while." I attempted unsuccessfully to straighten out my hair. It was futile.

"I couldn't believe it when Rose said that the car was in that storage shed." He looked over at me and shrugged. "Gio says you can hear her too?"

My heart began to beat faster. Terror, sheer terror coursed through me. I felt naked in front of him. Dad was the only one who knew. Not one of my siblings had ever uncovered my secret. Gio knew because we shared the experience. And now Max.

"Yes. I don't know what to say. I've never been comfortable sharing this with anyone."

"So that's why you didn't tell me?" His voice was softer than usual.

"I didn't know how you'd accept it." For some reason, I felt awful as though I had betrayed our friendship.

"I understand. It's not something that someone like me would readily be receptive to, right?"

"Yes." Gosh, this was uncomfortable.

"You can hear Conor? Is he, well, is he–"

I reached for his hand. "He is absolutely fine. He's with Mom. I usually hear them together. I hear others, but many times I don't understand, or it sounds like bad reception."

"Amazing. That is very special, Charlotte."

I watched his mouth combine those words. This was going better than I expected. "That's my secret. I only have that one."

Max's hand pulled away from mine as he extended his arm over my seat. He leaned in. "Only one?"

If I just don't look into his eyes, I'll be fine. I won't melt into this car and become part of its interior. I truly believed he took great delight in making me uncomfortable. He succeeded every time he did his little seduction thing. There were so many reasons to stay away from him. "Yes," I answered softly. There was one other, but I couldn't just blurt it out. "Would you like to come in and maybe Dad has dinner ready?" To invite a vampire into your home was dangerous, even death defying. Wait, he wasn't a blood sucker, he was the devil. He would scorch me. But he was a blood sucker…he was an attorney at heart! I began to laugh.

"What's so funny?"

I decided to answer with the truth. "You and me." I pulled away and escaped from the vehicle. I traveled up the sidewalk and could already smell the aroma from whatever Dad was cooking.

"Do you like the car?" Max yelled out.

"Of course I like the car. If I ever get to ride shotgun again, I need a scarf that flows, and really chic sunglasses like in the old movies." I saw a vehicle moving slowly in front of the house. Not again. But instead, Nate waved out of the window.

"You good, Boss?"

"I'm fine." Max waved him off as if he were a pesky fly. "Go home. Enjoy your night."

My smile disappeared. "Have you had more threats?"

"Constantly," he answered as if he were discussing what he was eating for dinner. He held my arm at my elbow. "It's not a big deal. It comes with the job."

"Really?"

Max winked. "Just like it does with a federal judge, right?"

I felt stupid. "Of course. It did happen now and then. I swear the main reason Paddy became a cop was so he could supervise my trips to school with his patrol car. I'd walk on the sidewalk, and he'd stalk me, driving about two miles an hour."

"He's a good brother."

"He's an annoying one." The closer we came to the door; I began to recognize the aroma. "He made Irish stew. You're going to love it."

Max opened the door naturally as though it was his own home. "I suppose I have to now that I'm Irish."

After an amazing dinner, Max proclaimed it wasn't that bad to be Irish. He had eaten two large helpings of stew, joined by fresh bread, sliced garden tomatoes, and a liberal helping of Dad's signature peach cobbler. Actually, it had been our mother's favorite dessert, but our father put his own spin on it. He always made sure to heap two scoops of vanilla ice cream on top, allowing it to melt over the hot flaky wonderfulness.

"Hey, Max, what are you doing next Friday night?" Dad handed our guest a small glass of brandy. "Try this. It is smooth."

Max smelled the liquid. "I don't think I'm doing anything. Why? Some dinner?"

"Yes, so you're in?"

I furrowed my brow attempting to think about the calendar. Suddenly, it dawned on me. "Dad, that's not fair." I looked over at Max. "It's my cousin's wedding. It's a wedding and reception, Max, not some law dinner."

Max sipped his drink slowly, enjoying it on his lips. "This is good. I'm in."

"No, you're not," I insisted. "You'd have to be my plus one, and that's just not something—"

"I'd love to, if you're asking." Those caramel eyes dared me from across the table. I vowed to not look directly into them, and yet I couldn't stop myself.

Max Shaw, there are no words, well there were a few words for the man, but none of them came to mind at the moment. "Fine, but you'll have to wear a tux. It's black tie, in fact no one is allowed to wear anything but black. You can wear a white shirt. No woman will be in white except for the bride. She's marrying our cousin Brandon Faherty."

Max finished his brandy, placing it on the table. He leaned across the table, still staring at me. "Charlotte, you haven't asked me."

I stood up quickly. I could spit fire as I read the room. Max was infuriating as he dared me. Gio was smiling widely, and my father was playing the part of the fool. "Fine. Max," I said sweetly. "Would you like to go to my cousin's wedding with me?"

"And reception," he added.

"Yes, and reception, the whole night."

My father and Gio turned their backs to us, but I could see that they were about to burst into laughter.

"All night, Charlotte?" Max whispered.

I was nine again and being bullied by Molly Walker. I decided I would act as though I was a child since the three men in the room enjoyed doing it so much. I seem to do a lot of that lately. "I hate you all right now."

I exited as the room erupted in hilarity. I found the dog sitting by Mom's chair. I looked at the sight, thinking she would appear, take my hand, and make it all better. Of course, it had been very funny, but I wouldn't give them the satisfaction. Perhaps Max was enjoying the coupling of us, but unless Max wanted that, it was becoming an old script not worthy of production into a full-length film. I'd have to have a serious talk with my father, and he'd have to have one with Gio. This needed to stop before I began to believe the storyline.

I was leaning my neck back to stretch some of the stress away when two large hands touched my back. From the energy, I knew it was Max. He was attempting to relieve the tension, but unknown to him he only created more in my body. My thoughts immediately went there…his hands on more than just my neck and tight muscles.

"Let me," Max murmured. "I'm sorry about that. You have to admit it was funny, but it was insensitive."

"It's getting very old with the two of them throwing us together."

His hands massaged slowly, hitting every knot in my neck and shoulders. I hadn't realized how much stress I'd been carrying this summer between Max's problems, and my decision to go after my long-lost dream. This felt so good, so very comfortable.

"Charlotte, I want to go. I've noticed we've been avoiding each other lately, and I miss your company. We'll have a good time, even if it's just watching Sean attempt to dance to rap music."

My entire body turned to butter. "That is fun to see. Oh, and Tom's clumsy steps aren't much better."

"Tom trying to dance is a comedy in itself."

"Did you know Meg signed them up for classes? The instructor refunded their money!"

"I'll dance with her. I'm a good dancer."

"Is there anything you don't do well, Max Shaw?"

"Truthfully?"

"Yes, truthfully?"

"Well, obviously family communication is iffy, but I'm not good with relationships."

I moved away from his magic hands and faced him. "I figured that all out on my own."

"You were always a smart little girl. It's getting late. I better get Gio home, and I'll see you next Friday. Text me the details. Wear something…black."

I smiled. The problem with Max Shaw is that I couldn't stay mad at him for very long. Well, he laid his cards on the table and warned me again. Now, it was my turn to decide if I would play the hand I had been dealt. And was this even a game that I could win?

Chapter Nineteen

Max was running late. His last text buzzed right before the bride walked down the rather lengthy aisle at the Catholic church on Broadway. I texted him back explaining we were on the right side about eight aisles from the front. I sat in between my father and Jane. Brad, Jane's husband, was out of town. Between her and Meg, Max's dance card would be full. If he ever appeared.

During the first reading, there seemed to be a commotion at the other end of our row where Sean sat with his date. I leaned over to see Max climbing over my siblings in a very undignified manner. It seemed Sean didn't want to move out into the aisle, Paddy told Max to climb over him, and Tom didn't even notice until Max punched him on the leg. Finally, Max stretched his long leg over his old friend and sat down next to me. His awkward smile melted my heart. It was always a good thing when Max didn't look perfect. It was actually more endearing, and he seemed to look more handsome if that was possible.

"I told you I'd make it," he whispered. "Sorry about the entrance, but I didn't want to go down the aisle, and your brothers–"

"And it will only get worse," I admitted.

"This dinner better be worth it." He waved at Jane and Dad. "Where's everyone else like Paddy's wife, Jane's hubby, the kids?"

"Brad is out of town for work, and Linda will meet us at the reception. Her doctor's office had late hours. Grandchildren weren't invited."

"Fancy and exclusive. Only five hundred of your nearest relatives." Max straightened the sleeves of his tux and tugged at his bow tie. His fidgeting disturbed Tom who nudged him into me. "Hey, knock it off."

"You were in my space."

"I was not."

My father was displeased as he peered down at us. He had that look. He used to have nonverbal cues that would quiet us when we were children. Apparently, we were all his kids tonight.

Max straightened up and smiled. In glorious fashion, my plus one had arrived. If just the last couple of minutes showed me anything, it was that we all still needed a babysitter.

The ceremony and Mass went on without any further disruptions, perhaps a few knowing looks between siblings, and our cousin Brandon was married to Miss Perfect in her size zero gown with her perfect hair and model makeup. Jane and I examined each other. She wondered why she had no boobs, and I wondered why I had hips. She nudged me and pointed at Max.

"He's perfect. I hate perfect people," she whispered.

I stifled a giggle. Even Jane now had a disdain for the perfect Max Shaw. I'd seen him on bad days with his eyes puffy and his hair out of place. I'd seen him fragile and unsure. I looked over at the man whose jacket sleeve continually brushed my bare arm and smiled. My plus one could definitely compete in the most perfect division of heaven's celestial beings. His brown locks had been recently sheared, there was no shadow on his face, neck or chin, and his nails were well manicured. His aftershave or cologne was light and not overpowering. Obviously, he hadn't rented the tux like my brothers did. Each crease and fold was to Max's body's specification. Yes, he was perfect, but I knew enough now to realize he was just as human as me.

As we knelt together, he smiled sweetly as he caught my glance. His sleeve pressed against my arm. I never knew kneeling together in front of God could be so intimate. It had to be the company next to me. Later, we all filed up to the altar for communion. Max stepped in behind me. I nudged Jane in the back and whispered.

"Is Max a practicing Catholic?"

Jane gave me a side glance. "I don't know. I didn't think so."

But he did as we did and knelt when we arrived back in our pew. His hands were tightly clasped in prayer. After a few more words, the happy couple were escorted by a bagpiper as a married couple for the first time.

"I don't think I've ever seen that at a wedding," Max said as we watched the recessional.

"It's an Irish thing." We all flowed out of the church and visited outside. I was able to stand back while my father took center stage. Everyone truly loved him.

"He's really in his element in the middle of the family, isn't he?" Max asked.

"Yes. He's a great man."

"That's a nice thing to say."

I looked up to see that Max had put on his sunglasses. "I mean it. I suppose that's why I don't mind living at the house again, but–"

"It would be nice to be on your own?"

"I've never really been on my own even when I had my house. I know it's hard to believe, but I'm the fixer for the O'Donohue family. I relay messages from my father to siblings; I convince them he's fine on his own; I make Sean talk to Tom, and I calm Paddy down when he's mad at Jane's husband. Sometimes, it's exhausting, but I'm the youngest, and I'm a girl. Someone has to do it in a large Irish family."

"So Gio and you have a lot in common?"

I could see he was kidding despite the cover of his glasses. "Yes. You better be worried."

"Oh, I am. You scare me."

"Good." I scared him? What a lovely thing to say. I was having a good night and felt more like myself than I had in a very long time.

"Are we ready to head to the reception?"

"Sure. I rode with Dad, Jane, and Paddy. It was an experience."

Max removed his keys from his pocket. "I'll get my car and pick you up right down there." He pointed toward the street.

As Max walked toward the parking lot, I gained Dad's attention. He was speaking with one of his former clerks, Brody.

"Charlotte, you remember Brody, don't you?"

I nodded. We were just talking about him the other night. "Of course. It's good to see you again."

Brody leaned over and gave me a peck on the cheek. "You are stunning, Charlotte. Any man would be lucky to have you on his arm."

"That's sweet. Thank you." I patted Dad on the arm. "I'm riding with Max to the hotel. Will you be okay?"

Brody interrupted before Dad could answer. "Are you dating Max Shaw?"

It wasn't his business, but he was Brody. He was an accessory of the family. "He's my plus one. Dad, will you be okay?"

Dad hugged me tight and kissed me on the head. "I'm going to be fine. Besides, I still have Jane and Paddy. We will see you both there. Don't bail on us."

My eyes flashed. "What else would we possibly do?"

"Knowing you two, I can imagine many things, and I try to not visualize any of them. A father should never do that."

"No, he shouldn't." I reached up and kissed him on the cheek. "I love you, Dad. We will see you there. It was nice to see you again, Brody." I walked away quickly before Brody could stop me for another uncomfortable question or to tell me he still wanted my house. Luckily, I could tell him we had two offers on the table at above the asking price.

True to form, Max pulled his midnight blue sedan up behind the couple's limousine. I received a few whistles, well the car did. It was just this past January this magnificent car pelted me with snow and ice. As I negotiated down the steps slowly, I was surprised that Max had come around the front of the car and held open the passenger door. More whistles ensued, but this time it was for my handsome plus one.

"Ms. O'Donohue," he said as he assisted me into the car. It was obvious that long, formal dresses weren't my usual form of dress. I tried not to tug here or there, but I wasn't used to a one shoulder gown. What had I been thinking when I purchased this little number? I know. I fell in love with the crystal clip that held the scarf flowing down the back. I slowly dropped into the seat, sending my feet flying up. I smoothed my dress quickly and made sure that all of it was in the car.

Max only smiled. I guessed he expected me to do something wrong. After all, he only knew me as the awkward little sister for years.

As we drove the short route to the hotel, I enjoyed the light jazz music he was playing in the car. "It's the new hotel, right?"

"Yes."

"Are you feeling well?" Max lowered his glasses to check with me while we were stopped at a red light.

"Uh huh. I'm not used to being around so many people."

Max chuckled. "Says the woman who is the youngest of six children with thousands of cousins."

"Yes, and all those cousins were in that church, and more will be at that party. I'd rather be in my pajamas with my popcorn than in a party dress that I feel like I've been sucked into."

"I understand. You've had a long week at work. You can always leave after the dinner."

"I cannot." I acted indignant. "What about the cake? I want cake. I starved myself for two days and have this girdle thing on just so I can eat it."

Max held up his hand. "Okay. Got it. No leaving until we eat cake."

"No leaving until no one will notice. If you leave early, they all talk about you. Well, they'll be talking about you no matter what. You're like a celebrity with all of them."

"Really?"

"Of course. You're on television every now and then, and with over twenty attorneys in the family, you'll be lucky if they aren't asking for your autograph. You are a superstar with young lawyers in this city."

"I'll have to be on my best behavior." Max parked in the garage, and we took the elevator to the massive ballrooms.

I checked in to find our table. We were all together. Lovely, all ten of us. How comfy! My father wasn't a small man, and Paddy was one of the tallest and largest men in the room. Tom and Sean were the same height as Max. With all these six footers, Jane and I would appear to be dwarfs.

I found Max waiting in line for drinks at one of the bars. "They have us all together."

"Good, I'll know the table then." He turned and handed me a white wine. "It's a pinot, or you can have my cab."

"No, this is perfect." Somehow muscle memory reminded me how to hold my small bag under my left arm while I held my glass in my right hand. I tried to stand straighter to improve my posture next to Max.

My plus one was subtle, touching my elbow to guide me away from the throng of hellos from relatives I hadn't seen in maybe a year since the last wedding. "Let's go over to the windows to see the view."

It was quieter there. "It's a beautiful hotel. The sunset will be amazing from this location. But we'll be in there." I watched as the doors to the ballroom opened and guests began to march in. A server stopped in front of us with several choices of appetizers. Max grabbed my glass.

"Get us a couple."

I smiled at the server and chose two stuffed mushrooms to place on my napkin. I laughed at poor Max. He had no hands available. "Here. Open." He did as he was directed. I plopped mine in my mouth and then took back my lovely glass of wine.

"I suppose we could go in. I think I saw Paddy heading that way."

"Yes. I saw Dad too. The gang's all here." We finished our drinks and began to join the party, but first Max stopped me.

"By the way, that dress is amazing. I love your hair pulled up. It's nice to see your neck. You look gorgeous."

"Wow, is that all?" I joked.

"For now." Max discarded our wine glasses on a nearby tray and softly touched my bare arm. His head lowered to look at the crystal brooch at my shoulder. "This is lovely." His breath was warm on my neck before he pulled away. "Ms. O'Donohue, allow me to escort you," Max announced. He took my hand and placed it onto his arm, presenting me to the room.

I needed to ask someone to crank up the central air or add extra ice to my water glass. The flurry of compliments from the most handsome man at the reception left me hot and definitely bothered. Our party of ten settled in. We were in a good spot, only inches off of the dance floor, and with a straight route out of the ballroom for any escape. Bathroom runs were especially important during a long night.

"Max, it is really good to see you here," Meg commented. "You are a brave man."

"I came for the free meal."

Laughter filled the table, but Max was completely solemn. "I mean it. I love free meals, and I'm here with a beautiful woman so it's a win-win."

The comedy team of the O'Donohues all looked around for the beautiful woman, as did I. Max quickly pointed at me.

"Nice. You are being very kind and charming."

Max's mouth found my ear so only I could hear. "You expect this out of me, so I'll just say it. I'm not being kind. You do look beautiful, and I'm trying to get lucky."

I had taken a drink of water and almost choked. I put my napkin up to my mouth. "I completely expect that out of you."

"But what if I mean it?"

"Eat your salad. I don't know if I'm ready for, for–"

"I love it when you stammer and babble. That's when I know I've made you very uncomfortable. Charlotte, just relax and have a good time tonight. I will." He added a flirtatious wink and a devilish smile.

I almost took his statement as a challenge. Apparently, Rose wasn't the only one in his family who enjoyed her little games. Thankfully, the evening began. It was a lovely meal, and the toasts and first dances were that of fairy tales. Jane and I remarked on every detail of the bride's dress as my brothers and Max discussed football schedules and shooting ranges. Poor Linda was stuck in the middle of her husband and Sean. As soon as the dancing began, I knew she would track down her friends at one of the other tables. At one point Max stood up and we lost him in the crowd. He returned, placing a piece of wedding cake in front of me.

"They'll be serving it to everyone, but I didn't want you to miss what you came for."

I thanked him and shared it with Jane. I touched his arm. "Jane and I have to go to the restroom. We'll be right back. Will you survive the crew?"

"Of course. Do you want another drink?"

Jane touched his back. "They have been serving more champagne since the toast. I'll have that if it comes around."

"Me too," I answered. "Thank you." As soon as I left my chair, Paddy's wife Linda filled it and began to point out different guests to Max.

Thank heavens Jane waited to speak until we arrived in the outer area of the restroom, and she didn't mention my date's name. "Oh, my goodness. He looks like he stepped out of a movie, and you look so good tonight. That dress is amazing. What was he whispering in your ear, or was he nibbling? I couldn't tell."

"He was whispering. He was just asking about who someone was." I lied to my sister easily. Anyone in need of a professional liar? I'm your girl. I was a student of fibbing with a degree in obfuscation. "I have so many elastic layers under this thing, an entire infantry unit couldn't get through."

"I'm thinking it's just one person who could."

"Jane!" I looked into the mirror across from us and my cheeks were as red as my neck. "I need to go to the bathroom." Jane followed behind entering her own stall.

"He can't possibly be acting. Can he?" My sister's question was annoying. "The way he looks at you is so very comfortable, but sexy. He leans his head over to listen to you. To talk to me, he drapes his arm over the back of your chair, and I thought I saw his thumb rubbing your bare shoulder. I'm getting hot just watching you two."

I flushed the toilet to drown out my sister's voice. I washed up and headed to the outer room again, leaving her behind. My face was cooling off, but other areas of my body were definitely warming. Even when I thought I was in love, I didn't have these feelings. "You and Brad need a date night. Seriously, Jane!"

"It's lust, pure lust." Jane looked down at me. "Don't you feel anything?"

I shielded my face with my hands. "I'm feeling everything, Janie." One sob escaped my mouth. I couldn't hold it back any longer.

"Oh, honey," Jane said as she sat down on the bench next to me. "It's okay. You're not a young, naive girl just out of school."

"But I feel like that. He not only gets under my skin, he sets it on fire. I have never felt like this even with the man who will not be named. I promised myself I wasn't going to fall for him because I'm just afraid that he's playing with me. I'm the snack of the week, and he's a well-fed exotic cat."

"He wouldn't do that to you," Jane assured me. "Now, let's get you cleaned up." She retrieved a tissue from a table and dabbed at my makeup. "You deserve a wonderful time,

Charlotte. Go ahead and let go. Don't think about family honor, or what someone might think. You're a grown woman, and he's a man. Yes, he acts like a kid sometimes, but every man at our table does, even Dad. You have been taking care of our family for so long, take care of yourself, and let Max treat you the way you deserve. And if he gets out of line–"

"I'm very good at throwing liquor and decking a man."

"There you go." We shared a laugh.

"Jane, if I did it to this one it would be assault on a federal officer of the court."

Jane gasped. "Maybe you just dump him first, don't deck him. Enjoy the sex and move on with a very large smile on your face."

By the time we reached the table, I had put myself back together and my spandex was restricting in all the needed places.

"Did I miss anything?"

Max shook his head. "No. That Brody guy came around to visit with your dad, and he was very upset he missed you. The champagne is coming around and they're bringing the cake to the tables. Paddy and Linda are out there dancing. He's not bad at the slow ones."

"He used to waltz with Mom. She taught him. I'm not sure what happened to Tom."

"Which do you prefer?"

My eyes widened in confusion. "Excuse me?"

"Dancing. What kind of dancing do you prefer?"

I was relieved. "It depends on the song."

We were amused as Meg yanked on Tom's arm. The band was playing one of her favorite songs. Instead, my father saved my brother and took her onto the dance floor.

The next song began and Sean rose from his chair. "Oh no, here we go," Jane commented.

"Is it really that bad?" Max watched the couple walk away from the table.

"Yes," Jane and I answered together. And it was. Luckily for Sean, his date was one who permanently stood in one place as she swayed, moving her arms slightly like the early robot toys.

"They're perfect together." Max's comment elicited a snort from Jane, and I just hid my head on Max's shoulder. His lips were near my forehead. "Seriously, they are." He lightly kissed my hair and returned to watching the show.

The party was in full swing when Max stood up. His hand moved down in front of my face. "Dance with me, Charlotte. Come on. It's time."

"This isn't my song. It's a slow dance."

He began to pull my chair out. "Lucky for you, I'm very good at slow dances. I always take my time."

"Oh Lord," Jane said out loud. She pushed my backside out of the chair. "Go. Do it for all of us."

And there I was on a dance floor in Max's arms. We were the center of attention. He was the handsome stranger, and I was cousin Charlie. My entire family, literally my entire family, watched as Max tipped my chin up. "I don't see any of them when I'm looking into your eyes."

"You don't have to see them at the next funeral or wedding, or even at Christmas."

"Then put your head on my shoulder. Close your eyes and enjoy the music. I have you, Charlotte. Trust me."

Oh no. Trust. Yours, Charlotte. Really? My voices were confident. I wasn't. Was I really going to have Max love me? Could he love anyone? "I'm going to trust you. Please don't let me down again."

"I'll try not to, but let's just dance."

It was much better with my head on his shoulder, and with my eyes tightly shut. I couldn't see anyone, but I could feel Max's strength. His hands were comfortably splayed against my back. This was becoming real, but my little attorney brain was yelling at me. *"Charlotte, this is just the Max Shaw dating experience. Enjoy the night, that's all you have. Please keep your arms and legs in an upright position."* Jane had been very clear that I should take advantage of anything the man offered, but I was fighting back feelings for him, deep ones that had taken root years ago. My attempt at denial was failing.

How could I have been so blind? I had that little sister crush on Tom's friend. At first, he was just the nice boy who held my hand when we crossed the street to go to the swimming pool. But a few years later, every time he came upstairs, I just had to say hello. Tom and he always shut the door to the room, sometimes abruptly in my face. They talked about football and girls. I was still just a kid in grade school, and they were the high school football jocks.

I was manifesting a crush into love. I needed to think sensibly. At the same time, the song was over.

"That was nice," Max whispered.

I nodded and retreated to the security of the table. Max joined me. "Poor Jane is just sitting there. Is it okay if–"

I would be mature. "Of course, please. She really does love to dance. Go on."

I watched as the delighted Jane took the floor with Max and took the floor they did. Leaning my chin on my hand, I just watched. I did a lot of that. It was more comfortable in the shadows. Tom, Sean, and Paddy ditched their jackets and ties, but Max seemed to appreciate his tux as a second skin. I could only imagine how many times he escorted a deb to her grand presentation to society.

"With inflation, it's now a million for your thoughts." My father sat next to me. "What are you thinking, or who are you thinking about?"

I leaned my head on his shoulder. My father was the second most handsome man in the room, and he was wearing his own tuxedo too. "I'm thinking about me, actually."

"Ah, I thought it might be some guy in a custom tuxedo."

I sat up to admit my silent musings. "Dad, I've been thinking I don't do much for myself."

"Interesting."

"Yes, it is. I went to college because I was expected to. I originally did the whole law school thing for you."

My father gently touched my back. "You shouldn't have. Your mother and I didn't care, as long as you were happy. Look at your brothers and even Jane. Jane doesn't use her art degree. She volunteers at the food kitchen, raises her children, and her husband, I suspect, and she's a grade school principal. Sean and Paddy went into law enforcement. Tom used his business degree to begin a real estate agency. Conor, well... but you, I thought you were the sure one."

"I was just acting. I think I've been the most uncertain of all of them. I've taken the easy route. I took the job Tom handed to me when he needed help."

"That's the other problem, you're always placing all of us ahead of your needs and wants. You helped with the fallout from your brother's and mother's deaths. Didn't Tom and you plan Mom's funeral? It's still a blur."

I nodded. I looked out at Jane who was having the time of her life with someone who actually knew how to swing dance. "She's having a great time."

"Charlotte, when Mom was sick, you nearly put your life on hold, and then you were there for me after she passed away."

"I dated. I almost married the man who will not be named."

"I can't even remember. I never liked him."

I tapped his arm playfully. "You never told me."

"No. I learned a long time ago it was best that you all made your own mistakes. I made my own."

Jane and Max remained dancing through another song. The tempo was now a quick salsa, and my plus one was up to the task. I watched Meg, Paddy's wife, and Sean's date join them while the brothers forged a quick path to the bar. "Now Max has a harem."

"He's a good man, deep down."

"You and Gio have to stop setting us up." I clapped to the music as the women surrounded my date.

"We know what is good for both of you. Max needs you, but he may not know it yet."

"He's not ready, and I'm not sure I am either."

My father tilted his face until I looked him straight in the eye. "But it was nice to have a shoulder to lay your head on, wasn't it? There was no agenda, no plan when you two were dancing."

"What are you saying? You usually aren't so obtuse. It must be a law thing because Max speaks the same riddles to me sometimes."

"I'm saying." He stopped and took my hand in his. "It's time for you to do what you want to do. A father shouldn't know anything about his daughter's love life, but it's way past time for you to bust out. Be who you want to be, and you're old enough to certainly do what you want to do. If you end up pregnant–"

"Dad!"

"Judge? What have you done to my date?" Max asked as he and his women returned to the table breathless from dancing.

I narrowed my eyes and gave my father my mother's look. I had perfected it and only used it when totally necessary.

"I haven't done anything to your date. I was talking about what you might–"

I kicked my father's leg under the table.

"Ow, I was discussing what you might do with the other bedrooms on the second floor."

Good answer Dad, even though it had a double meaning. You may live. My eyes remained slim slits. My father knew he was in big trouble. He would be a lucky man if I ever spoke to him again. Pregnant? Even though we hadn't even had sex, with Max Shaw you possibly could become with child just standing too close.

Max removed his jacket and his tie. "It's getting warm."

"You have no idea," I muttered as I watched his lovely fingers unbutton his custom-made white shirt. His gold cufflinks were exposed. They looked old and had the letter S on each one.

"Charlotte, another wine, or something else? I need something cold. What would you like?"

"How about–" We were interrupted by Tom and another woman who looked vaguely familiar.

"Max, do you remember Penny who used to live down the street from us?"

Penny embraced Max quickly. "It's been years." She stepped back. "You look amazing, and you're a federal prosecutor? Your dad must be so proud."

While they reminisced about junior prom, my mind raced to his real father. Was the man proud of who Max had become or did he truly see him as a hindrance?

Penny pulled on Max's hand. "You really need to see all the girls again. We're sitting right over there."

But Max's feet were firmly planted. "Maybe later, but I've neglected my date. Penny, do you know Charlotte O'Donohue?"

The woman's eyes squinted. I could feel her checking me out from head to toe. Did she really look under the table to see my shoes?

"Weren't you Tom's little, nosey sister?"

I stood up like I was on fire. "I still am, but I'm all grown up now." I looped my arm possessively in through Max's as though he was my most prized possession.

Max grinned awkwardly but murmured through his teeth, "Down tiger."

"Yes. I see. Well Max, come over to the table when you can. You and I used to spend so much time parked on our block, remember?" Penny winked.

"I do. We were just stupid kids back then thinking we were all grown up."

"It was fun. Come around." Penny kissed his cheek and waved as she sauntered away. If I swayed my hips like that, I'd herniate a disc.

Tom clapped his hands. "That was interesting. Sorry about that, Max." Meg beckoned him back to the floor despite his bad moves. It was a very slow, romantic song, one that held a special sentiment for them.

"They danced to it at their wedding." I sat back down and took a drink of water. It was hot in here.

Max pulled me up. "Oh no. We are dancing. Come on. You can rest tomorrow."

In his arms I completely forgot about Penny what's her face and her high school make out sessions on our block. The next song was fast. I removed my shoes and Max threw them near our table. Before long we had an entire grouping of O'Donohues, including Dad, jumping up and down like the children we were.

Dad and the boys shared shots with the groom's father. Jane and Meg were huddled across from me probably discussing my lack of a sex life. Poor Sean's date was at another table in deep conversation with one of our cousins, and Linda was visiting with the groom's family.

I yawned. Max moved his arm around my chair. "Are you ready to get out of here?"

"Oh please. The next thing my male relatives begin is the singing. It's always shots, then songs. It's terrible. You will adjust your opinion of my father."

Max laughed, but I was dead panned. "I'm serious. It's awful. Mom never allowed him to sing to any baby."

Max stood up and grabbed his coat off the back of his chair and handed me my shoes. "I better tell someone we're leaving, right?"

"No, I'll tell Jane. She'll have it passed around before we hit the garage."

After Jane and Meg comically winked and giggled at us, we waved our goodbyes and headed for the garage. Once inside the sedan, my head throbbed. "I could go to sleep in this car. It's quiet and much more comfortable than sitting at that table."

"I have to admit, that was a party. You all know how to do it right."

"Until they begin singing," I joked. "They'll drag you into their ceremonial insanity one day, and you'll see."

Max pulled out onto the street, and we drove through the Power and Light District. It really wasn't that late. The bars were still packed, and visitors spilled outside on a warm late summer night. Next week would be Labor Day, and the annual Irish celebration. Summer would officially be over.

"You should come to the festival next weekend. It celebrates just the Irish. There's bands, food, and you'll learn a few jigs."

"You all have your own festival?"

"Of course. The Irish were integral in the establishment of Kansas City," I answered proudly.

"I'll have to check the calendar. You all get the entire weekend?"

"It begins on Friday and ends on Sunday evening. Jane volunteers, and Paddy is on the committee. There's food, lots of beer, and wonderful music. One of our local bands travels the nation, so the entertainment is very good."

"Being Irish is very popular in this town."

"Yep." I looked down at my feet. They were swollen. "I'm never getting those heels back on."

"I'll carry you to the door."

"No, you will not. You'll hurt yourself."

"I don't think so. Before you go into a debate with me, I want you to know I had a fantastic time tonight. Being with you is easy, Charlotte. Again, you look amazing. That dress is–"

Max never finished his sentence. Instead of any more discussions, we remained silent, enjoying the light music playing. I watched him drive, and occasionally, Max glanced in my direction. In this quiet, it was the perfect ending to a perfect night. While we weren't bickering or joking, it did seem we could be the perfect couple. When he pulled the car up in front of the house, I hadn't realized my hand lingered on his collar, two fingers running through his hair. He was right again; it was easy to be together.

Max turned the vehicle off and removed his seat belt. I prepared to leave the car, but before I could touch the handle, Max's hands caressed my face, holding me still as he kissed my left cheek and then my right one. Slowly, he seemed to be teasing me with the route his lips were taking. "You can't deny there's a connection between the two of us. Charlotte, I'm blurring our friendship line."

I nodded. "Uh huh," I murmured, but I didn't protest. My thoughts were only of the way I was feeling being so close to him without anyone watching.

I didn't stop Max. Friendship be damned. My arms found their way around his neck as he pulled me closer over the middle console. His hands quickly landed on the sides of my body.

"I just want to touch you," Max whispered in my ear. He began to caress until he reached the side of my bare shoulder. I heard the zipper, but my lips were too busy enjoying every second of this man's delicious mouth on mine. His lingering touch offered me a sensation I missed. I had only one thought…I wanted to be even closer to Max.

"I've wanted to do this ever since I dumped water on you," Max murmured. I began to argue, but the words wouldn't come out of my mouth. My lips were too busy.

Deftly, a warm hand caressed my freed breast. Max's thumb found its way kneading softly. I clutched him tighter as I moved my body to mold into his. His slow fondling countered my eagerness to be touched by him. His mouth left mine and traveled a trail down my neck. The light feathery kisses not only touched my body, but my soul. This man with all of his faults was perfect in every way. Honestly, we did have a connection, one that probably frightened both of us.

Occasionally, I giggled softly as his lips tickled my skin. One side of my body was completely exposed to his touch. "Oh Max," I gasped, sounding like some heroine in a romance novel. What else was there to say? At least I wasn't stammering. He certainly was good at everything he did. With every excruciating slow touch, Max created a frenzy in my body. Here I was making out in front of my parents' home. Making out on this block just like he had with what's her name. And that's when reality tore into my fantasy.

I pulled back quickly, leaving Max nearly falling into my lap. "I can't." We were both breathing heavily.

Max wiped at his lips as I nervously zipped up my gown, covering my bare skin from his eyes. "You can't or you won't?"

I began to search in my bag, pulling out a small bottle and uncapping it. My reasoning was sound, wasn't it? "You've made out on this block before with Penny, remember? And God knows how many girls, how many women have succumbed to those evil hands and lips of yours."

Max threw his hands up and collapsed back into the driver's seat. "You have got to be kidding. We were in high school, Charlotte. It's been years, and you can't hold all my past relationships against me." He grabbed my hand as I debated my next action. "Stop. It's just sex. If you would prefer, we can just talk."

"No. I can't be near you. It is not just sex for me. I won't be burned again. You are evil." I squeezed the bottle, and the liquid flew out onto Max's jacket. My hand flew up to my mouth. Max was making me lose my mind.

"What the bloody hell? What is that?" Max wiped at the wet marks on his lapel and shirt.

"It's holy water. You need a full-on exorcism but consider this exorcism lite. Maybe it'll cool you off."

Max's laughter filled the car as I gathered up my shoes. "Do you always carry that with you?"

I continued to look down as I pulled at my heels. "Only when I'm out with the devil."

"We're back to that? What else do you have in that little purse to combat evil?"

"If needed I have a little cash to get me home and my phone."

Max smiled. "Well, it was funny. Wet but funny, and a little nutty. You do make me laugh."

"I'm so happy I entertain you," I growled. I haphazardly attempted to push my shoes on my feet, but it was futile. I'd have to make a run for it in bare feet. "Max, I need to be more than just your entertainment. You can't trifle with people's feelings, with their bodies, and not expect them to get hurt–"

"Stop," Max demanded. "Are you talking about me or someone else? You can't compare me to the guy who let you down. In fact, I won't be compared to anyone. When you're with me, I want you to think of only me. There are never any guarantees, and if you're expecting me to be as sure as you about every action, every relationship, well it's very annoying. Just take a chance for once in your life, Charlotte."

Max's eyes pleaded with me. It wasn't just about sex, but I wasn't sure what he offered, wanted, or if he even knew what it might be. I opened the door, and Max released my hand. "Max, I took a chance back in March during a parade, and look where it got me. Right here. Dad told me I needed to place myself first, and I'm doing that right now. I won't be a one-night stand, or the solution to your needs. I'm pretty sure I need to think about this one, **friend**."

"**Friend**, I see. Will we revisit this, or even discuss it, table it, or will we be uncomfortable with each other for a few weeks again? Have you decided that for us as well? You seem to be in charge of whatever this is." His tone was sincere, but he was beyond disappointed.

"**We** need to decide," I murmured.

Max turned and gripped the wheel. "Charlotte, I don't know if anyone bothered to tell you, but sometimes you do make mistakes." His cold stare as he turned to me again led me to believe he was calculating his options. "Maybe, just maybe, that other guy wasn't the right one. Maybe you made a mistake. The right guy can change everything, but I'm not sure you'd know him if he sat next to you at dinner. Think about that one, friend."

I bit my lip to quell the tears. I didn't need advice or a lecture from Mr. Player. "I know you'll be at dinner Sunday, and I want you there. No matter what does or doesn't happen between you and me, you are part of this family whether you or I like it. None of us would have it any other way. Goodnight, Max. I had the best princess night ever. Text me when you get home, please."

I shut the car door and never glanced back. I heard the window lower, and I stopped.

"Charlotte, when you're ready, I hope the right man will be there for you. I hope you figure out what you need."

I continued running away, something I was very good at doing. My bare feet slapped at the concrete as I fled. I didn't want him to see me cry, and I didn't want to know what he was doing right now. As soon as I entered the house and was met by Mickey, I heard the car speed down the block. Suddenly Mickey jumped into Dad's chair and began to howl mournfully.

"What in the world are you doing?" I looked out the window and saw the full moon. "You've never howled before?" Full moon and howling? I completely understood. The vampire had crossed a line, and the werewolf was warning him off. "Lord, all that is missing is a ghost or two." I waited. The house was silent. They were probably still at the wedding.

Chapter Twenty

"We brought the dessert," Max announced as Gio and he entered the house Sunday. He held the boxes from one of our family's favorite bakeries high in the air. His eyes met mine first.

"I'll take them to the kitchen."

"I made sure there were a couple of peach tarts, and even the lemon ones you like."

"Thanks, Max." My smile was forced. It was necessary to make sure this dinner was as natural as always; except we were probably being nicer to each other than usual. Gio's gaze went from Max to me, and back to his grandson.

"What's up with you two?"

"Nothing," Max answered slowly.

"Hmm, nothing? Charlotte, are you going to fess up?"

I smirked. "Gio, you're imagining things. Max, Dad's in the kitchen."

I escaped quickly, but I could feel Gio's beady little eyes on my back. His scrutiny wasn't needed when there really wasn't anything to say.

I moved the tarts to platters on the sideboard for our after-dinner treats. With no grandchildren at the table today, there'd be more than enough, and I might get to have both of my luscious favorites. Max had remembered again. He could be thoughtful. Even his text when he'd made it home Friday night had been caring. He never apologized, but he did admit that maybe his timing had been all off. It was as though our timing was always off.

Before I fell asleep Friday night, I'd gone over the words he'd thrown out. I'd felt hurt at first, but my heart told me he had been correct. My ex wasn't the right man. I wanted to get married. I wanted to be a mother. The year we became engaged, I'd gone to fifteen weddings of friends and relatives. I'd also attended five baby showers. Obviously, love was in the air, and it had polluted my psyche. Besides, that's what you did. You dated, fell in love, became engaged, married, and began your family. A career along the way was a bonus.

I heard Dad walk down the hallway that night. He stopped by my door and went on to his bedroom. When I finally fell asleep, Mom visited with me. She and I were sitting outside at a small table. There were roses and hydrangeas surrounding us. On this sunny day, we were drinking iced tea. A plate of strawberries and cheeses set between us.

"Charlotte, you need to step back and analyze the situation. That's what you do best, but sometimes you over analyze. Will you please stop that?" My mother's soft voice made a reprimand sound comforting. It was lovely to see her in color, to hear her voice, and to smell her flowery perfume. Or was it

all the flowers? This was a nice dream after such an abrupt end to an evening that had been so promising.

"I ruined everything, Mom," I admitted. "Why can't I just take what he's offering?"

"Because you want so much more. You always have. He can do it. Just give him the time."

I shook my head. "Mom, I just don't know. I think I'll concentrate on my law practice. Maybe I'll go out with Brody?"

"No." My mother quickly sipped on her tea and turned away. *"Not him. Look."* Her hand extended to direct my attention to a yard. A man was crouched down, holding onto the hands of two small children.

"That's a cute little girl and boy." In a navy-blue dress, the little girl giggled at the other child. The boy blew on a dandelion, its seeds scattering into the wind. He handed one to the man, and he blew on it in one breath. "That's sweet."

Mom glanced back at me. Her added smile warmed my heart. *"Don't you remember, Charlotte? If the one you love scatters the seeds in one breath, that person will love you back."*

"I don't remember. How could I forget that?" My dream continued with the man chasing the two children. Their giggles filled the air, and his laughter was joy filled. I could only see his back. He wore a fitted, crisp white dress shirt and dark pants. "Mom, who is this?"

"Him, just be patient."

We watched the scene play out. The little boy fell and began to cry. The man doted on him, picking him up in his arms, soothing his fear. The little girl sat down in the grass and began to cry as well. Finally, the man turned.

"Charlotte, honey, I need you." It was Max.

"Charlotte, honey, I need you." This time, Max and the children vanished, and my mother was saying the same words. *"Charlotte, I'm worried."*

"Me too, Mom. That was so beautiful, and it all disappeared so quickly."

My mother nodded. *"Remember, it all can disappear in an instant. With the snap of your fingers, life can be taken away."*

I woke, gasping for air. "Mom," I yelled out, but there was no answer.

"Charlotte, honey, are you okay?" My father was outside of my bedroom door, and it was morning.

"Yes, it's just a bad headache. Sorry. I didn't mean to wake you."

"May I come in?"

"Sure." I wiped my eyes as Dad entered and stood at the edge of my bed.

"Bad dream or a visit?"

I managed a slight smile. "I'm not sure." I shook my head. "No, it was a dream. Mom was worried." I fudged and didn't tell Dad the rest of my story. "It's hard to shake off those feelings of–"

"And this has nothing to do with Max?" My father sat down on the edge of the bed just like he used to when I was a little girl.

Before I answered, I took a deep breath and clenched my hands under the sheet. "It has everything to do with me, Dad. Max and I always banter back and forth, and we had one of our discussions last night. He said some things that hit me hard." Dad's face was unchanged as I continued. "I listened to what you said. I want my law practice. I want, well that's the part I'm not sure about."

Dad's expression finally changed. His face lightened. "You're not sure if you want Max. All of us have thrown the two of you together, but we had the best of intentions."

"Not Paddy."

Dad laughed. "Not Paddy. That is true. If you want the boy wonder then talk to him, not your father."

I leaned back on my pillows. "Now that's the problem. Max wanting me, with my conditions, may never happen."

"Ah." Dad lowered his gaze. "Then, you have to decide what will make you happy. That's all I'm concerned about, Charlotte." When Dad's head raised, his eyes met mine. "I'll support you no matter what."

"Thanks, Dad. I love you for that. I know I'm not the most patient person, and I have this habit of having to be absolutely sure about everything. Oh, and I hate making mistakes that come back and bite you in the butt."

Dad began to laugh again. It was annoying. "You aren't patient? I've never noticed."

I threw one of my small decor pillows at him. "You aren't helping."

"It's hard realizing our faults, isn't it? Honey, you've been running headlong into every situation since the day you jumped off the front porch and broke your nose. You face planted because Tom was leaving you behind."

"He was going to the movie I wanted to see and wouldn't take me along. I was five!"

"A very determined five. You've probably been the most cautious of all of your siblings, and you always had to have those perfect report cards. Not every human being is perfect."

Analyzing oneself was difficult. Having your father agree with the self-depreciating analysis was annoying. "I know. I know what I want to do with my life. Now, I need to figure out if I need someone on that journey and if that person is Max."

Dad suddenly stood up. "Now you have a plan. Shake it off. I'm going to make us some breakfast."

He left the room before I could answer. I tried several times to talk to Mom or Conor, but on this Saturday morning they were silent. Why would Mom be worried? Was she just concerned about me, or was there something else coming our way? I shook off the wary warning in the shower. By the time I was sitting at the kitchen table that morning, I began to plan my independence from expectations.

I heard my father's boisterous Sunday dinner welcome toward Max and knew all would be fine. Dad would do as I had asked and not let on that anything had happened on Friday night or Saturday morning.

Dinner was uneventful. The conversation revolved around next week's festival. I had a full day of work on Friday and promised to be there on Saturday and Sunday nights. Max commented that he wouldn't mind stopping in to embrace his new Irishness. Dessert was served. Jane and I handled the cleanup, and Gio joined us as we finished up the last of the pans.

"I hear the wedding was very nice." He sat down at the kitchen table in his usual chair.

"It was," Jane responded. "We all danced so much we were completely exhausted. The cake was great. The hotel was amazing. They had a lovely meal too. The bride's dress was very lacey. They had close to five hundred guests. Unbelievable. Max sure can dance."

Way to go Janie. Babble until he gets the hint that we're covering up something. I could see suspicion in Gio's eyes. The man had kept himself alive by his awareness of his surroundings and knowing a liar when he saw one, or even two of them. When Jane began to wring her hands, it was all over.

"And did you have a good time, Charlotte?"

The question had come. "Yes, I did. Your grandson was a perfect gentleman." Until he became very handsy, and I lost my nerve.

"Really? That's interesting. That's not what he said."

"What? He talked to you about it?" As I turned to face him, I saw the satisfaction on his lips. "You horrible little man!"

He pounded his fist on the table. "I knew something happened. What did he do? I'll bury him somewhere, and they won't even realize he's gone for a month or two. By that time, I'll be in Bolivia."

I threw the towel at the elderly person. "You can't go to Bolivia. You probably don't even have a passport. I'm not in the mood so don't play me."

Jane's jaw clenched. "Excuse me, I'm going to leave now." I attempted to pull her back, but she bolted like a wild horse.

Gio pointed at my father's usual chair. "Sit."

Yes, I did as I was told. "It was a lovely night, really Gio. Max was amazing."

"And what did he do?"

I sighed. "I got scared. We messed up the entire friendship thing we had going. He told me a truth I probably needed to hear. I'm looking for something Max isn't ready for yet."

"I wish you'd stop that," Max reprimanded as he appeared in front of me. "You are always so damn sure. You don't know what I am or am not ready for, Charlotte O'Donohue. Let me tell you something, you're still my best friend."

My eyes widened. How long had he been listening before entering the kitchen? I began to answer, but Max held up his hand. "You are going to listen to me. You have surprised me. I wasn't looking for all of this…this family stuff, this closeness, this everyone knows everyone's business. Obviously, my family has lived with secrets. I've lived with secrets. I've been alone, and now I'm in this crowd. You need to take me as I am. I don't have the luxury of getting things wrong or going back in time to fix all of my sinning. I need to do it right the first time, from now on, so just have a little patience, damn it. And stop being so sanctimonious. As I said the other night, you made a mistake with that guy. He wasn't the right one."

Gio and I sat silent in front of the professional talker. He had given his summation and apparently pleaded his case.

Gio watched us. "Well, that went well. What about it, Charlotte?"

As I stood up, I answered him. "I'll try to be less sure and sanctimonious. I appreciate what you were telling me the other night. It hurt to hear it out loud, but you were right. You're my best friend too, Max." I kissed his cheek as I passed by to join my family.

Sunday passed by with no other outbursts. By the time the next weekend came, all anyone in our family was worried about was if they would run out of the Italian sausages they served at the festival. Of course, Sunday dinner was canceled. We attended the open-air Catholic Mass and breakfast with a couple hundred of our friends and family members.

I hadn't managed to attend until Sunday. My little practice had a huge week, and I was able to manage the payroll without dipping into my savings this month. It was a long day of visiting with relatives and seeing friends who turned out to enjoy Irish music. The crowd swelled during the day for the last concert of the night.

I found a place to sit as I finally had my first cold beer. Paddy had a lawn chair for Dad, but I didn't mind sitting a little back from the band on a concrete barricade. I saw Max before he saw me. I could've just ignored him, but I waved. He looked very informal wearing shorts and an FBI shirt.

Max returned the wave and headed in my direction. "Gio didn't want to come. He said there'd just be a bunch of Irish people here." Max looked down at me. "Where's the beer?"

"Over there." I pointed toward Tom's concession tent.

Max left and returned with his drink. "Where's the judge?"

I motioned toward the stage. "Right down there with Meg and the grandkids. He's waiting for his favorite band."

Max's eyes wandered as he looked over the crowd. "And Paddy and Sean?'

"Paddy is helping with security, and Sean has to work his real job. His shift isn't over until midnight so he's not happy."

"This is really something. Every year, huh?"

"Every year. At least it's a little cooler this time. Last year it was over one hundred degrees." Small talk was interesting.

"Charlotte, I need you to come over to the house when you have time."

My sunglasses shielded me from any true eye contact with my friend. "What's wrong?"

"I just want to get your opinion on some colors for those upstairs bedrooms."

"Your designer could do that."

"Yes, she could, but I want your input. I trust your opinion. She left me with samples and boards with her ideas, but I'm thinking about putting a bed in them and shutting the door for a while. The living area is almost completed as is the dining room, and Gio's suite is on schedule to be finished before Thanksgiving. I'm getting renovation burnout."

"You did take on a huge project." Max watched the crowd. "Max, you've done a wonderful job. Your grandmother would be so proud."

"Do you know that for sure? Did she say something?"

I leaned into him. "I haven't heard anything lately because I haven't been over."

Max nudged back. "If proximity matters then come over. I miss you telling me off."

"Why? Am I the only one who does it?"

Max smiled. "You're the only one except for Gio who has ever done it."

"And lived?" I joked.

He nodded slowly. "Well?"

"I'll come over next week. Hey, I made payroll this month. How about that?"

He seemed genuinely happy for me. "That is fantastic! Great job. Everyone knew you could do it, except for you. I'm really proud of your work."

Humbly, I replied my thanks. "The band is starting. It's going to get loud."

Darkness set over Kansas City, and the lights from the stage blazed over thousands of people enjoying the music. Almost two hours later, the band left the stage, and another festival was over until next year.

"Well, what do you think?"

Max and I had stood through most of the concert, and even danced together. "That was a good time."

"Are you happy you're Irish now?"

"Part Irish, and yes. I'm feeling a lot better about all of that."

Several loud bangs filled the night. I looked around, but no one moved. Nothing seemed to be wrong here at the venue. "Maybe someone dropped some of the equipment backstage?"

Max's demeanor darkened. "No. Those were gunshots. They may have echoed in this building canyon, so maybe they were a few blocks away? We need to get to your father, Charlotte."

My hand was grabbed by Max as we began to wind our way to Dad. Max pointed at several police running behind the stage and down the street.

"Judge, are you okay?"

Dad had his folded lawn chair under his arm. "I'm fine, but those were shots, Max."

"I know. Why don't you two stay over there, under that umbrella? I'll be back for you."

I grabbed Max's arm. Mom's warning haunted me. "Don't go. The police and security will handle it."

Max placed his hand on top of mine. "It doesn't seem to have anything to do with the crowd here. Charlotte, I'll be fine. Stay here with your dad, and I promise, I'll be back in just a few minutes, or I'll text you. Trust me."

I nodded, but I gulped. I didn't feel right. I heard someone. I pulled at Max's arm as though he were my final lifeline. "Max, my mom says something is wrong. Max, she says something has happened to Sean."

Max kissed my forehead. "Charlotte, let me go. I'll find out what has happened. Stay here, and don't tell your father anything until I know for sure what is going on. It could be nothing."

"You believe me, don't you?"

"I never doubt you." He pulled away and ran through the crowd as the police began to direct the crowd away from the blocked north streets. Most of the crowd was dispersing easily with no event of any kind. Whatever those shots were, it had nothing to do with our annual celebration.

It was almost twenty minutes before I saw the text. I shut my eyes and tried not to cry. "Dad," I began as my voice broke. "Max says we need to get to the car. Let's go."

My father nodded. Neither one of us said anything as we headed to the parking garage. A police officer at the entrance stopped us. "Judge, we are going to get you out of here as fast as we can. Follow that officer on the motorcycle."

Dad thanked him, drove his car, and followed the police escort. "Charlotte, where are we going?"

"Max said he'd meet us at the hospital across the way."

"I see," my father said calmly. "Let's say a prayer, please."

"Okay, Dad." He began to recite the Our Father. I mumbled as best as I could while holding back tears. Now, I understood my mother's warning.

The officer led us directly to the emergency room entrance. Max and Jane were waiting for us there. As we rushed up to them, Max held me. "I saw Jane and brought her. I thought your Dad would need as much support as he could get."

"Max?" My father needed information.

Jane began to cry, and I hid my head in Max's chest. "Judge, there was an incident about four blocks away. I don't know all the specifics yet, but Sean's been shot. They are preparing him for surgery right now. They're waiting for you. Go."

Jane ran with my father, and I remained with Max. "Does Paddy know?"

"Yes, he stayed behind to help. There were several people on the sidewalk. A young woman was grazed, but Sean took the shots."

"Oh my God," I yelled. I balled my fist and hit Max. "Why does this stuff happen to us?"

"I don't know, darling." We both heard Max's phone, and he answered it. "Hey. Where are you? Okay. Do you have everyone? Do you need me to come back and pick you up? I have Jane, Charlie, and your dad. He's in there with Sean right now. Tom, there's police beginning to swarm this place. Okay. I'll text with our location. We'll see you as soon as you can get down here."

I removed myself from Max and wiped my nose with my arm. "I really am the snot nose sister." We shared a smile when there wasn't anything to smile about. "Sean is such an idiot. Why did he need to be some kind of a hero?"

"To save a woman. Charlotte, I want to tell you something, and I'm only telling you. No one needs to know about this yet. Do you understand?"

"Max, you're scaring me even more than I am already."

In complete seriousness, Max took my hands and bent down to look into my eyes. "Charlotte, Sean had to talk to me. He told me he knows who killed Conor. Whoever it was, was on that downtown street tonight. I don't know if that person shot your brother, or if Sean just saw the killer when he was on patrol, but he knew who it was."

I nodded. I understood, and yet my entire world seemed to be completely imploding. "I won't say anything to anyone."

"Good. Now, let's just think about Sean surviving surgery and continuing to be an idiot. He does it so well."

I sniffed back more tears. "He's a professional." When Max smiled at me, I broke down. My knees weakened, and I began to collapse, but Max's arms were there to hold me upright.

"Let's get inside and sit down to wait for your dad and Jane."

It was the beginning of another longest night of my life.

Chapter Twenty-One

Tom and Meg arrived almost an hour after Sean went into surgery. They dropped off her children and made Brad stay at the house until further notice. Max began to gather intel from various officers and paramedics. Firemen who had a truck at the festival came to the hospital and blocked the news crews as they congregated. Several noticed the U.S. Attorney pacing back and forth. They thought they had a scoop on a non-existent story. The only news here was that another policeman had been shot, and another O'Donohue son was in jeopardy of losing his life.

A coffee cup appeared in front of my nose. I looked up to see Max held a tray with enough coffee to go around for all of us. "Thank you."

"All of them are black. I figured it could be a very long night."

Tom grabbed one of the cups. "They haven't released Sean's name, have they? The family will be crushed. I need to call uncles, aunts. Max, have you told Gio?"

"Damn, no. Here, hand out the coffee. I'll call him now."

I leaned my head on Jane's shoulder and closed my eyes.

Meg rubbed my back, and I nearly fell asleep. It was almost two in the morning when Linda arrived. Police continued to mill around the outside of the emergency room. Our firemen had left, but the news crews remained waiting for one of us to go past the sliding doors.

I opened my eyes to see my father stand, greeting the police chief and the mayor. We watched. Our patriarch was every bit the judge. He was stoic and matter of a fact. He was no nonsense and gracious. What could he be feeling inside? I clamped onto Jane's hand. "Have we heard anything from the surgical team?"

"No, not yet." Jane looked intently down the hallway. "I want to go home as soon as we know anything. I need to be with my kids. My in laws are sleeping over just in case."

I understood. Just in case…just in case Uncle Sean never played football with them again or took them out for pizza. I sat up and began to plan. Jane needed to get home. Tom had showings tomorrow, well later today. Paddy looked like hell. He wouldn't want to leave, but Linda could make him. He would surrender if I promised to stay. Eventually, Dad would need fresh clothes, his razor, deodorant, and another pair of shoes.

I was supposed to be in the office to catch up on paperwork, but that could be done when Sean was stable. I only scheduled consults this week and wouldn't be in court for a couple of weeks. Dad and everyone would need breakfast in just a few hours.

Max returned and patted Tom's back. "Gio is upset, but I told him to stay put. He'll probably show up at the house and begin cooking for all of you."

"Max, I've been thinking that as soon as we hear about the surgery, Jane needs to go home to her kids and husband. Tom needs to get some sleep. He has showings today. Linda and Paddy should go home. We'll need them later. I need to grab Dad a few things. We won't get him to leave so he'll need clothes and other shoes. He's still wearing sandals and that shirt."

We all looked over in his direction. Max and Tom began to laugh. The judge was very proud of his Irish shirt with the words *Kiss me, I'm Irish, or just kiss me!* Tom's laughter was stifled as he faced Max's shoulder. Quickly, his laughs became sobs. Max embraced his best friend and walked him over to another side of the waiting area.

"Charlotte, I thought you were sleeping, but you were planning, weren't you?" Meg asked.

I didn't answer. I watched as the mayor and chief left Dad. Tom and Max offered him a coffee and sat on either side of our father while Paddy paced. It seemed as though the men took their turns wandering away and returning while we females sat patiently and waited. No feeling was as bad as helplessness.

We caught a few minutes of sleep until daylight began to stream through the doors. Apparently, some of the hospital traffic was diverted to another entrance, but now and then an ambulance would pull up with an emergency. Around six in the morning, one of the surgical team came through the door to speak with all of us.

"It's been very slow. I don't want to alarm you or get your hopes up. The surgery should be over in another hour. He is holding his own. He's very strong so that is to his advantage. When he's in post op, the surgeons will discuss the details."

She said everything, and she said nothing. We nodded like little bobbleheads. Paddy stood in the middle of all of us. "Now what? They could've taken him apart and put him back together again by now."

"This isn't a game, Paddy. It takes time to cut through Sean's thick skin," I argued. Dad was the first one to smile. Again, we laughed until we cried.

Sean's usual police partner arrived with breakfast sandwiches and fresh coffee about thirty minutes later. A spokesperson for the department dropped by to have Dad approve of what they were going to say in a statement. Max insisted they not release Sean's name or his relationship to a former retired federal judge and the brother of a murdered sibling.

Finally, two surgeons came out to our waiting area. One sat next to Dad and began to explain Sean's injury. He'd taken three shots. One bullet remained lodged in his body near his spinal column and another above his vest was removed. The third round hit his leg leaving significant shredded muscle tissue and ligaments. Thankfully, he didn't bleed out. The upper shoulder and neck areas were concerning. They were waiting until the swelling went down to assess the injury to his spinal column.

When hearing tragic news, we'd been through it enough. I knew how each of my siblings would react. Paddy used profanity and retreated into himself; Tom's bottom lip trembled. He remained calm until Meg kissed him. Tom crumbled, crying like a baby in his wife's arms. Jane cried and called her mother-in-law. After mom's passing, she became very close to Brad's mother. If Sean had been here, he would look for the nearest bar, and Dad would be Dad. He would be strong and quiet. I would plan and organize. I would cry a little and wait until I was alone before I completely fell into pieces. Right now, the option of going to the nearest bar had the best appeal.

Max watched me. I could feel his gaze. I couldn't tell what he was thinking, but he'd said to trust him. We now had our own shared secret about Conor. If Sean pulled through, we could put our brother's murder mystery to rest. If Sean joined Conor, we would be back at square one, only this time it would be multiplied in a tragic way.

The police chaplain visited, and a hospital liaison took us up to another waiting area for our privacy. Max followed us but was constantly speaking on his phone or discussing in hushed tones with other police friends of Sean's who touched base with the family. One by one, my siblings took off to check on their own family. We even convinced Tom to meet with his two clients. Max handed me his phone at one point. Phoebe wanted to assure me she would keep the office going, and that she could sit with her former boss.

Max dropped into the seat next to me, holding my hand. "Charlotte, what do you need me to do?"

"Nothing. You've done so much. Go home. Check on Gio. I need to get Dad and me fresh clothes, and I need to check on Mickey. Jane's husband has let him out twice today, but I bet the poor dog hasn't been hugged." I looked down at my watch. It seemed as though there was no time within a hospital.

"Are you sure?" Max bent down to see my eyes. "I'll stay here."

I looked up and smiled. "You have been so kind. Thank you, but Gio will be worried. You need to give him a recap. I'm sure you probably were going to catch up on work today. Go home. I promise I'll call you if anything changes, and you'll tell me if you hear anything, right?"

My question received a nod as Max stood and left my side. I needed to trust Max, but I wondered if he did learn about Conor's killer, would he really read me in on it?

Finally, Dad was allowed to go back to the intensive care unit. When he returned, he looked like he had aged. I called Jane, texted Tom and Paddy with the little bit of information he offered. Sean was alive. Sean was a fighter.

Now it was just Dad and me. I managed to wrap my arm around his large, strong shoulders. "Dad, I should go home and get fresh clothes and check on Mickey."

"Poor Mickey. He'll wonder what's happened," the strongest man I knew muttered. "Yes, you should go." He dug deep into his pocket and removed his car keys, placing them into my hand. "Charlotte, you should take a break. Take your time. If I get hungry, I'll get something here. The nurses showed me where I can grab a coffee at their station. I'll be fine."

As I walked through the emergency entrance, the rain pelted my face. Apparently, it was to be another wet Labor Day. I looked over at one of the young policemen near the door. "I'm Judge O'Donohue's daughter. I have no idea where his car is. My brother Detective–"

"It's right there."

The car had never been moved. "Thank you. Where do I park when I return?"

"Right there, Ms. O'Donohue. How's your brother?"

"He's hanging in there."

"I'm praying for him."

"Thank you. He'll need every prayer he can get."

By the time I reached the house, it was raining harder. There were flood warnings beginning around the city. It didn't surprise me when I noticed the news van parked on the other side of the street, but I ran into the house before they could leave their vehicle. In the afternoon, the released statement named Sean and our family. They may have thought I was just a friend checking on the house. Mickey greeted me enthusiastically in the front hallway.

The dog was unusually loving, realizing that his constant companion was missing. I fed and watered him first before heading upstairs to pack a small bag for myself, and to change my clothes. I instantly threw them into the hamper. My only other option was to burn them. I headed into Dad's bedroom to gather a fresh shirt, slacks, socks, underwear, shoes, and a few toiletries.

I had to search in what used to be Mom's side of the closet to find a small bag to pack them in.

"Charlotte."

"Oh Mom, we need you. You warned me. I just didn't understand. How could I?"

"Pray."

I dissolved into a puddle of tears, sitting on the floor alone until Mickey joined me. "Mom, what are we going to do?"

"Love."

"Mom, why does this keep happening?"

"Charlotte, trust."

I did, but I didn't. I had this desperate feeling, just like when Conor was murdered. If Sean was to have the same fate, I had no idea how we would survive. How could Dad possibly go on? Even a strong man had a limit to his survival of tragedy and agony. Didn't he?

As I pulled myself together, I looked around my parents' bedroom. Dad kept it tidy, and he had made very few changes since his wife's death. Her robe remained hung on the back of the door, and her prized jewelry box still held a prominent place on the dresser. The family photos she loved so much were all around. My favorite was their wedding portrait. Mom was so young and beautiful, and Dad looked as though he was scared to death. I suppose I inherited her surety to do the right thing and to say what needed to be said. But I was so tired of carrying that load. How did she do it and retain her grace and sanity? She always said she had a good partner.

Finally, I made my way downstairs and made sure Mickey had a quick trip outside and was settled in for another night. One of Paddy's sons would come in the morning on his way to school to let the dog out. I suspected he volunteered for the job so he could play hooky. He was heading into his senior year in high school, and in his mind, he really was finished with academics until college.

As I locked the front door, I turned into several bright lights. Not only were television reporters surrounding me, but there seemed to be other reporters. I shielded my eyes from the glare and headed to the car. I heard question after question, but I said nothing.

"Ms. O'Donohue, you've had one brother murdered, and now you have another hanging onto life. Do you think your family is cursed? Do you think this has something to do with one of your father's judgments before he retired? You have another brother who is a detective. Has he done something? Was your brother the target of retribution?"

I threw the bags into the car and started it up. I patted at my tears as the wipers' noise on the windshield masked my sobs. I reversed slowly and drove away. Were we cursed? Was that what all of this was about? Did Dad do something? Did someone hate us so much that they were targeting us one by one? Could our relationship with Max be threatening all of us? Or were we cursed because I could hear those desperate souls who were trying to relay messages through me?

When I arrived back at the hospital, one officer directed me to the same parking place. I put my head down and ran into the building. Security asked for my identification, and I was led up to a private waiting area. Nate, Max's friend and Gio sat with Dad. Nate stood as I entered the room.

"We brought dinner. I hope you don't mind. Gio fixed up sandwiches and some Italian soup. Pretty good. He brought enough for an army like your family." Nate directed my attention to a table full of plastic containers, paper plates, and utensils.

"That's wonderful. I forgot to pick up anything after I was at the house. Thank you." I gave my father a quick kiss and did the same to Gio. "Dad, Mickey is fine. His care is covered through tomorrow morning, and I have fresh clothes." I set his bag down at his feet and placed mine over in an empty chair. "I brought your phone charger too. It must be dead by now."

He removed his phone. "It is. Before it died, Edward Shaw called. He'll have the FBI check into the shooting. It was good to talk to him. I guess Max told him."

"Max thought you might want to talk to an old friend," Gio said quietly. "Charlotte, eat something. I couldn't smuggle any hooch in, but there's good coffee there. Nate picked it up at one of those drive thru places."

"Your soup smells good, and I bet I can find a microwave. It's so wet outside I'm chilled."

"The microwave is just around the corner," Gio directed. "The nurses said we could use it. It did cost me a couple of sandwiches, but I don't mind. They do a lot of good work."

"Oh, and Father Mark dropped by. He wondered if we needed anything," Dad added.

The soup was warm enough for me. I suspected it was Gio's own recipe for minestrone mixed with Italian wedding soup. The aroma alone made my empty stomach growl. I looked over the sandwiches, but first I needed to get warm and try to forget about the reporters' comments.

I sat down across from the men and began to eat while Dad looked into his bag. "Charlotte, is everyone as good as they can be?"

"Yes, Dad. Everyone is accounted for, and we've established a phone chain, so we don't have to make any more calls than needed."

"Your mother used to–" Dad looked up. "Sorry, yes, good."

Gio patted my father on the back. "You don't need to apologize. Charlotte is a lot like your wife. I remember her fondly."

Dad nodded but continued to search the bag. "Oh good, you packed my razor. By tomorrow I'll really need this."

"Dad, do we have any updates?" I finished my soup and began to graze the table. Gio had thought of everything including pickles, condiments, and a tray of brownies. Before I selected my sandwich, I began to eat my dessert.

"No, well, they come in and say nothing has changed. I was able to go in for five minutes. I hate to see the ventilator." Dad pulled out the folded shirt. He looked down at what he was wearing and smiled. "I didn't even realize I was wearing this stupid shirt."

Nate smiled. "You look good in green, Judge."

"Yeah," Gio chimed in. "Much better looking in green than those black robes you used to wear."

Dad stood up. "All right. I'm going to change right now."

I pointed at the shirt in his hand. "There's a nice sweatshirt in there that would be better for night."

"We were thinking your dad should go home and get some sleep," Gio said quietly.

Dad turned on Gio. "No. I'm not leaving until he is out of the woods."

"Dad, Gio is right. You can't stay here much longer without making yourself sick."

My father didn't exactly agree with me, but he didn't reprimand me either. "Charlotte, that is a good idea…for you. You should go home and sleep tonight. From past experiences, we all know this isn't a sprint. It's a marathon, and I'll need you fully rested. Then, maybe tomorrow night I'll go home, and one of you kids can stay. What about that?"

He was shrewd. "Fine. If you promise that if I go home, you'll go home tomorrow night when one of us has the shift. Do you promise?"

"Sure."

"No, I know you better than that. Promise correctly." I took another bite of my chocolate wonder. "Come on."

The judge looked over at Gio and Nate. "She's bossy, isn't she?"

"She apparently knows you very well," Nate answered.

"Fine. I cross my heart, and if we had a bible, I would swear on it. I know when I'm beat in more ways than one. I promise, as long as one of my children is here tomorrow night, I will go home and sleep in my bed with my dog."

"Perfect. We have a deal."

All of us sobered up when one of the surgeons entered our space. "Judge, if one of you would like to go in for a few minutes we can make that happen."

My father's eyes lit on mine. "Charlotte? Do you want to see him?"

I gulped and nodded. I put aside my food and followed the doctor back to the intensive care unit. I pinched my arm to prevent myself from passing out. As I entered the room, I became increasingly overwhelmed. I suppose my nausea was from past experiences when Mom was ill and in the hospital. Now, as I saw Sean hooked up to every imaginable tube and machine, my knees swayed a bit. I quickly sat down on the small stool next to him.

His eyelids were dark, and his lips were almost white. Sean always had the prettiest mouth. It looked like a little tight bow. Mom used to call them Cupid lips. I managed to slide my hand through all of the lines to touch his hair. I expected him to reach up and grab my hand, telling me to stop touching him. He always hated being touched by anyone.

"Oh, Sean. Why did you have to be a hero? And who did you see? I wish you had told Max before you ended up like this. You will get better, right? Sean? I better not see you or hear you ever."

"My sweet boy." I felt my mother's warmth near my right shoulder.

"Mom, please help him. I don't know what Dad will do, what any of us will do if we have to go through this again. Sean is bigger and stronger than Conor was. He will pull through."

"Charlotte, stop."

"No, Mom. If I don't stay strong, keep believing, then everything will fall apart."

"Charlotte, in God's hands."

I began to weep. Maybe if my tears rained down on Sean's face, he would wake up. "Mom, please."

"Go to your home."

"I promised Dad I will."

"No, your home, Charlotte. Where you belong. It is time. I'll be here with him."

She was gone. I could feel it. Mom always said I worried about the future too much, but the days that might be coming if Sean didn't make it out of the hospital could change everything and everyone. We were cursed. At some time, a pact had been made by the devil…the devil. What had Max said? I always had to be sure; to keep everybody together. Mom had left me with that position.

There was one day in November when I was with her. She was so ill, the cancer ravishing through her body. We positioned the couch so she could rest on it and watch the leaves turn into their beautiful colors before the dark days of winter arrived and lingered. But that day, a cold breeze filled the air, and we saw a few flakes of snow.

"Charlotte, am I imagining that? I wanted to see snow one more time. I know I won't make it for Christmas."

I patted her hand. "Don't say that. Of course you will."

"My sweet baby. Do you know your father and I didn't plan to have you? You were a miracle."

I giggled. "Did you plan any of us, and don't you say that about every baby?"

"Well, I do, but your father, never mind. We went to this New Year's Eve party and even stayed at a downtown hotel.

My sister was in town, and she stayed with the children. Paddy and Jane didn't think they needed a babysitter, but we knew if they were in charge the younger boys probably wouldn't eat that night. We went up to that room and well–"

"I don't want to hear this." I placed my hands over my ears and began to recite a prayer about my guardian angel.

"Stop that." Mom slapped playfully in the air at me. "You need to hear this. Your father was so sweet and romantic. We did a lot of kissing, and he was always so gentle, but that night was very special. He carried me to bed. My goodness. I was breathless. That's what I want for you. I want you to be romanced, to be kissed like his and your life depend on it, and I want you to catch your breath that first time with the man you love."

That afternoon I learned so much, and I was given the responsibility to take care of our father. Mom warned about Paddy's strength and temper, Jane's timidity and lack of self-control, Tom's tendency to worry way more than he should, and Sean's impetuous nature. And of Conor, she said she would search for him in heaven first and hold him forever.

A nurse asked me nicely to return to the waiting room. I kissed Sean and whispered that Mom would be there for him, one way or another. I held in my tears and all my fears as I met Nate in the hallway.

"Look, Charlie, Max wants me to stay with your dad tonight. I think it's a good idea until we know what is going on. No one, no one is allowed near Sean. There's a policeman at either end of the hall on this floor."

"So, he's told you?"

"Yes. Gio doesn't know, but he wants to stay the night too. We can't talk him out of it, so you should get a good night's sleep. Maybe you could call Max and update him personally? He's at the house reading over some legal stuff."

"I will. Thank you, Nate."

As I entered our private room, Dad and Gio were laughing about a strip joint downtown that all of the mobsters used to go to. "I leave for just a bit, and you two are discussing the good old days?"

"What else is there to do?" Dad replied. "I've been praying so much I think I heard God say he was trying to take a nap."

"I've thought over the years that God does take a nap now and then." Gio's comment was met with looks of surprise. "Why shouldn't He? He has to get tired of all of us."

"Charlotte, get out of here. Go home and take a shower and sleep."

"I will in a bit." It really wasn't that late. I wasn't sure I could sleep after seeing Sean, but I could use a warm shower. I felt cold from the inside out, and after listening to someone from beyond, I always felt colder, numb as though my physical body was being chipped away to bear only my soul.

Another nurse came in to check on us and tell us that Sean's vitals remained stable but at times were erratic. She was honest, telling us that it was touch and go, and it could remain that way for several days.

I listened to Dad and Gio's stories. Nate began speaking about his time on the aircraft carrier with Max. My eyes could barely stay open even though tales about Max Shaw were highly entertaining.

"Charlotte, go home." My father's voice startled me, and I jumped in the chair.

"Yes, okay." I kissed Dad goodnight and thanked Nate and Gio again. I was leaving the room as a nurse brought in more pillows and blankets. They were settling in for the night.

As I headed home, my intent was to go to the house, shower, and hide under my covers.

How could it keep raining this hard? Streetlights were blurred and as night had come on it was increasingly more difficult to see the yellow lines on the pavement. Thank God not many people were on the roads at the end of a holiday.

I sat at a red light off of The Plaza. My tears flowed as I remembered Sean's poor body. "Mom, please help him." I began to pray.

I hit my directional signal to turn right. Even my nose was running. I kept wiping my eyes with my sleeves. Where was the tissue when you really needed it?

I needed more than a tissue right now. I needed a shower and just one good stiff drink.

I began to organize what I needed to do. I'd post a text to Jane on the communication chain. She would relay the message to siblings, family, and friends. I should also update Max, but Nate and Gio probably had already done that. I hit the wheel.

"I hate this!" Feeling this helpless again was unbearable. The car behind me honked. "I'm moving you idiot. I'm having a crisis here." But the driver couldn't hear me. My windows were up, and thunder was masking any screams.

Even Mom wasn't comforting. She was more confusing than helpful. She told me to go to my home. I turned my car and pulled over to the side to collect my thoughts in front of one of the area's restaurants.

Mickey and I would be fine alone in that house. I would collapse after my shower and sleep until mid-morning. But I wouldn't. I knew me by now. I'd make coffee and be up half of the night. Maybe I could get some of my work done? There was a burning discourse within me. I had no words for it, or nothing to quell it. This shooting had shaken me.

I steered back into the storm. I drove aimlessly around the area until a police car pulled up next to me and hit its siren. I put down my window as rain came in on me.

"Yes, officer?"

"Pull over. We'll need to see your registration."

"It's my father's car. It's registered to Judge O'Donohue. I'm his daughter, Charlotte. Sean's little sister."

The officer sitting in the passenger side nodded. "Sorry, Ms.

O'Donohue. We just wanted to make sure. With your brother hurt, we were just checking it was a family member with that car. Everyone is on alert. May we escort you somewhere?"

"No, thank you. I'm just going to my home. Thank you."

"We're praying for him."

I shut the window before I became a blubbering idiot again. My act of invisibility wasn't working tonight. Even the police noticed me. I drove slowly until I reached a half flooded large intersection.

"That's just what we need, a damn flood. The basement will fill. What more?" The wiper on the passenger side was slower than the one on the driver's side. "Seriously? Is this a test of some kind?"

I continued to cry and scream out. "All I want to do is go home. My home. I want to take a shower and feel warm. I want to know it's all going to be okay. I'm just so tired of doing this alone, of not knowing–"

I stopped my rant suddenly and dried my tears. I listened to the intensity of the rain pelting the windshield and felt the strong wind toss the car slightly. It was peaceful in the middle of a storm, at least it could be. I wiped my nose with my hand as several drops of liquid fell. I was probably in shock, but at the light, I turned left and began to drive with purpose.

Despite my moral grounding, and my fortitude of always doing the supposed right thing, I knew what my real fear was now. I was suddenly sure, yet alarmingly afraid of the decision I was about to make.

I drove around the block, avoiding impassable water swollen lanes until I pulled into the large parking area. I looked up at the house and saw a few lights were on, including a couple upstairs. Grabbing my purse and the bag I had packed, I locked the car and ran up to the door, drenched before I hit the doorbell. There was no turning back now. I knew what and who I wanted. The gravitational pull that was Max Shaw was too intense for my heart. To be with him would place me in the spotlight. Next to him, people would see me, and I would never be allowed to be invisible again. Would he be worth the sacrifice of changing my very life?

But Max was right. I had made a mistake the first time I thought I was in love. He had been the wrong man, and it had been the wrong time. This was the right time and deep down in my heart I knew he was definitely the right man. Now, the question was, did Max see us the way I did?

Chapter Twenty-Two

I waited patiently, only beginning to doubt my decision when I heard the lock turn and the alarm switched off. My eyes focused on the knob like Mickey's when he was about to receive a treat. Once the door opened, there was confusion on both sides of it. For me, I had decided I needed help. It wasn't just my hormones flaring, it was need. For once, I hadn't over thought this. I'd only driven around the block once, and as my stomach began to rumble nervously, I realized I should've driven at least fifty miles before standing before this door. Impetuously, Max was the one I ran to, drove through flood waters to see. He and I were at an impasse. We could go on forever with me dreaming about him, and Max treating me special now and then. We would continue bickering and bantering. Or, one of us could be courageous to pull the other out of darkness. Right now, I wasn't sure which one of us was more in the dark.

"Charlotte? I couldn't believe it was you on the security camera. Get in here. You're drenched." Max pulled at my rain jacket and brought me in. "What's wrong? Is it Sean? Are you hurt?"

His anxiousness was sweet. That's why I came here, came to him. Those tempting eyes and his charm were sexy as hell. It was who Max was deep down that pushed my faith and virtue aside to collide on a course with temptation. But I needed someone to care for me, and he seemed to be the perfect man to do the job. I was just tired of being alone in every way, especially tonight. "I'm not hurt. Sean is the same, and everything is wrong." I wiped at my nose again. What was I really expecting? I probably looked like the bride from hell right now or a lost soaked puppy.

Max seemed to be relieved by my answer. "Let's get you out of that raincoat." He began to pull at my jacket, placing my purse and bag on the floor. He pointed down at my shoes. "Kick those off. They're soaked."

I did as I was told as he moved them to the side of the door. "Are you hungry? How about some coffee? You're probably cold." Max began to walk toward the kitchen, but I grabbed his arm to stop him.

"I've had enough coffee to last a lifetime. Max, the other night in the car–"

"I'm sorry about that. I tried to apologize in that text, but I should've done it in person. I have no words for how rude I was with my accusations. I was getting the wrong signal from you, and I realize I overstepped my boundaries–"

I placed my hand over his heart. "Life is too short for all of that stuff. I'm ready. Do you want me?"

Max blinked twice. "Excuse me?"

I moved my hands on either side of his face. He was trapped. "You were right about my mistake. You are you, and you most certainly aren't my ex. You led me to believe you wanted me."

Max remained silent. His eyes held my gaze, but he said absolutely nothing.

Oh shit. Why hadn't I overthought this entire idea? I pulled away and took a couple of steps back. I could flee very easily, but it would take an embarrassing amount of time to slip on my shoes and raincoat before I could hit the door for my escape. "Max, do you **want** me?" I stamped one bare foot for emphasis.

Max bridged the gap between us. "Charlotte, have you really thought this out? You're probably upset because of Sean and driving in the rain."

I nodded. As some of the droplets of water on my hair dropped down into my face, I wiped at my eyes. "I can't tell you how much I've thought about this since the day you saved me from falling on the ice. I just never thought we, you and me, never mind. Do you **want** me? Please don't make me spell it out or ask you again."

Max's eyes softened. His hand swept my wet hair from my forehead. "God help me, but yes. Charlotte, you're all I've been thinking about, and you're so beautiful when you're wet and unsure."

"Then–"

Before I could say another word, Max's hands shifted to my waist as he pulled me into his embrace. His face hovered just above mine, lowering it to touch my lips with his. His soft kiss was sweet, and something I never expected from Max Shaw.

"Let's get you out of those clothes." Max broke his hold and grabbed my things. I chuckled quietly. I expected that he'd want me naked, but not this soon. When I put my hand in his, I naturally followed him up the stairs to his bedroom.

The only lamp on was the one near the chairs in front of the large window. Max headed toward the massive bathroom to bathe it in light.

"You need a hot shower, Charlotte. I'm going to put your things in this empty closet. Is your phone in your purse? I can charge it for you. You don't want to miss any calls about Sean."

I stood in the middle of his master bedroom and dripped. My hair was heavy as it hung down onto my back. My shirt was drenched, and my jeans were soaked from running in the rain. "Rose, you don't watch, do you?" I whispered while Max was talking about towels. I didn't receive an answer.

He came back into the room and pointed at my feet. "You're making a puddle."

"Oh no. I'm so sorry. I shouldn't be here. Your new rug–"

Max tugged at my arms. "Where should you be? Alone? No. Don't worry about the rug, but let's get you warm."

Unexpectedly, he swooped me up into his arms and carried me into the bathroom. No one had ever done that to me, except for Paddy. I refused to go inside when he said I should. I was ten and wanted to ride my bike one additional time down the street. When he finally lost his temper, my dear brother swooped up both the bike and me. I was unceremoniously thrown over his left shoulder.

Max's gesture was more romantic, more movie-like. He was probably just saving his rug, but when he deposited me onto the floor, his hands remained around my waist. "Charlotte, look at me."

Again, I did as I was told.

"You are in shock. You're hardly blinking. Did you have a problem driving?"

I nodded. "I hit flooded streets. A police car stopped me. They thought I'd stolen Dad's car. They're praying for Sean. I had to drive around the block to get to you. I think Dad has a wiper that's bad and one of his headlights may be out."

"I'll check the car in the morning, or when this rain eases up. The courts are closed tomorrow, and I've already alerted my staff to work from home. This is a real emergency."

I nodded again, but I had no words. When was the last time I had nothing to say? I felt cold all over and only repeated Max's words. "It is a real emergency."

Max watched me for a few seconds and began to act. "Charlotte, honey, I'm going to get you out of these wet clothes." Max's hands unbuttoned my jeans. I heard the zipper go down, and as Max tugged, I watched. Eventually, he told me to step out of each leg.

"Are you sure you're not hungry? Maybe some food would help?"

Max lifted my shirt over my head, and I stood in front of him in my panties and bra. I began to come out of my fog as I noticed that my set didn't match. My panties had red hearts on them, and my bra was the staple white one I bought online. "I ate at the hospital. Gio brought his soup and the sandwiches. That was very nice of him. They're staying with my dad. Did I tell you that?"

"No, but I knew. Gio called. Nate texted." Max was over by the large shower, checking the temperature of the water. "Do you prefer hot or warm?"

"Warm." Chilled, I began to shake. "Max, I'm so cold."

"Let's get you in. There're large towels on each side."

My feet wouldn't move. Max stood in front of me, rubbing my arms. "Honey, you're freezing. Let me take care of you tonight." Max pulled off his own wet shirt. I blinked in surprise but realized I'd ruined his clothes as well. He reached under one of the shower heads once more. "The water should be perfect for you, I hope."

I was losing my nerve as I looked over his chest. His middle was flatter than mine emphasizing a six pack of toned muscles, and light brown hair nestled on his chest trailing down below his waist. I'd intentionally come over here tonight to have sex with Max Shaw. What kind of a person was I? I was here when my brother was hanging onto life.

"Max, are you just being nice because of Sean?"

"You should know me by now, Charlotte. I always do what I want to do. As far as being nice, it seems to me you've never accused me of that. Do you know I trust you more than myself?"

"No," I answered softly. "Why? I can't be trusted."

Max shook his head. "Really? You keep my secrets."

I nodded. "I'm good at keeping secrets." I wasn't feeling right. Maybe he was right, and I was in shock?

"Let's get you in here." Max's extended hand offered an invitation. It's funny how your mind works. I remembered my catechism from grade school. The devil had once been an angel and the favorite of God. I nervously smiled but walked toward my fate.

In the middle of the shower, I faced the wall and remained dry. Max hadn't activated the large square head in the middle, and neither side shower head hit my body. I looked over my shoulder to see him still standing there. Max smiled shyly through veiled eyes. "I'll give you your privacy."

As tears began to stream down my face, I sobbed out loud. "Please stay." I thought I could bend but never break, but here I was completely falling into pieces. "Max, I do need you." One of us needed to say it.

Max's silence was unnerving, but his actions were swift. I looked back again to see him pulling off his own jeans and boxers. I felt his hands on each of my shoulders. His lips burned into my neck, nuzzling under my ear lobe. "Let me." His murmur sent a chill throughout my body. Max unhooked my bra and slipped it off of my shoulders throwing it onto the growing pile of clothing outside of the glass doors. His fingers ran a feathery trail down the sides of my body, landing on the trim of my panties.

My chills were replaced by warm tension as for the first time this man slowly pulled down my panties without one insult or chuckle. He tapped each leg when he wanted me to step out. I still faced the wall, with my hands covering my breasts and my naked back in his view.

I finally heard a familiar chuckle. "Charlotte, you can't shower facing the wall." Max's hands returned to my body. He turned me by tugging on my upper arms. "How's the temperature?"

"Good." Max activated the large middle shower head, a cascade of water falling on us. He began to use a bar of soap on my upper body, intimately running it all the way down to the curves of my hips and bottom. The soap appeared in front of me.

"I'm going to wash your hair." Before I could protest, Max's hands were in my hair. In his close work, I could feel his naked body against me. "Does that feel good?"

"You have no idea," I whispered.

"Is that a yes?"

I nodded this time. I closed my eyes and allowed Max to care for me. His touch was a healing salve on my fear. My body was content, bending into him uncontrollably. My eyes opened when he turned my body to face him. I held the soap as a small barrier between us. A coral reef wouldn't be a large enough space. "You know, I'm still indifferent to your charm."

Max's low laugh made me smile. "Keep telling yourself that, baby. But, if that's the case, then I'll have to try harder. I have a reputation to keep intact. Close your eyes." He placed me under the shower and rinsed my hair. I felt him remove the bar from my hand. Max tugged on my arms removing what little of my privacy I had remaining. I felt his lips on mine. I hadn't been kissed this much in years. But Max didn't settle on my mouth. He began a tour of my body.

My eyes shot open as the tip of his tongue attended to one of my breasts. My body wasn't playing hard to get. It was shouting to come and get it! I reached up to grab him, but with Max's head lowered, my hands landed around his back. Surprisingly, my touch elicited an involuntary flexing in his muscles. As I caressed, they flexed. Did I do that to him? "Max."

"Do you want me to stop?" Max waited a second and continued on his determined track. His hands trapped me around my hips as he continued to attend to my body.

"No, but I don't know. I'm so sorry."

Max looked directly into my eyes. "Are we okay?"

I gave him a quick kiss. "We are more than okay, but here I am with you while Sean–"

"While there's nothing we can do," Max answered quickly. "Charlotte, I can't let you go back out there. You're currently stuck with me."

We blinked back water as we stared into each other's eyes. "I know it's dangerous to try to go back to the hospital, but I'm feeling so guilty–"

Max kissed my forehead. "I'm going to give you some time alone. Would you like a glass of wine?"

"Yes, please." Max nodded his acceptance and stepped out of the shower. I shyly watched him dry off and wrap a towel around his waist. He left the bathroom, leaving me alone under the water. This time I leaned up against the wall and tried to catch my breath.

"What have I gotten myself into and especially tonight?" I crossed a rubicon swelled from flooding rains to be here, to be with Max. Any shock I had from my drive had passed. This Max was sweet and adoring. This is the Max I loved.

I managed to turn off the water, grabbed the largest towel, dried off, and wrapped it completely over my body. I haven't waxed or shaved, and I look like a drenched rat. I shook my hair out and noticed a brush and blow dryer on the counter. I began to put myself back together when a glass of wine appeared in front of me. I looked up to find Max still in his towel and sitting on the bathroom counter.

"You look like you're feeling better," Max said. He took a drink from his glass.

"I do, but I might need a second glass."

Max pointed out into the bedroom. "I have a wine fridge in the bedroom."

"Of course, you do," I murmured. Again, I saw confusion on his face.

"Charlotte, now that you aren't in shock, do you want to tell me the real reason you're here? I know you probably have some divine plan."

His voice dripped with sarcasm, and it infuriated me for some reason. "I told you. I couldn't do it anymore, being alone. I didn't want to go to that empty house. I'll admit that after all of these years, and the last few years of tears and fretting, I just don't know what to do. I pray–"

"Of course, you do. Sometimes that gets you into trouble."

Why did he always provoke me? "And it stops you from doing something stupid."

"Ah, me. You're the one who came here," Max reminded me. His statement cut the wind from my debate.

I finished brushing my hair. I unplugged the blow dryer and began to search for my bag and purse.

Max jumped from the counter and countered my movements. "Your stuff is in the closet, but I'm not allowing you to go out in that weather."

I tugged at my towel to make sure it would remain in place as I raised my arm to reprimand him. "Allow? You don't allow me to do anything, you narcissistic–"

"Ass, devil. I've heard it all before. Any other terms of endearment?"

I found my bag and began to rifle through it. "I'm thinking. You wear all those descriptions as a badge of honor, don't you?"

"I've been called worse." Max sat casually on the bench near me. "You have such finesse and are so much more descriptive with your vocabulary than the others."

"And there's another problem," I interjected. "How many women have you been with? Should I have you tested or something?"

Max laughed hard. "Sweetheart, not that I have to share with you, but thanks to you and your family, I haven't been with anyone since I arrived in this city. Does that make you happy?"

Strangely, it did make me happy. I nodded. "Now I understand why you were so desperate the other night. It didn't matter if it was me or someone else, it was just who was available. I was an easy mark after all that romance. I knew it!"

Max shot up and moved my bag away from my shaking hands. "No. You know better. It was that damn dress. It was dancing with you, spending a wonderful night with your family, and again, God help me, it's you." Max's soft grip on my arms made sure I didn't move. "Honey, I'm sorry, but I won't make promises to you. I wish I could. I'm not a good bet."

I looked up into his eyes. "Don't you think I know that? I don't know the future. I wish I did. I wouldn't be so fixated on constantly improving my work, helping with my family, feeling so damn responsible. Does that make sense?"

"That's who you are, Charlotte." Max's mouth lowered, and he released my arms long enough to take one hand to tip my chin up to his. "I avoid commitment like civilization avoids a plague. I can't help it. I'm not sure if you can help me overcome my problem or if I'm destined to be alone. With the complete understanding, and under pain of some law I will find, you will never divulge to anyone that I'm a complete psychological mess. Got it?"

I smiled and gave him a quick kiss. "Got it. Max, a few people already know that...my dad, Gio, Tom, Meg, your personal assistant, and I suspect Phoebe and your dad know too. But, Max, do you understand what I'm offering you? Don't you dare say a good time." Dad always did say to trust your intuition and never give up. My gut was telling me I was going to have to fight for what I wanted, even if at the end of the battle I only had fond memories.

Max turned off the light in the large closet. He took my hand, walking me through the bathroom as he drenched that in darkness as well. "Charlotte, I know. You're offering me much more than just one night. You make me think about the future. Come to bed. If you want to go back to the hospital in a few hours, I'll drive you. I will get you there."

My heart quickened, and I nodded slowly. Here I was, the usual ring on the finger kind of girl, placing my hand in his and following.

When we arrived by the bed, Max had already turned back the covers. The bed was ready, but was I? The last and only time I'd been with a man was with the one who would never be named, and he'd been my one and only. I thought I was going to live the fairy tale my parents enjoyed, but within weeks the story ended in true soap opera fashion. Max wasn't him, was he? No. He'd already made me feel more than I ever had with, what was his name?

I couldn't remember the past. I barely remembered my name as we sat down on the edge of the bed, and Max began to kiss me passionately. He made my name sound like an angelic chorus.

"Trust."

I heard Rose's voice and pulled away from Max.

"Did I do something wrong?" Again, confusion was etched on his brow.

"No, you're doing everything right. I need to trust you even if it's just for this one night."

Max kissed the top of my right shoulder. "I think we can have more than one night and definitely more than one time."

My hand went up and touched his face. "I care so much for you it scares me. But I'm here while my brother is fighting for his life."

Max turned my chin back toward his gaze. "Charlotte, don't you think that Paddy fell into Linda's arms tonight? I bet Tom and Meg made love and fell asleep while listening to this storm rage. It's okay. Don't be haunted by those voices in your head."

I wanted to tell him that everything was stacked against him if I believed those voices in my head. I needed to trust them, but most importantly myself, even if it was just this one night. I entwined my hand with his and leaned over to kiss him as hard as I could. I found his lips but toppled both of us unceremoniously onto the bed.

We both laughed at my awkwardness as Max found the edge of my towel and pulled it off along with his own. There was nothing between us now. Max cupped my face. "Charlotte, do you know how much I want you?"

Given what happened in the shower, I had a fair idea. I tilted my head. "Really? What do you want from me?"

"Absolutely everything, but we could just talk. I'd be disappointed, but I won't take advantage of a vulnerable Charlotte," he murmured.

I touched his face and languished in those beautiful caramel eyes. "I don't want to talk."

In one quick moment, I was on my back and Max hovered over me, examining every body part I'd tried to hide before.

This was all too serious. My mind began thinking…I hadn't shaved my legs, waxed any part of me, I probably needed to brush my teeth, did I turn off the car lights…

Max's finger touched my lips. "You're thinking, aren't you?"

"I'm not."

Max chuckled. He placed a kiss on my shoulder. "You are lying. Do I want to know what you were going over in your mind?"

Smiling, I touched an errant lock of hair on his forehead. "No, it was silly."

Max nodded. He stopped and heatedly looked down at my body. "Every inch of you is perfect."

I wrapped my arms around his neck and laughed. "Wow, you are really desperate and filled with an overload of blarney."

Max shook his head. "No. You are…" His voice trailed off. He stared at me in the low light as he seemed to be searching for something, or maybe the right word to make me happy. Obviously, everything he said and did in the bedroom was calculated for maximum effect. "Charlotte, you're mine." He leaned down closer and began to kiss me slowly and deliberately. His large hands petted my hair and softly brushed my face.

I loved being kissed by him. I never knew a man could just kiss one concentrated area of your bottom lip and make you feel as though you were the only woman in the world. He took his time, never rushing, and he smelled so good. Now I knew his secret. I smelled like the same soap. I enjoyed the experience, and the more content and confident I became, I kissed back. Lacing my hands behind his neck, I played with the curls at the nape of his neck. A few strands were still a little wet from our shower.

As Max's heated kisses moved slowly to my neck, I moved my hold to touch his back. His muscles flexed, and he looked up quickly into my eyes. "I'm happy to have you touch me wherever you want. I'm a big boy, and I can handle it."

Before I had time to tame my mouth, I blurted out, "I noticed." I shut my eyes. "I'm sorry. That was rude."

Max's laughter filled the quiet room. "Charlotte, you do make me laugh."

"I don't think that's what I should be doing right now, do you?"

"You can do anything you want. We'll take our time."

Really? My only other experience had been no more than twenty minutes of kissing, nuzzling, and then bam it was over. My soft porn movies on the streaming channels showed a more lengthy depiction of hours of love making in various positions and locations. Obviously, that was fiction, but Max wanted to take his time?

Looking into his eyes always made me lose my train of thought, but tonight his gaze spurred me into clarity. "Max, you've already given me the date and seduction experiences. Is this the finale?"

Max didn't answer and definitely didn't give me time to change my mind. He just acted. His one arm slid under my back and pulled me on top of his body. "I hope it's just the beginning. Kiss me, Charlotte."

I didn't wait one second. This time, I wasn't awkward. I found my mark, lingering on those luscious lips. Our bodies were pushed together, and I began to feel something coming on.

"Ow. Darn it." I pulled away suddenly and sat up on the bed.

"What the hell? I haven't done anything yet."

I laughed nervously as I reached for my leg. "Cramp. I have a cramp in my leg."

"Here, let me do that." Max's attention moved to my inner calf muscle. His strong hands massaged. "Better?"

"Yes, thank you. I'm so sorry."

Max grinned. "This is going to be a long night, isn't it?"

I tilted my head in an attempt to at least be cute. "Is it? We're irrevocably blurring our friendship line."

"You did that when you came here tonight." Max stretched out next to me. He ran his fingers through my hair. "What is it about you?"

"I'm unassuming? I can literally become invisible within a crowd?"

Max kissed the tip of my nose. "We have to do something about that. You should stand out, be yourself, and show others who you really are."

"But who am I, Max? I'm just the little sister, my father's daughter—"

"Stop that." Max rubbed my shoulder, his thumb massaging near the base of my neck. "You're a very kind and intelligent woman who could possibly make me lose—"

He stopped. In the silence, we just looked at each other. We kissed, whispered words of affection and longing, and touched each other not just physically. At one point, our foreheads touched.

"Charlotte, it is time to blur that line forever," Max finally whispered. I only nodded as he began to hold me closer.

"That's probably the nicest and most frightening thing you've ever said to me."

Max kissed my cheek as he whispered. "So, no more calling me *Poop Head*?"

I patted his shoulder. "I can't promise that."

"Well, Charlotte, that doesn't seem fair."

"Max, who said that anything about us is fair?"

"Or makes sense?" Max's question went unanswered as I just looked into his eyes. "But we do work, Charlotte. Just let me show you."

I had no words. It was only Max and me now. I needed this. I needed him. When he began to touch me, my back arched instinctively. God knew I would never have done it on purpose. My body was betraying me and becoming Max's experiment.

My body trusted him even though I couldn't shut my mind off from wondering what the hell I'd been thinking coming here. My brother was fighting for his life only miles away from me. It would be dangerous to go out into that storm, but remaining here was the risk of my life. Max's passionate kisses flowed over my body. He murmured how beautiful I was. What did I want from him? And then he said the words I needed to hear.

"Charlotte, don't ever doubt that I want you."

Before I could offer some witty response to ease the tension, Max and I became entangled in the most loving human act possible, at least in my mind. His eyes never left mine; his touch was perfect. His beads of sweat landed on my hair, and his strong arms trembled. I didn't hear one voice, nor any judgment. I only knew that this man was leaving a mark on me that I would remember the rest of my days.

"Charlotte, good Lord," Max murmured afterward. "Are you okay?"

"Yes?"

Max's quizzical brow raised. "You're not sure?"

"I'm not sure I'll ever be just okay again."

"Was I–"

I liked vulnerable Max. "Do I need to bring a paddle with a ten on it for the next time?"

Max's laughter made me feel more relaxed. "You're going to have to wait a little bit. I'm good, but I'm not that good."

I felt the heat warming my face. Thankfully, in this dim light he couldn't see me blush. "And there's the real Max."

Max pecked me on the cheek. "Admitting that I'm not perfect?"

I lightly patted his arm, eventually resting my hand on his bare leg. "Sure. It's comforting to know the devil does have his flaws."

"But not for long." Max grabbed the comforter at the bottom of the bed and threw it over our bodies. He pulled a large pillow beneath our heads.

Max's hand searched for mine and caught it in his. Even though we'd just been intimately connected, hand holding seemed so much more. "Are we okay?"

"I think so. Just a few minutes ago I was that ring on the finger kind of girl."

"Obviously, you've changed your mind," Max said as he looked over at me.

"I was being selfish tonight," I whispered.

Max turned on his side and threw a protective arm over me. "Don't you think it was about time for you to take care of yourself?"

"I don't know. Max, that first time I had that ring on my finger and look where that got me." I looked directly at the man next to me. Laying side by side seemed so right, and he offered the caring touches I so desperately needed tonight. "In fact, I'm thinking I need to send a note to my ex."

"Really? What are you thinking in that pretty head?"

I kissed Max. "I need to tell him I now know how lousy he was!"

Max's throaty laugh warmed me. "Please let me deliver it for you. I could even bring him a manual with handwritten notes in the margin."

In our amusement, I tumbled into Max's arms. Our arms were locked, our legs tangled together. The laughter turned into kisses and murmured whispers. We eventually made our way under the sheets.

"Charlotte, I like you in my arms and in this house. You belong right where you are tonight." Max held me close, his hand softly stroking my hair. I nuzzled closer and desperately tried to stay awake.

"I'm home," I whispered. As I closed my eyes, my last thought was at the very worst of times, this was the man I wanted by my side.

Chapter Twenty-Three

Where am I? What time is it? I opened my eyes expecting to see Mickey sitting next to my bed begging to go out to do his morning duty. When I turned my head, Max was sprawled next to me. I touched his shoulder to see if he was real, or if I was having a magnificent dream complete with a wonderful man who had made love to me last night. Max was definitely real.

I looked out the window to see that the rain continued. I might not ever make it home. Home. I felt more at home here than I had in my parents' house since I returned from college. Even my little house never felt like it was mine. It had just been a place to lay my head and to pretend I was an adult.

I pulled the sheet up and snuggled next to his body. His warmth would be nice on a cold winter night. I'd have my own personal heater. Max stirred and opened his eyes to see me.

"Good morning, Charlotte."

"Good morning, Max."

"And how are we this morning?"

I kissed his chest as I moved his arm to lay on him. "We are fine, I think?"

"Yes, we are." Max outlined the side of my check slowly with one of his long fingers. "You know, you're my first."

I pulled back in confusion. "I am not. You're lying."

"I'm not. You are my first. You're the first woman I've ever woke up next to."

"I wonder what that should tell me about you."

Max rubbed his chin. "I'm not sure, but I don't want to be anywhere else but right here beside you."

I gave him a quick kiss as I wound a bit of his hair with my finger. "That was a lovely thing to say. It's still raining. I wonder what's going on at the hospital."

"I'll check." Max stretched to reach his phone on the side table. "I never sleep past six either, and it's a little past seven. There's a text from Jane. Sean is the same. She wonders if anyone has spoken to you since you went home last night. Everyone says to let you sleep. Oh, wow. Your nephew is at the house, and you're not there."

"Damn."

Max smiled. "I've got this. I'll text that you made it over here because of the flooding."

I grabbed his phone. "Don't you dare. I need my phone."

Max's brow rose over his left eye. "Are you embarrassed, Charlotte?"

"No, but I really don't want to deal with explaining this yet. Do you have a death wish when Paddy discovers I've been doing more than just looking at your home renovations?"

"That's a unique way of putting it." Max grinned as I shoved his shoulder, but I could tell he was going through the situation in his head. I just couldn't figure out what the star litigator was thinking. He looked dangerous when he did that sort of thing.

"You have a point. I'll get your phone. I have it charging in the bathroom." Max threw back the covers and jumped from the bed. I was offered a very nice sight of his naked backside. The man did indeed have muscles on muscles. When he returned, I received the unabashed frontal view of his naked body. Muscle memory took on an entirely different meaning. His body was muscled, taut, and sensual. Max didn't walk toward the bed, he prowled. The man knew what to do to a woman's body, and not that size mattered, but it didn't hurt either. Max cherished every inch of me last night. Was this the real Max?

As he got back into bed, he handed me my phone. "What are you going to text?"

"I'm going to say I made it over here early this morning because you were going to make breakfast and tell me how the streets were." I began to text.

"If it's that bad, why would I have you drive over here? I'd come and get you."

I finished my lie and prepared to hit send. "Why do you do that? That's the lawyer in you. You just give them an answer. They'll accept it. Our family is in crisis. We aren't thinking straight."

Max leaned on his arm and stared at me. "Is that what this was all about? Not thinking straight?"

"No, not at all. I wanted this." And I wouldn't tell him that my mother and Rose were working against him. I knew in my heart it wasn't only about sex. I wanted his arms around me, telling me everything would be okay. I wanted to believe every soothing word.

"Just tell them you never made it home last night because of the flooding and headed over here instead," Max suggested casually.

I erased my initial text and began one to Jane, using Max's simple explanation. "You're very good at lying. Should I be worried?"

"I only present a different view of the story." Max stretched his arm over my shoulders.

"You know, I've been thinking–"

"Of course, you have. Now what?"

"That it's sad that I'm the first to see you like this in the morning. It's good for me, but bad for them. You're very cute in the morning and surprisingly peaceful." I touched his hair where an errant curl cascaded onto his forehead.

He tapped my nose lightly. "You're very cute too. I knew that, but this morning you're glowing. It must've been the shower last night or maybe there's still some of that gold glitter I dumped on you months ago."

I ignored his comment. "They always say women glow when–"

"What?"

"Oh, crap. We didn't use any protection."

"You're on the pill, right?"

"No, Catholic!" I began to panic, but Max seemed unusually calm. "Besides, I wouldn't be glowing that quickly. Maybe I'm radioactive from something at the hospital?"

Max began to laugh hard. "Really? Radioactive? Charlotte, you are very entertaining."

"I bet you say that to all the girls."

Max sat up again. "Wait, this Catholic thing, what about your ex? You and he did–"

"Just a couple of times. He was working out of town. I needed that ring before we did anything, remember? When we became engaged, we went to a hotel that night. That was my first time."

"With him?"

I closed my eyes. "No, my first time."

"I see." His short remark seemed to hold some kind of judgment I tried to ignore.

"He left town after the bar event, and he's married to the girl he was seeing while we were planning our wedding."

"Did you lose all of your deposits?"

"Gee, Max. How mercenary! No, we didn't. I found out about the cheating the same day I looked at wedding dresses. It's a long story. I need to call Dad." Max watched me, and he knew I was avoiding all the messy details for more than one reason. He could make a man cry during cross examination. He knew when someone was holding back.

"Dad, how are you? How is Sean?"

"Charlotte, we were all worried about you. Where are you?"

"Dad, I couldn't make it through the flooded streets to the house last night. I could make it to Max's."

My father's sigh was one of relief. Bless him. "Oh good. You shouldn't be alone. Don't come here. We've been watching the news and so many streets are impassable that the city has issued an emergency. Sean is the same. There's nothing anyone can do now but pray. We're going to get some breakfast. Will you be okay with Max?"

Max heard my father's question. He rubbed my arm and placed a kiss on the top of my shoulder. "Yes, Dad, I'll be fine with Max. He's been very sweet."

"Oh good. Paddy's youngest is staying with Mickey so don't worry about him. If you have to stay at Taylor House, it's fine. Just be safe. I already have one son in a bad situation. I don't need my daughter injured in a car accident or hurt in the flood. I love you, sweet girl. I better go. Nate is getting a little hangry."

"Sure, Dad. I love you too." I chuckled as I ended the call. "It's funny to hear my father use the word hangry."

"Sweet girl. Your father has no idea." Max loomed over me and kissed me softly. "You are very, very sweet."

"Max, maybe I'm sacrificing myself to you to break the curse." I was completely serious, but the man was having none of it.

"Stop it, Charlotte. There's no curse. Sacrificial lambs are only in the bible, and I'm not the devil. But I can think of so many very sinful things we can do on a rainy day."

There wasn't time for me to respond as the sheets were thrown off quickly. Max pulled me up with him. "Charlotte, I want you as much as you want me." He studied my mouth, his own lips so close we were almost touching. "I know what it took for you to come to me last night, but I'm so very happy you did. You're where you should be."

"Max, why you?" I grabbed his face with my hands.

"I don't know, but I'm sure happy it is me. No more words, counselor."

Afterward, I stared up at the immaculate tray ceiling. I could feel Max's eyes on me. He was playing with a few strands of my hair. "Why did you pick that light fixture?"

"I liked it."

"Oh."

Max kissed my shoulder. "You don't like it?"

"I might have gone with a more traditional chandelier, but it is your bedroom."

"Anything else you want to change?"

I glanced over at his smiling face. "No. Everything is pretty perfect."

We just looked at each other for several minutes before Max broke the silence. "I'm hungry, what about you?"

"I can always eat. You know that."

He kissed me quickly and jumped from the bed. "I'm going to cook for you. I have never done that for–"

"A woman who has spent the night?"

Max tugged on his jeans and threw on a shirt. "I've never cooked for a woman. They never seemed interested in a night at home, so I always took them to restaurants."

"What?"

"We went to their place or out. If I stayed over, I woke early and left. I had work to do."

"But not today." I stretched out in the large bed. When I ended up on his pillow, his scent lingered. "I told you there's nothing better than sleeping in when it's raining."

Max completely ignored my comment. "I'll do a little work later, after we've eaten."

"I have my laptop in my bag. I could too, I guess."

Max nodded and came back over to the bed, crawling over to me. "Do you want pancakes or an omelet?" He kissed me quickly.

"You can make pancakes?"

"Blueberry or plain?"

"Blueberry, please."

As soon as he left me alone, I jumped out of bed and headed to that devine bathtub. I longed for that bathtub experience, but that would be rude without permission. Instead, I stepped into the shower and enjoyed the solitude. I began to think I was an idiot. But I had been the one who made the decision, and my regrets had nothing to do with making love with Max Shaw.

I dressed and began to head downstairs. The smell of vanilla wafted up from the kitchen. I looked down the hallway. I thought I heard a man's voice. No one else was in the house with us. We were alone, but I felt a sensation that unnerved me. I felt cold inside. I shook it off and almost ran down the one flight of stairs.

"Charlotte."

I froze. Rose was saying my name. What if she wasn't pleased with what happened in the house last night? Would there be retribution?

"Charlotte, yours."

I smelled coffee as I began to walk into the kitchen. I saw Max smile. He was serving pancakes onto two plates at the island.

"Charlotte, your home." Rose, I need to pay attention to Max, I thought.

"Charlotte, target."

My eyes flared. "Max, what have you discovered about Sean's shooting?"

Max poured coffee into two mugs and handed me one. "Sit and eat. I've already checked in with the police chief. Your brother was targeted, in fact they have witnesses who heard a man yell Sean O'Donohue."

I jumped onto one of the chairs. "Oh, dear Lord."

"Yes, so whoever Sean saw, he does know, and he knows that the same man killed Conor. I'm not sure why he wanted me to know instead of Paddy. Paddy was on-site first, and your brother wouldn't tell him."

Max sat next to me and began to eat. I poured syrup onto my pancakes. "I love sausage and pancakes. You didn't tell me about the sausage."

"I like to surprise you." He seemed to be studying me.

"What?"

"You aren't glowing anymore. We must do something about that."

"I took a shower. I wanted to take a bath in that magnificent tub, but I didn't want to be a bad guest."

"You could've. Maybe later we should give it its inaugural spin? I'll light the candles, pour the wine, and add the bubbles."

I blushed. Even after last night's activities, his suggestion piqued my interest and heightened my embarrassment factor. "You are outrageous."

"No, I'm very much a happy man. This is a good day. I'm sorry for Sean, but I'm happy you are here, friend."

I shoved him hard unexpectedly. Max nearly fell off of the chair. "Who knew you could be so humorous? You may not be my biological brother, but you certainly act like all of them."

Max's voice lowered. "Except for last night and this morning."

How would I apply makeup if my face was constantly red while I was with this man? "Well, except for that."

"I'm going to my office, but we can set you up in the bedroom, kitchen, dining room–"

"Has the desk come yet for the sitting room?"

Max's eyes softened. "It has. I bet Rose would like that. I'll give you the password and set you up. Bobby Mack approved of all of the electrical outlets, and there's one right there by the desk. Oh, and I texted Phoebe too. I hope you don't mind. I told her you were working from home."

"Didn't she think it was strange that you were texting her?"

"No, I don't think so. She knows we're friends."

"Ah yes, that word again. After last night, I'm beginning to think of friendship in a totally different way." I began to eat slowly as Max acted as though he'd been starving in the wilderness before he was found by the rangers. "Are you that hungry?"

Max's thin smile truly evoked the devil. "I worked up an appetite doing something in my bedroom." He winked in an exaggerated manner.

I rolled my eyes and enjoyed my pancakes and sausage. He finished before me and began to clean up, filling my cup with more coffee. I finished my food and placed my plate and cutlery in the dishwasher. I sipped my coffee and watched Max think. He leaned on the kitchen counter staring out into Rose's room.

"I think I'll check the security cameras from some of the bars on the street where Sean was patrolling. Maybe I can catch the guy who asked where he was. I'll get on that this morning."

"The police will do that," I answered. "Heck, Paddy has probably already requested the footage. You should check with him. Max?"

He looked as though he was miles away in his thoughts. "What?"

"I'm more worried about why Sean was targeted, and perhaps by the same person who killed Conor. Last night, reporters were at the house and one of them suggested in a not very nice way that our family was cursed. I lost it. I didn't respond; I just fled."

"I would say that's silly, but considering you have conversations with my dead grandmother, curses aren't out of the realm of your reality. As the devil, I do understand curses, possessions, and other forms of demonic behavior. I deal with it almost on a daily basis as a prosecutor. By the way, the holy water didn't work."

My eyes filled. "Not funny. What did we do to have Conor killed and Sean hurt? And Mom died so quickly. Whatever we did, we need to make amends."

Max placed his cup on the island and brought me into his arms. His hands lingered around my waist. "It will be okay. I'm sorry I joked. I do see the very worst in people. That reporter was out of line. Charlotte, you and your father, heck, your entire family are some of the very best people I have known. Even though I had my career and family reasons for returning here, I was happy to see all of you again. I missed the family."

I didn't respond. As I listened, I settled into him. We stood in the kitchen quiet for a few minutes, just me in Max's arms. In moments like this, I was confident in my decision last night, but soon the doubts would come. I assured myself that I would survive when Max said this wouldn't work. We would see each other occasionally, as had been the original plan, and we would smile and be cordial.

"Well, I'll be the adult," Max whispered. "I need to get to work. How about we meet back here around one for lunch? Gio has more of that soup in the refrigerator."

"I do love that soup." I reached up and offered him a kiss. He was more than willing to be the recipient of my attention.

"To work with you woman. Let's get you set up." He patted my backside as I began to walk away.

"Watch it, or I'll tell Paddy what we really did last night."

"And this morning. Don't forget this morning," Max joked.

In just a few minutes I was set up at the new small writing desk, and Max had headed to his upstairs office. I began to check my emails, sending a quick one to Phoebe with instructions on rescheduling a few of my client meetings. I was working on adoption documents when Jane called.

"Charlotte, are you safe?"

"Yes, you saw my text, right? I've already talked to Dad this morning too."

"So, you went over to Max's last night?"

"I tried making it back to the house, but so many streets were flooded. I saw an easier path to Max's. I had to drive around the block to drive south on the street in front of the house." I wasn't lying, just fibbing.

"Why Max? You could've made it to our house. We're closer."

I leaned back in the chair. Jane, why do you have to know everything? "Well, I was very upset, and I wasn't thinking. We stayed up most of last night." Yes, we did. "I'm working downstairs, and he's working upstairs. Is everything okay?"

"Yes. I hate this, not being able to get down there. Paddy will be visiting. He has a shift today. So many streets are closed. Did you see that The Plaza is flooding again? Oh my gosh, the interstates are closed with so much water ponding. They don't think it'll stop until Wednesday."

It seemed as though Jane believed me and moved on to the state of our world. Until…

"Charlotte, are you spending the night there again?"

"Janie, I don't know. It depends on the streets. It sounds like we all have to stay put. I hate that for Dad and Sean."

"There's nothing we can do but pray. I'm getting a call from Tom. I'll call you back."

Before I could even say goodbye, Jane was gone. I returned to my work. What kind of a sister was I? All we could do was pray, and I was making love with Max Shaw while my brother struggled to live. I stared at the screen.

"Charlotte."

"Oh, Rose, what am I going to do? I've made a mess of this."

"Love."

"I do, but all that was last night was selfish behavior."

"Max is yours."

"Okay, I'll trust you. Mom told me to come here, didn't she?"

"Your home, Charlotte."

"So, you're okay with this?" My human question was tedious and infantile.

"Charlotte."

God was watching even if Rose wasn't. I was going to hell.

I shook off my thoughts and made a few inquiries to clients to confirm information. With the entire city shut down, they welcomed the call and appreciated that I wasn't sitting around watching the emergencies going on all over. My family had its own emergency, and there wasn't a damn thing I could do about it.

My back was stiff. This chair was lovely, but a French Provincial style didn't lend itself to sitting at a desk for hours. I walked to the window and stared out. The wind had picked up, and the rain was moving from side to side. I heard a siren blaring outside.

"Are you ready for lunch? It seems chilly in this room." Max entered the sitting room without me even noticing.

"It doesn't feel cool to me." I lied. Rose was here. I was surprised that he could feel it. "What time is it?"

"Almost one. I finally watched the news coverage. Now, there's a tornado in the area. The storm is a remnant of that large hurricane from Texas. They've already canceled court for tomorrow, and my offices will be closed. Let's have that soup."

Max walked on. I trailed behind. Reality was beginning to set in. "Max, we can't just play house."

Max pulled out a large pot from the refrigerator. He looked around and smiled. "Who says we're playing?"

"Really? You're okay with me here?"

"Of course. What's the matter? Are you having buyer's regret?" He continued to set the pot on the stove to warm it.

"It's not that. You've been wonderful to me. I needed you. A little guilt is setting in."

Max stood at the island, both hands splayed on the countertop. "Will this pass by the time I get that romantic bathtub scene set?"

I sighed, and I saw him grimace. He wasn't happy with me. "I'm not sure. I feel guilty about enjoying my life while Sean is in such dire straits. I feel guilty for not being at my father's side every minute through this crisis. I feel guilty because I came here for exactly what happened. And then there's the whole sin thing."

"Well, we have a problem then." He lifted away from the island and came around to where I was standing. He tenderly grabbed my shoulders and made me face him. "Charlotte, I can't do this anymore."

I pulled out of his embrace, and he allowed me to leave his arms. I expected this. I could probably make it to the house. The streets couldn't be that bad if Paddy made it into work. "Okay. I completely understand. Bipolar love is confusing…I want to, I don't want to–"

But my hand was taken in his, and I was quickly back in Max's arms, flush against his body. "You always rush into a determination. Listen to me. I can't keep doing **this**. I care about you very much. I'm not sure where this is going. Give me a few days to enjoy a relationship, will you? What I can't do anymore is not care about you. I can't let you go. I need to see where we are headed. I want to be with you in every way. I'm being as honest as I possibly can, Charlotte. Love scares me. I've seen my parents miserable. I've seen how much someone can lose, like poor Rose and Gio. He is still unequivocally in love with her. My mind doesn't comprehend that sort of commitment."

"Yet, you seem to be unphased by my ability to speak to Rose, my mother, my brother, others–"

"There's others? Oh Lord. Wait, my grandmother didn't watch us–"

I giggled. "I'm not sure how that works, but she doesn't seem upset."

"She's talked to you today?"

I avoided his eyes. "Yes."

He tipped my chin up. "Is there anything I need to know or prepare for?"

"No."

I was saved by the boiling pot. Max stirred the soup. "What did she say?"

"Nothing, really." How long could I avoid telling him the truth? I just could.

"Charlotte, you are such a bad liar. You'll have to fix that if you ever decide to become a public defender. Spill."

I stamped my foot, and Max was seemingly amused by my little childlike move. "Fine. She said stuff about love and this house. That's it. Not much."

Max couldn't hear her, but Rose was yelling my name. "Charlotte, I need to check this house for drafts. Did you feel that cold breeze?"

"Yes, it's your grandmother."

"Really? Hi Grandma. I wish you would tell Charlotte to tell me the truth." Max pretended to take me and my antics in stride.

I heard laughter. Rose was laughing. It was a delightful, light sound. I came around the island and took the spoon from

Max to take a taste. "Needs a little more heat, but you, Max Shaw don't need any at all. You are plenty hot." The spoon ended up somewhere on the top of the stove as I wrapped my arms around Max's neck and pulled him down for a kiss. "Max, you don't have to say anything, but if this is love, I was really wrong with the first guy." I kissed him again before he had a chance to reply with something that would hurt my heart.

But against my lips, he whispered, "You'll have to teach me how to love. Be patient." Max pulled away quickly in confusion. "Did you feel that? Can you smell that?"

"You said there's a draft, and I smell the soup."

"No, I smell roses. It's the day after Labor Day during a storm, and I smell roses inside this house, and it felt like someone just hugged me, and it wasn't you."

Oh, Max, you poor guy. You don't really have a chance of making it out of this without being happy. Your grandmother will haunt you until you are.

After a few more hours of work and a delicious dinner of leftovers that evening, we headed into Max's newly finished living area. We watched the news coverage of the storm. The rain continued as did the emergencies around town. There was a brief mention of Sean's shooting, and a statement from the police chief. Max held my hand as we watched.

"Charlotte, we will find out who did this." Max was so certain.

"I don't know. We've all had our suspicions about who murdered Conor, and nothing has come to fruition. Not one piece of evidence has helped to discover his killer. Tom, Sean, and I have exhausted the questioning of friends, and those who were there that night. Paddy has even looked into the case, and unless he's holding out on us, he's found absolutely nothing."

"You haven't had me on the investigation." Max flashed a wide smile as he pointed to himself.

I shoved my body closer to him. His arm was soon around me. "You really are too confident. I'm surprised no one has taken you down a peg or two."

Max switched off the television and looked down at me. "I have this nagging suspicion that you might be the one to do it."

"I thought I entertained you."

"You do, but you also challenge me. It can be annoying, and it can be endearing." Max stood up and headed into the kitchen. I followed.

"Wait, you can't say I'm annoying and endearing and leave. That's not allowed." I found him unloading the dishwasher. When I saw his wide smile, I knew what he was up to. "You don't have to keep pushing my buttons."

Max finished his task and stood in front of me. "But it's so much fun." He wrapped his arms around me, holding me in his embrace. "I'm going to prepare my bath seduction scene. Give me ten minutes and come on up."

I looked out the window. "Where am I going to go in this storm?"

"It does seem you have nowhere to go but up." He pointed with his finger to the second story. He kissed me quickly and walked away. "Ten minutes."

As soon as I was alone in the kitchen, I felt the cool breeze encircle me. "Rose?"

"Danger."

Yes, Max was dangerous, but I was sure she wasn't speaking about her grandson. "When or who?"

"Find the killer."

I impetuously stamped my foot. "That's what we're trying to do. I'm sorry, but you're not helping."

"Protecting."

I shook my head in frustration. "I know. You've given me warnings, and they are much appreciated, but I don't understand what is going on.

"Danger is so close."

"Really?" In this weather no one was close to Max and me. I just wasn't understanding. "Rose, if you could just drop a name that would fix everything." There wasn't an answer, but I heard music upstairs. Max was preparing his seduction. I took a deep breath and wondered if I'd survive what I had begun. Just last night I had come into this house asking for him to be so much more. I picked up my phone and saw Max's text telling me it had been ten minutes, and the water was getting cold.

Smiling, and a little afraid of what I might find upstairs, I began my trip to his bedroom. When I stood on the second-floor landing, I felt a stream of air float by me. I walked toward the bedroom but stopped when I heard a noise upstairs on the third level.

Distracted by another text from Max, I shook off both incidents. When I arrived in the room, the bed's bedspread and top sheet were folded back. There was one lamp on in the room, and barely any light in the bathroom. As I crept in slowly, the darkness was lit with candles on the shelves above the bathroom and a few around the edge of that magnificent tub.

Max was already soaking, toasting me with his full glass of wine. "You have a lovely white in your bottle, and I have a red. The only thing missing is you. How'd I do?"

He'd done very well. It was almost too much, but when a dream comes true, shouldn't you live in it, relishing every second? I came closer to the tub and saw the bubbles. "You know you did very well. You really do know how to treat a girl."

"Again, I've never done this for anyone else. I'll even close my eyes so you can get in the tub with your modesty intact."

"I believe my modesty left the building in the shower last night. It walked out with my virtue, my upbringing–"

"I get it. Just get in and stop talking." He took a sip from his wine and placed the glass on the side of the tub. "I'm closing my eyes now. Don't let me go to sleep."

I began to undress quickly. "Max, you need a hot tub in the backyard. Maybe to the left of the patio."

"Nope. The hot tub will go by the pool on the right."

I giggled. "A pool now? My, you really are settling in." I was down to my underwear. Now, I was the one who was surveilling him. His eyes were closed, his head leaning back on the edge of the beautiful tub. I unhooked my bra and removed my panties. My hasty drop into the water created a wave of bubbles that hit Max in the mouth.

As he rubbed the water off of his face, his eyes flashed. "What the hell did you do, surf in?"

"I got in. I guess I didn't realize the tub was this deep. This really is wonderful."

I closed my eyes and began to relax despite Max's legs moving on the sides of mine. "Are you enjoying Max's seduction soak?"

I smiled but still didn't look at him. "Uh huh."

"Good. You do seem to love this tub."

Hearing the word love drip from Max's mouth sent a tremor throughout my body. I finally opened my eyes and found my glass of wine. I didn't glance in his direction even when I took a drink and returned it to its place. I closed my eyes again as if that would protect me from really being naked, in a tub with a man. The water became disturbed; I felt him closer.

When I opened my eyes, I was staring into those caramel orbs. "Hello."

"Hello Max."

"I was lonely all the way over there."

I laced my arms around his neck. "You poor baby. Were you afraid?"

"A little."

"I thought you liked being alone."

"I'm afraid of you. Please don't tell anyone. It could be our secret."

I studied his face. He seemed sincere, but I heard my brothers' voices telling me he was a player. And he was so delicious. "We seem to be adding to our list of secrets. Why on earth would you be afraid of little old me?"

"I'd rather not say. It messes with this entire romance thing I've got going." His crooked smile made me laugh out loud.

"And now what, Max?"

"Dessert." In an instant, my body was pressed against his, and Max Shaw kissed me as though he was really devouring me. His hands wrapped around my back, nestling me into position. When his mouth left mine, Max seemed to gasp. "You are sweet. We shouldn't be…I shouldn't be corrupting you."

"What are you doing? I showed up on your doorstep, remember? One of us had to pull the other over the line."

His brow arched. "Tug of war?"

"Yes. When you're ready, I'm not. When I'm ready, I get scared and run, but not this time. I'm a big girl, and I've made my own decision. Maybe I want dessert too!"

"Well then…"

Later on that night, Max and I talked before we slept.

"You're here just because of my tub, aren't you?" Max murmured.

I touched his leg. "No, I'm here for your money. Is that what you wanted to hear?"

Max shifted onto his side, flush up against my body. "Your honesty is gratifying. The trouble is, unlike other women who never said that my money was the reason, I know you're lying."

"And how do you know that Mr. Shaw?"

Max traced up and down my arm with his finger. "Because you don't like spending money, and you could care less if I have millions."

I laughed, and the sound filled the room. "Your trust, your foundation does. You have family money."

"I have my own too. I've been very lucky in investments."

It was beginning to be harder to keep my eyes open. "Sure, Max." I patted his arm. There was a stillness in the house for the first time since I arrived. The rain had finally stopped, and a few streets were beginning to open. Our reality would change.

"Max, playing house is about to end for the two of us."

Max nuzzled his mouth against my neck. "Again, who says we're playing?"

I giggled nervously. "An hour ago, we were certainly playing at something. This can't continue."

Max shifted his arm over me. "Why not?"

"I'm not sure the guilt will pass."

Max lowered his mouth to the top of my right breast. "Has it passed before?"

"No. I usually feel guilty until the next time. Do you remember when they used to joke about Catholics, especially us Irish, drinking on Saturday, and confessing on Sunday? That's me."

"Then we tell everyone." I tapped him on the head.

"Ow. What was that for?"

"Just pay attention. Oh, and no more of those burning, knowing glances or those light touches with those long fingers of yours. While I'm making rules, that tongue of yours… Well, all of this makes my temperature rise, and I can't hide it."

Max modeled his mouth in the most devilish, seductive smile he could manage as he hovered over me.

"I said stop it. We both need time before we tell everyone, especially my family."

Max collapsed on his back next to me. "Your family. Is it an Irish, Catholic, large family thing that you all know each other's business, or is it just the O'Donohues?"

"It's all of that. We may not all treat each other like we love and care about each other, but we do, and we are very good at togetherness when we have a tragedy."

Max extended his arm above my head. "My family seems to praise alone time. They raised me to be on my own."

I heard anguish and lament in his voice. Snuggling up to him, I placed my head on his chest. "This lone wolf act of yours is very depressing. I'm sorry, but honestly you haven't been alone since you returned here."

"If I'm honest, that was part of the reason I did come back. I knew you all would be here, but I didn't realize how overwhelming your caring would be, and how that hovering extinguishes solitary thoughts."

"And that's why I frighten you?"

"I really don't want to talk about it."

I pulled away and sat up in bed. "That doesn't work for me."

"Charlotte, you need to understand—"

I shook my head. "I wasn't raised that way, and you know it. When I came here in the storm, that was the most impetuous thing I've ever done. When I make a decision, that's it." I thought for a second and added, "Even if it is a mistake."

Max sat next to me. He grabbed my hand and brought it up for a kiss. "Charlotte, let's just take our time. I've had a weird year. I have a grandfather I never knew about, and a father who isn't my biological father, and another man who chooses power over a child, well an adult child. I have a mother who never shared any intimate details. I've been shot at, someone has attempted to burn us alive and take this house down, and there's enough secrets in this house to keep a magician working for years. And then there's you with your honesty, your skill of listening to dead people, and now your caring. I'm a little overwhelmed, so I'm asking you to have patience. Also, be honest, and if I'm not meeting up to your expectations, you will have to tell me."

I had no words. I kissed him on the cheek. "Fine, for now. But you need to know I won't continue to spend the night with you and creep into my father's home before he wakes up in the morning. I won't be dishonest, no matter what."

"I understand, Charlotte. We'll have to take this day by day while Sean is in trouble. And we'll have to keep our secrets."

I patted his cheek. "I suppose. What don't I know about you, Max?"

When there was no quick answer, I looked up into Max's face. He was expressionless. "There is something? What? Does it involve me or maybe my family? If you know who is doing this to us, please tell me."

Max's arm strengthened around me. "I don't know, but we will find out. No, I have been keeping something under the radar since I arrived."

"Do I need to know, or is it about your job?"

"You should know, but it is about my job. If we ever do announce to the family that we are seeing each other–"

I giggled. "All of each other."

Max touched my nose. "Yes, that. Charlotte, I reached out to someone I could trust before I came here to Kansas City. You can't share this information with anyone. You can't mention it to any of your family, not one of them."

"Fine. I understand this is very hush hush. Are you sure you want to tell me?"

"I need to. The reason why your brother Paddy was called on the day you found Mr. Martin's dead body was because he's my inside man."

I pulled up and leaned over Max. "Paddy? Seriously? You trusted him over, well, over anyone else?"

"Yes. I don't want you thinking that what we have has anything to do with the work Paddy is doing for me."

I patted Max's chest. "Or you're scared to death that Paddy will think you are using me! That's what this honesty session is about, isn't it?"

"He scares me."

I laughed out loud and landed back on my pillow. "He scares everyone. We will deal with Paddy together, only if we absolutely have to, and only then will we tell him. We should probably wear helmets."

"If he finds out, he is going to be pissed."

"He'll feel betrayed. He will get over it. Besides, you're used to threats, aren't you?"

Max began to answer me, but my phone rang. "It's got to be about Sean." There had been no change, but they were beginning to wonder if Sean would ever wake up.

Chapter Twenty-Four

After another day of home-based work, kitchen activities that had nothing to do with cooking, and another evening bath that resulted in me leaning against Max sharing stories of our childhoods, it was time to venture out into the real world. It was before dawn on Thursday morning when I drove back to the hospital. I followed Max's car as I drove my father's. Max was continuing onto work, and I desperately needed to see my dad. Sean began to wake in the middle of the night. His pain was unbearable. Earlier this morning, he had yelled out for Max.

It was the first real time we were coming in as a couple, holding hands and walking briskly into the private waiting room. Gio sat beside my father and noticed our hands. His wide smile warmed my heart. For all I knew, Rose and he plotted the entire conspiracy. How Rose could plan this storm would be another mystery.

"He's awake," Dad announced as he held me. "Max, he wants you. He's desperate to see you."

"Okay, Judge." Max nodded to Gio and kissed me quickly on the cheek. "I'll find out what's going on." He scrambled to the nurse's station.

"Go with him," Dad directed.

I ran to catch up with him. We were led into Sean's small curtained area. His eyes remained dark, and he was still hooked up like a superhero undergoing a full transmission upgrade. Max nodded for me to go nearer. He stood behind me at the bedside.

"Sean, it's Charlie. Max is here."

Sean's eyes flew open and looked directly at us. "Max."

His voice was so low it was barely audible. We bent down to hear him.

"Max."

"Sean, I'm here. What is it?"

"I need, I need to tell you…"

I took Sean's hand in mine. "Sean, just tell us."

"Max, I know Conor's killer. I know. Shot."

"Sean, just say the name, and I'll take it from there."

Sean's eyes closed briefly and shot open once more. "Max, I know."

Now I was confused. I glanced at Max. "Why won't he say?"

"Maybe it's too hard or too painful, Charlotte."

"We love you, Sean," I said, touching his hair lightly.

One tear escaped from his eye. I grabbed a tissue and dabbed at it.

"Max, I forget."

I thought I could hear Max's heart fall onto the floor to join where mine had already crash-landed. He remained calm.

"Sean, it's okay, brother. You will remember. You need to rest and get better. Take your time. We have time."

"No, Max. Danger. Max, danger close."

I stepped back in shock and nearly took out one of Sean's pieces of equipment. Max's eyes followed me. "Charlotte, what is it?"

"Rose said the same thing over and over. I thought it was all about the senator, but now–"

Max continued to coldly assess me as though I was one of his preys on the witness stand. "Tell me, what did Rose say?"

As I answered, Sean repeated the same words. "Danger, Max. She said it was close."

"It's about me, not your family," Max stated calmly. "Good. Now, I can go to war."

The man saw this as a good thing, but I kept thinking about the curse. Perhaps the curse was on me? Was that the tradeoff for talking to the dead? Everyone I loved could be in danger, and now Max was the target?

Chapter Twenty-Five

On my way home from work that afternoon, I stopped by church. I sat in my favorite back pew and looked up at the cross hanging over the altar.

Sacrifice took so much courage, or stupidity depending on your frame of reference. Dear Sean sacrificed his body to protect innocent bystanders. Mom worked so hard bringing up her family, and her reward was a shortened life. And Conor, God only knew what he had gotten himself into. Ultimately, his lifestyle determined how his life ended.

Closing my eyes, I began to pray out loud. "Lord, I didn't ask for this. If my behavior is creating this curse, this punishment, I will make amends. I'll do everything I can to not hear the voices. Maybe there's medication I can take?" Even my whispered supplication could be heard in the empty church.

"Charlotte, it's not you. You help people."

When I opened my eyes, Conor casually sat in front of me. His arm was lightly draped over the back of the pew. I wanted to touch him, but I knew from past experience there was nothing to touch. "Oh, I've missed you."

"I've missed you too, but you know we're always here."

"Seany needs you. He's in bad shape."

Conor nodded. His smile faded. Moving his arm away, he turned his metaphysical body to look toward the front of the church. *"He is in our arms."*

I sobbed out loud. "Help him. I don't think Dad's heart can take another loss like this. Max is doing his best to figure this out–"

"Max. He has secrets."

"Conor, what is it? I've asked you before who killed you. You never can answer. Why did Sean only want to talk to Max?"

My brother stood up and began to fade. He smiled as he looked back at me.

"Careful, Charlotte. Max has secrets. He will know about me. The danger is close."

My brother disappeared before my eyes. I came here for solace and for answers to my prayers. Instead, I had more questions and uncertainty. Sean only wanted to speak to Max, and now I knew Max had his secrets. What did they say…it was better to know the devil you knew versus the devil you didn't? The real question was, did I know the devil at all?

Chapter Twenty-Six

The next morning there was a chill in the air. Dad stayed another night at the hospital despite his promises. I took care of Mickey in the morning, toasted a muffin with a dab of peanut butter, and even made myself a large cup of coffee. I felt very much the adult. Last night, I was a child. Max texted me three times and left four messages. Finally, after looking at my phone each time, I texted that I was very tired. I would speak with him the next day. It was now the next day, and I had no intention of calling Max Shaw. I had to get my head around Conor's statement.

I seriously didn't know what to think. "Damn ghosts. They never tell me everything," I said out loud as I grabbed my things and headed to work. The sun shone so beautifully through the orange and red leaves changing each and every day. But before I even reached the end of the driveway, clouds were forming. We were expecting light rain today. Since the storm, the fall days had been magnificent as everything dried out. It made me think of the rose garden in the park. As if the car had a mind of its own, it made the turn and began a route away from my office.

When I parked, I noticed a few joggers and groups of walking mothers. A couple of them pushed babies while taking the trail. I slowly walked to my bench. A few of the garden's caretakers were already busy trimming the bushes. By November, the beauty of the garden would disappear until next year. The fragrance from the season's last roses was intoxicating, and the colors transformed my spirit. My heart lightened. Even though Dad was exhausted, Sean was still in dire straits, and I was confused as hell about every part of my life, this place offered peace in the storm.

I sat on my favorite bench. This place gave me the closeness to Conor that I desperately needed. When I visited the graves at the cemetery, I never had that connection as I did in any loved one's favorite place. For Rose, her sitting room was where her spirit was the most comfortable; for Mom it was our home.

I sat in peace for a few minutes. Once the volunteers were working on the other side of the fountain, I reflected on what I needed to know. "Conor, please tell me about Max," I said out loud.

I waited for a response with my hands clutched in prayer.

"Just ask me."

I whipped my head around to see the man I had been avoiding. "Max."

"Is this where you always go to hide?"

I bit my bottom lip. "I come here to listen."

"May I sit down or is this a private party with your voices?" Max pointed at the empty area next to me. He was attired in one of his dark blue suits with a gray and blue striped tie. He looked tired, but ready to begin his day at the office.

I nodded and continued to stare straight ahead. I heard him sigh. He bent over and grasped his hands.

"I guess I should've asked if I could approach the bench given the fact we're both attorneys."

I managed a slight smile. "Cute."

"You've been avoiding me," Max stated without any emotion in his voice.

"No, I've been busy."

"You've been thinking, overthinking. You and I have that in common. You're moving away from me. I've done the same thing to you."

I offered a side glance. "I'm not. I–"

"What do you need to know about me? What do you want, Charlotte?"

I shifted my body toward him in a confrontational manner, but his soft, tired eyes quieted my response. "Just like you, I need time, Max."

"For what? Are you and the group going to begin investigating again? I want you to think about this very seriously. This could be dangerous; it is dangerous."

"Don't tell me what I can or can't do. You aren't allowed that liberty just because we slept together."

Max smiled. "Ah, it is buyer's remorse. I wondered when that guilt of yours would rule your head."

"It's my heart I'm more worried about. By the way, how did you know I'd be here?"

Max moved, his arm setting comfortably on the back of my bench. "I know you, and I followed you here. I was coming to see you this morning at the house, and you pulled out of the driveway as I was driving down the street."

I nodded. I searched his eyes. I was beyond annoyed at myself. Why didn't I know him? I thought I did sometimes, but now… "Max, you have more secrets. You tell me the ones that you don't care about," I blurted out.

"Doesn't everyone? Some of the secrets have not been my doing, remember?"

My hand instinctively reached over and held his. "You've had a rough year just like all of us."

Max stared down at our joined hands. "I can handle it." Max nudged a little closer. He held my hand a little tighter. "Charlotte, what do you need to know about me?"

"You've been very understanding about my special talent. I appreciate that."

Max shook his head. "I don't understand, but I trust what you tell me."

I bit my lip, and Max's eyes followed my action. His gaze on my lips created that same old warmth in my body. His attention also made me stop my behavior. "I need the truth from you. Please."

"Anything, Charlotte. If I can, I'll tell you whatever you need to know."

"If you can," I murmured. That's all I could hope for with this one. "Max, Conor says you have secrets. He also says you know about him. What do you know about Conor? Does it have to do with Sean and the shooting, or with his murder? Please tell me, no matter what."

Max shifted on the bench. Our hands remained together, but he was clearly distressed.

"You do know something, don't you? How long? You knew something the night I came to you, and you said nothing? How could you?" Two of the volunteers looked over at us with concern. My temper had gotten the better of me, and I stood up quickly shaking my finger at Max.

Max shook his head. "Please sit down, honey. Let me answer you."

I reluctantly sat, but further from him than before. I needed to be certain and receive answers first.

"Yes, Charlotte, I have secrets. You have your own. I know you haven't told me everything about how and why your engagement ended. I'm fine with that. It was your business. I can't talk about my job. I told you about Paddy, but every day there's information I can't share. If that's a secret, then yes, I have secrets, and I'm not going to share with you. I'm sorry. I've never been rejected by a woman, but I'll understand if you want to call it quits before we even really begin."

"So that's it? What about Conor? What about all of those secrets?" I spit out the questions.

"I have no idea–"

"Conor said Max has secrets. Max will know about me. What do you know about my brother?"

Max seemed to be searching for an answer. He was probably developing his fabrication as he stared into my eyes. "I don't know how to answer you."

"Think, Max."

"I'll know about him? What will I know? Charlotte, I honestly have no idea. Your father doesn't say much. I only know what you and Tom have told me. Maybe I should read the newspaper articles?"

"Maybe you should. He was very adamant that you would know about him." This was getting tedious. "Max, forget it." I felt a drop of rain on my jacket. "I need to go to work, and you should too." I began to stand up, but Max pulled me back down.

"Wait. Let me do one thing to prove to you that I have no idea what you're talking about." Max pulled out his phone and made a call. "Nate, Max here. Where are you? Okay. Look, meet me in my office. I have a job for you. I need you to look into the murder of Conor O'Donohue. Yes, Charlotte's brother. There's something we're missing in all of that. I'll see you within the hour."

Max stared at me while more raindrops fell. Apparently, we were under the one cloud in the sky that was emitting precipitation. I finally gave up.

"Thank you. If you really have no idea then I appreciate that you're going to look into it, plus maybe it all has to do with Sean's shooting."

Max cocked his head. "Maybe. Supposedly. Charlotte, I'm opening up an investigation that could lead in so many different ways. You may not like what I discover. Will you accept that?"

I nodded. My chin began to tremble, but I went back to biting my lip to stave off the tears. "I'm sorry I didn't answer you yesterday."

"It's okay. I get it." Max's hand grasped mine. His thumb intimately touched the inside of my palm. "I've missed you."

"Good."

Max's laughter was light. "You are such a–"

"Melon Head?"

"No, I was going to say you are such a tease."

My eyes flared in indignation. "I am not a tease and never will be. I'm not a flirt either."

"Yes, you are."

I looked down at our hands. Max's thumb had worked its way up to my wrist. "You are the devil. You make me sin."

It began to rain. It was beyond sprinkling. "No, I just have a different definition of what heaven feels like."

I ignored his comment, but it was nice to hear that being with me was divine. "We need to get going. We're going to be drenched."

Max stood up and offered me his hand. "It won't be the first time. Come on, dance with me."

"Charlotte, he's asking you to dance in the rain. Take his hand."

I blinked with open eyes. I placed my hand in Max's, and he quickly pulled me up into his arms. He waltzed me near the entrance of the rose garden. We continued our silent dance under the portico where we could be dry. He kissed my neck. "Charlotte, I'm trying to be the man you deserve."

"Just be you, Max."

"Sometimes on some days, that Max is very much like the devil. Can you live with that man?"

I pulled away from his shoulder and looked directly into those caramel eyes. "I don't know."

"That was an honest answer. I suppose we just take it day by day."

I nodded my answer.

"But you have to know you're the reason why I'm still here. You're the reason why I'm fixing up that old house. I want you to be happy there." Max's voice was soft and low as he pulled me close. We remained in each other's arms for several minutes.

We eventually ran to the cars when there was a break in the downpour. I watched him drive away. I loved him, but there were secrets. Even his declaration of why he was still here was puzzling. Was I really the only reason why he remained? Was he really renovating his home, so I'd be happy there? There was danger and uncertainty. The future held so many hurdles for us and for our families. There remained a murderer who enjoyed picking off O'Donohues. There was a power-hungry man who seemingly was intent on unraveling Max's career or threatening him at every turn so he wouldn't divulge a very delicate secret. And there could be a curse that I alone could remove with enough sacrifice and penance.

I pulled away from the park slowly. Max had found me there. Now, I was trusting him. Though for me, it was past time to go to work in more ways than one.

What's Next for Charolotte...

Charlotte O'Donohue is facing joy and tragedy. She may have just begun a relationship with the love of her life, yet her family's challenges are always in her thoughts. With several mysteries surrounding her, Charlotte has made the decision to go to work…to find a murderer and to save the man she loves. She only hopes her discovery comes soon before another O'Donohue is placed in peril, or she loses Max Shaw forever.

I hope you are enjoying this series. I've based them on the serial soap operas my mother used to watch every weekday. Characters often become a part of you, and that's exactly what my mother felt. One night at dinner, she was unusually quiet. Our dad asked what was wrong. She commented without emotion that Rick had died. Dad and I were concerned. Was there a funeral or visitation we had to go to? How did Rick die? Mom shook her head. "He's not really dead. He's only lost his memory. I think he's in a Broadway musical, but he'll return to the show in September."

The O'Donohues include some real personalities, and I hope you feel as though they are part of your family for the hours, you're reading my novels. At the very least, Judge O'Donohue will always give you some ideas for your dinner menu! Happy reading as always!

Sign up for C.L. Bauer's newsletter at www.clbauer.com for monthly updates, giveaways, and contests. You can always contact her at clbauerkc@gmail.com, or on the many social platforms including Goodreads, Facebook, Instagram, and Twitter.

C.L. BAUER

"I always wanted to write romances. I read them, and our mom loved her soap operas. But at night, our family watched mystery and detective television shows. I was influenced to go in a different direction when I began my adventure in writing. I love a who done it that adds in a little humor, romance, and keeps you guessing."

C.L. Bauer's first cozy mysteries, A Lily List Mystery Series, debuted with The Poppy Drop featuring Kansas City florist Lily Schmidt. A spin off, A Lily List Mystery Exclusive introduced readers to the popular character, Gretchen Malloy. The premier event planner never met a pair of stilettos she didn't love!

Kansas City, Missouri native C.L. Bauer comes from a background in journalism and has received numerous awards as the owner of her family's wedding and event flower business, Clara's Flowers. (Many stories in A Lily List Mystery Series are based on true events.)

With Charlotte's Voices Of Mystery Series, C.L. Bauer has incorporated her love of mystery and romance with a bit of the paranormal. It's a little naughtier than your usual cozy, and with the introduction of the spirit world you'll never know what or who is just around the corner.

To contact the author or schedule special events/book club appearances, email clbauerkc@gmail.com. Visit her website at www.clbauer.com to join the newsletter for news about publications, contests, and upcoming events.

Other Books by C.L. Bauer

The Lily List Mystery Series
The Poppy Drop
The Hibiscus Heist
The Tulip Terror
The Sweet Pea Secret
The Magnolia Dilemma

A Lily List Mystery Exclusive
Stilettos Can Be Murder
Stilettos On The Run

Charlotte's Voices of Mystery Series
The Haunted Lost Rose
Haunted Decisions of the Heart

www.ingramcontent.com/pod-product-compliance
Lightning Source LLC
Chambersburg PA
CBHW060856210726
48293CB00006B/1835